THE CHINA
DECLARATION

THE CHINA DECLARATION

THE CHINA AFFAIRS

BOOK 4

BRAD GOOD

This book is dedicated to Queen Elizabeth II.
May the memory of the Queen live on forever.

CHAPTER 1

Jack Gold got out of the shower and looked at himself with dismay in the mirror. He'd never been one to care much about his physical appearance. He was beginning to suspect it was because he'd always managed to stay in shape whether through his long-time practice of karate or the fast pace his life had taken these previous years.

So much had happened since he'd met Jojo that it was sometimes hard for Jack to reconcile the slow, more mundane nature his life had now taken.

It wasn't that long ago I was in the Control Center he thought, instantly recalling exactly how it felt when he'd been there. It seemed improbable the way his life was suddenly more akin to something out of a high-octane action flick. Sometimes Jack wondered if it had all been a dream.

Yet if it had, he would not be here now, living in a boutique hotel and married to the daughter of the sitting president of China. If it had been all a dream, he likely would not be standing in the bathroom, looking at the twenty pounds he had gained in the mirror he'd just wiped the steam from.

He'd gained exactly as much as Jojo had gained during her second pregnancy. Since having children, sleep and exercise had been much harder to come by despite their live-in nanny, Sherry. Jojo's aunt and uncle had been visiting from Suzhou to help out her dad President Wang, was always coming and going along with a constant train of Jojo's friends. Unlike in America, a new child in China was not just a new family member but a cherished heir and member of the social strata. Two kids— first their daughter, now a son—meant something for everyone. It was also a great excuse for everyone to bring food.

Jack's dad and brother had not visited. Beijing was too far away from the west coast of America. He didn't mind. They often visited via FaceTime. But the contrast to Jojo's family and friends—and their constant presence—could not be more distinct.

Jack helped whenever he could by getting meals for Jojo and taking care of Kai, their daughter. Jack Jr. always slept in their bed as Jojo insisted since it was Chinese custom. It was exhausting waking up in middle of the night and always being attentive. And to Jack it seemed a little bit ridiculous. The baby was so young he did not recognize much except when he was cold, hot, hungry, or needed a diaper change. Occasionally on these sleep-deprived nights Jack entertained the thought that kids should be delivered to their parents when they were over two years old—that would be great.

Jack threw on a pair of jeans, a black cotton t-shirt and then descended the stairs. He could see Jojo holding Kai. Next to her was her father and her friend Jennifer, cooing over the child. Jack felt like an outsider entering an event that he was not invited to.

"Jack," Jennifer said, turning to him. "I saw a picture of your mother. Kai looks just like her—with some Chinese mixed in."

He grinned. He'd heard so many such comparisons to every member of both his and Jojo's family. "She's my daughter, unique and beautiful in her own right."

Jennifer looked at Jojo. "He knows all the right things to say."

Jack sat down in a chair across from them. Since he last spoke at the CCTV Building, everyone had left him alone. The population felt a renewed sense of well-being as the economy motored along and property prices had until only very recently continued to increase, which had been one of the most promising signs of all. Property accounted for seventy percent of all wealth in China.

President Wang looked at Jack. "How are you doing?"

It felt strange to have the question directed at him; it had been a long time since someone had asked. His father and brother had not. The family and friends who visited were (understandably) most concerned with Jojo and the children. Truthfully, Jack didn't know how to answer. What he did know was he was not meant to be a stay-at-home dad. This was simply not something that made him happy. He needed to do something but did not have the slightest idea what.

Before Jack could answer Wang, Jojo chimed in. "Honey, you shouldn't be afraid of doing other things. You have taken great care of us. Think about yourself."

Think about himself. This wasn't something Jojo would have said in the past. She'd felt the opposite, in fact, that their relationship was always taking the backseat to the needs and concerns of the country, made up of over a billion citizens Jack would never personally meet. Yet she had stuck with him through it all. He looked down at his soft midsection then up to Wang. "I need to get in shape."

Wang chuckled, patting his own midsection, which was much bigger than Jack's. "Welcome to the club. Good luck making that go away."

The front door opened suddenly. No knock, or at least not one Jack heard. His good friend Ari walked in and negotiated his big, heavyset frame down the few stairs as everyone turned his way. Jack jumped up and gave his friend who was now more like a brother, a big hug.

"Ari!" he exclaimed. "Come sit down. I think you've met Jennifer. And of course you know President Wang."

Wang leaned forward to shake Ari's hand. Wang did not speak English well, warmly smiled and said, "Hello."

Ari sat down after shaking hands with Wang and took in the entire scene. "You don't look busy enough, Jack. When is your third child coming?"

Jack suppressed a smile. Ari had four children; it seemed to Jack that all Jews had big families, "We were just talking about how out of shape I am. Imagine what a third child might do to me?"

Ari let out a loud laugh and looked down at his own bulging stomach. Jack did not want to join that club, though he wouldn't proclaim such a sentiment out loud. Jojo bounced Kai in front of her and in Chinese, for the benefit of her father, said to Jack, "Why don't you convert one or two of the rooms upstairs into a gym?"

That wasn't a bad idea. The boutique hotel they were living in was not being fully utilized, as there were five extra rooms, only two of which were ever used by guests. "How about we convert three rooms into a nice gym?"

Jojo frowned. "I was thinking two. That will leave us three rooms for guests."

"Three rooms would make a really nice place to work out."

"Okay, you win. Three rooms it is. But I get to convert them and design everything for you. That'll be a fun little project."

"You have great taste and know what I like. It's a deal."

Jojo looked at her dad. "I'll send over some guys tomorrow," Wang said.

"If you are serious about getting back into shape," Ari said to Jack, "why don't you visit Israel and join the IDF training? We could assign one of the lead instructors to you."

"Israel!" Jojo said. "How long would he be there for?"

"It's a month-long program. It'd be fun and you can't get better training anywhere else in the world. You and the kids can come too, of course."

Jojo translated what he said into Chinese for her father, then turned back to Ari. "No. Jack is not leaving for an entire month."

"Fair enough," Ari said. "How about we send someone out here to train him, then he can visit Israel for a week or so for in-person tactical combat shooting training? It'd be a shame to miss out on that."

Jojo smiled. "That sounds better."

Though Jack was doing little in the way of formulating this plan about himself, he liked what he was hearing. "I wish President Sutton were still in office. He could help with someone from America and maybe Japan."

Wang leaned forward. "Yes, President Sutton could have. I miss my interactions with him. I actually spoke with him the other day. He and Cam are enjoying their time in Florida. They said to send their regards to the both of you."

President Sutton had lost his bid for a second term. His successor, President Glendon Smith, was a progressive hands-off operator who thought America should collaborate with all other countries and not impose its will globally. His liberal ideas appealed to a number of America's different factions and Smith promised a "level playing field" and "equality of opportunity" which was a message people were ready to embrace.

"Anyway, I'd offer something similar with China's special forces," Wang said, "but honestly they do not compare to what Israel has to offer."

Jojo was beaming as she sat on the sofa holding and bouncing Kai in front of her. "Jack is just a big boy. Now he gets to play." She gave Jack a stern look.

Jack knew what that meant. "Okay, I'll only go visit places for one week at a time." He was thrilled with this unexpected development. He'd get to train with some of the best people in the world. It wasn't just about getting in shape. Jack was a third-degree blackbelt, but his skills needed to be honed and improved. Perhaps, more importantly, his brain was out of shape. Martial arts at a high level required practice, thinking, and creativity. It required using your brain instinctively. That's what excited him. That's what he missed—what he felt he had lost.

"You'll need a partner for all the training," Ari said. "And I'm sorry to say I'll have to decline your offer, but it'll be best if you have someone to practice with while being instructed."

"Where is Davis?" Jack asked. "He has been on vacation for weeks now." Jack knew his longtime bodyguard would cherish the opportunity and suspected he too needed to get back into shape after so much relaxation.

Jack looked at Ari. "You really think you can get someone to come here to train me?" He was a little skeptical. These people had their own lives, they were important, and why was Jack so special?

"Jack, the Israeli prime minister would be delighted with the idea. Plus, they'd be thrilled to have you visit Israel again."

Jack's mind was already at work forming a plan. One month of training here followed by a visit to Israel—he'd be a changed man.

"Well, now that settled, what have you been up to?" Jack asked Ari.

"Some interesting stuff, actually. I was approached by a laser communication company. They've developed some new technology that will enable communication with astronauts in outer space, using lasers. I'm focused on using the system to bounce lasers back to Earth to provide ultra-fast internet to major cities."

"How fast is the connection?"

"20Gbps, with 99 percent up time."

"That's fast. Elon's Starlink is only 500Mbps and that's their premium service."

"It's a game changer. That's why I decided to get involved. There are all sorts of applications for such fast internet. Israel is good at this sort of technology."

"What's the business model? How will you make money?"

"Close to seven trillion dollars of foreign exchange transactions occur every day globally. They need a fast and reliable connection—and they'll pay for it. Starlink requires too many satellites. And it's slower. We'll have receivers placed in all major cities by the end of this year. We'll put institutional customers on a subscription fee plan, except the price will be much higher than normal plans. There are also military related customers we're talking to. They like the security features."

"What about other customers who might need fast internet but who are in more remote locations?"

"We'll get to them eventually, maybe three to five years down the line. Providing the service to our military is a priority. We'll be placing receivers in secondary cities eventually." Ari glanced at Wang. "No plans for China yet."

Jack was fascinated. "What would it take to place receivers in China's more isolated cities in the mountains for use by schools and hospitals?"

"At the right time that won't be a problem. Regulations will be the biggest hurdle. Later this year we'll have all the satellites in place. But positioning receivers in all the towns is not enough. Once a beam reaches a city it can be diverted to other areas within the city and two-way communication is possible. Still, infrastructure needs to be built out connecting customers to a nearby receiver or cell site. In most cases, China does not have such cable laid out."

Jack looked at Jojo, who had also been listening intently as she held Kai on her lap. Jack nodded for her to translate what had just been said to Wang.

He turned his focus back to Ari. "What do you think it would cost to connect remote Chinese cities to get it done earlier, for educational institutions and medical facilities, along with the cables connecting them to a laser node?"

"I really don't know. Someone would have to do a study to figure it out. My best guess is a few hundred million."

"A few hundred million." Jack had been wondering how he might be able to use the one billion dollars sitting in his Luxembourg bank account. Money that had been deposited in the account in exchange for Jack no longer participating in a transformative project for China. Neither the US or Chinese government acknowledged the money existed and so, by default, it belonged to the account holder–Jack.

He hadn't given any real thought of what to do with such an enormous sum of money. But now he had a few ideas. "If I can arrange the investment," he said now to Wang, "will you agree to the concept of helping isolated hospitals and educational institutions in China? Mostly those in isolated mountainous areas. They can ramp up remote medicine and teaching. China can leapfrog the rest of the world technologically."

Wang sat back in his chair, clearly not anticipating having to address such issues while visiting his grandchildren. "I'll have someone from our

Ministry of Health and Ministry of Education contact you for a discussion."

Jack could tell Wang liked the idea, but as a prudent leader he could never commit too quickly to something. "Maybe you join that meeting," Jack said to Ari. "We can see if something can be worked out."

"Sure. Sounds great. Let me know." Ari stood up. "Anyway, I should be going, I was just in the neighborhood and wanted to drop by to see my buddy." He shook Jack's hand and then turned to Wang. "President, it's a pleasure as usual. Jojo, you look amazing. Good job with your kids." He looked at Jack and grinned. "All *three* of your kids." There was good-natured laughter as everyone bid Ari goodbye. Though his visit was quick and unexpected, Jack felt buoyed and engaged in a way he hadn't been in a while.

CHAPTER 2

Not long after Ari's visit, Jack received a phone call from the Minister of Education's office, requesting his and Ari's presence at a meeting along with Madam Li Dequan, the Minister of Health.

Rather than just have two white guys go, Jack had invited his former assistant Susan, who agreed to join them after he briefed her about the project. Exiting the elevator, the three of them were escorted to a well-appointed conference room with walls of frosted glass. Both ministers were seated near the middle of the long boardroom table and in the midst of a conversation. They looked up as Jack walked over to them, immediately stopped their discussion and stood. "Hello, Jack, it's nice to meet you in person," said Huai Jinpeng, the Minister of Education.

"Nice to meet you." Jack gestured to Ari. "This is Ari, my good Israeli friend who you may have heard of. And this is Susan, who worked with me on the province planning project."

Everyone shook hands. Jack, Ari, and Susan made their way to the other side of the table and sat across from Huai and Li. From an appearance standpoint they both seemed like nice, well-educated people.

"Thank you for taking time today to meet with us," Jack began. "We have an idea that we think will help satisfy the missions of your ministries. In other words, we hope we can assist in developing and implementing plans for educational and health reform." Jack had researched their websites and used the same wording he had seen there.

Ari had earlier sent Jack all of the technological plans for using lasers to communicate with outer space and how these could be bounced back to Earth, providing high speed internet. They were solid plans with the intent for mass production of transceivers so as to drive down costs. They made money to offset the costs of equipment manufacturing by charging a nominal up-front fee and monthly subscription fees. The technology had been patented around the world so it was well protected, even in China. Jack had also read some articles about the company and the comparative advantage of their technology. They were clear leaders in the industry. Someone could come up with a better solution, but they'd be at least a few years behind.

"We think the technology can be used by schools and hospitals, particularly in hard-to-reach mountainous areas. A laser can be pointed from outer space to a particular area from which cable wire can then take it the last mile to schools and hospitals. Teachers and doctors can be beamed from anywhere in China and the world, depending upon what you want, to share their expertise."

Jack showed a chart he had printed out from Ari's materials that illustrated exactly how things would work, though right away he could tell that they didn't need it—they understood.

Madam Li asked, "How much will it cost to lay the cable from the receiver to the end user site?"

"We would need to detail that out depending upon what you think are the priority areas. Maybe we start with a few particularly isolated regions and go from there."

"Jack," Huai said, "you know we submitted our plans and have funding for approved initiatives. Is there a monthly fee for the service?"

"Normally there would be a fee but let me back up a little bit. I'm not involved in this venture to make money. I have no stock or salary. In fact, I'm willing to pay for laying the cable and any monthly fees. I've always wanted to do something to help elders and children in China's remote areas. I'd expect Ari's company to provide all equipment at cost, given our lofty goals."

Madam Li coughed. "That's nice that you'd be willing to make a donation, but would it be remotely close to covering the costs? I suspect laying cable and buying routers and computer screens will not be cheap."

Jack decided to turn the tables on them. "What if you detail those costs from your standpoint. We can go from there."

There was skepticism on their faces as Huai and Li spoke to each other. Jack did not feel they were being rude, rather, they were just being professional and efficient. Jack had avoided their question. They were probably wondering why they should detail costs when they were unsure if Jack hand enough money.

Hesitantly Jack said, "If we have a detailed plan and your commitment, I can personally commit up to $500 million. I'm very serious about getting this project done. That should be more than enough to fund the project."

Madam Li's jaw dropped. Minister Huai blinked and said nothing. It was not often people walked into their office making a generous offer.

Once again the two ministers politely chatted in low tones that Jack could not quite make out. Finally, Madam Li spoke. "Your offer is generous. This technology could put us on the leading edge of remote learning and medicine. Jack, we have to be honest with you. The timing is just not right. I can't go into anything more than that. We are grateful for your visit and your offer. If you have some materials please leave them. If things change we can study them and get back to you."

Jack was dumbfounded. He had offered them everything for free. How could the timing not be right? He stood when the others did and leaned across the table to shake hands. As he did so he could see a slight sadness in their eyes, but he did not know why. Before heading out Jack nodded to Susan to stay behind and find out what she could. They had worked so closely before she knew instinctively what he wanted. Ari and Jack made their way out and took the elevator to the lobby.

"Where is Susan?" Ari asked, glancing over his shoulder.

"She stayed behind to see if she could learn some more."

"What just happened in there?"

"Let's wait till Susan comes down."

A few minutes later the elevator door opened and Susan walked out. Ari couldn't contain himself. "Can you tell me what is going on? How could they say no if they didn't have to pay for anything? Did they want a payoff, money sent to their kids in Australia? And, Jack, where did you get $500 million dollars?"

Susan looked at Ari. "I spoke with them. They have lots going on right now. It's not in the planning cycle."

"Okay," Jack said. "Thanks. We should go."

"It was a nice try," Ari said as they exited the building.

"Sorry it wasn't better news. At least they didn't drag things out."

They both shook hands and Ari took off. Jack looked over to Susan. "Care for a walk?" Jack asked. Davis, recently back from vacation, was waiting just up ahead by the black SUV he'd driven them over in. Jack motioned to him that he'd be a little while longer.

They found a sitting area near the building and Susan sat down on the side facing the traffic. Jack joined her. "What did they say."

"You have to promise me this is confidential. You can't tell anyone."

"Okay. I promise."

"Minister Li and Huai are good people. I know of them from my work with President Wang. When I asked what was going on they said it was a *timing problem*. I asked them to clarify. They know I worked in Wang's office and were forthright. They said one word: *Election*."

Jack frowned. "What do you mean, *election*?"

"Rumor has been going around that President Wang will announce presidential elections. That they will be held in a few months."

"What are you talking about? Why would Wang hold elections? Wang might not win if he holds elections?"

"President Zhao served two years, and Wang is coming up on three years. Combined, that makes a five-year term. Presidents are allowed two five-year terms. Wang is finishing his first term. He believes in China's constitution that stipulates the National People's Congress should elect the president. The timing is bad, though. China's property market is softening so his re-election is not certain."

"And the ministers didn't want to move ahead with the project because of the fear that Wang might not be re-elected?"

"Exactly. It shows that they are unsure who might win. And they know what you've done for the country and wouldn't want you to spend money that might not end up getting put to the use you intended."

If Jack hadn't been sitting down, he would have. Everything he had done he now realized would have been useless if not for the vision and dedication of Wang. Now, without Wang, it could all fade away. All this effort for nothing.

"How am I going to keep this from my wife, or not mention it to President Wang, my father-in-law?"

"Fine then. Just don't mention me or the ministers."

"This is big news. Is there anything else I should know?"

Susan hesitated. "There is one thing you'll want to know."

"What is that?"

"If Wang loses the election, it'll likely be to Li Keqiang."

"I thought he was under house arrest?"

"He is but he can communicate to the outside world. He has come up with a plan for the government to invigorate the major property developers that involves China and some banks paying off the debts of major developers. This means buyers who already paid for apartments that have not been built will get their money back."

That in turn meant the property market would get a huge injection of money and prices would continue to go up. All apartment owners in China would like that.

"I see. We know how this plays out. Okay, I've got lots to think about."

"I expected you'd understand faster than anyone. At least they were gracious in seeing you and letting us know the truth."

"It gives me no satisfaction whatsoever. But thank you. It was nice seeing you and I appreciate you taking the time to join us today."

"It was my pleasure. Reminds me of the old days when we went to all those provincial meetings." Susan smiled. "Never a dull moment."

They said their goodbyes and Jack walked over to Davis. "How'd it go?" Davis asked.

"Not what I'd expected. Nice people though."

Jack looked in Davis's rearview mirror and thought this was as good as any time to ask. "Ari is going to arrange for an IDF instructor to visit and train me for a month. Training starts in two weeks. I need a partner for the training opportunity of a lifetime. Are you in?"

In the mirror, Jack saw Davis's eyes squint from the smile he knew was on his face. "Jack, that does sound like the opportunity of a lifetime. Please let me think about it and check with the Bureau."

"Sure," Jack said. He knew Davis wouldn't pass it up. But then again, he had been certain that his offer of half a billion dollars wouldn't be turned down either.

CHAPTER 3

They were in the backyard on the grass near the swimming pool. Jack threw the sturdy rope toy for Mini to retrieve. Rather than take the dog to a Chinese obedience school Jack had read several books and worked with Mini never punishing him, only using positive reinforcement. The dog was smart. One night at a small party, Mini had tried to herd all the people, lightly nipping at everyone's ankles. Jack undid that habit with a few instructions and some treats. It never happened again. Jack made sure he knew all his commands in both English and Chinese. Maybe Mini was the first bilingual border collie in the world.

The black and white dog eagerly dropped the rope, not on the ground but into Jack's hand. If it weren't for Mini, Jack knew he would be even more out of shape. The dog had endless energy. They constantly played ball in both the back and front of the house. Just when Mini looked tired, Jack would give him some water and they would start again. The entire neighborhood knew Mini and saw Jack during his endless walks, with the dog always along Jack's left side, never out of pace with him.

"Jack, *Nǐ hǎo le méiyǒu?*" *Are you ready?* Jojo yelled from upstairs window.

"Yes. We're ready!"

Jack looked at Mini. "Put your toy away. We have to go."

Mini immediately put the rope toy in a plastic bowl on the other side of the pool then ran to the back entrance of the house.

Jack put on his jacket then walked in. Only then did Mini follow him—Jack, as the head of the pack, went first.

Jojo was coming down the stairs wearing a bright yellow form-fitting dress. Both Jack and Mini stared as she descended.

Jack said the only thing he could think of. "Ooh-la-la."

Jojo smiled and smoothed the front of her dress. "Are you bringing Mini?"

"I thought it'd be okay if he joined. They'll be no kids there to pull his tail or try to ride him."

"Has he exercised enough so he'll be relaxed for the evening?"

"We went for a walk and then played fetch out front and in back. He's cool. See the way he's looking at you? He thinks you look beautiful too."

On cue, Mini barked in agreement. Jack had trained him to bark whenever he used the word "beautiful."

"Well, it looks like I'll be escorted by two gentlemen tonight. Dad will be happy to see Mini, for sure."

Davis was there with the door open for Jojo on the driver side. Jack and Mini got in by themselves. Jojo said, "Welcome back Davis. How was vacation?"

"It was good not to see Jack for a while. That was the most pleasant part of my vacation."

"It looks like you worked out a lot," Jojo said. "Nice muscles, Davis. Did you have a chance to go out on any dates?"

Davis was uncharacteristically silent. Both Jack and Jojo looked at each other. Jack said, "Davis, it's not polite to not answer a lady's question."

As the car pulled onto the main highway he said, "Yes, I went on a date."

"Only one date? Is this confidential information you are sharing with us?"

Davis said nothing.

"I bet you went out with Rio," Jojo said. "That Chinese agent you met in Dali. Was the date with her?"

Davis had always been guarded about sharing details of his personal life, though given everything they had been through, Jack felt there was no harm if the personal and professional lines crossed a little. But no further details were forthcoming.

Jack settled back into the seat. "So, what's tonight all about? I know you have planned the entire evening but I really don't know what it's about."

"It's my dad's sixty-sixth birthday. In some parts of China, that's an important year. Six is a good number. I've called all the relatives. There will be a six-layer cake. Unfortunately, there is no good place for fire-crackers."

"What do I say to your dad, just a simple *Happy Birthday*?"

"That's fine."

They pulled into Zhongnanhai and all three got out. Mini immediately moved to Jack's left side. Jack held Jojo's hand as they walked toward the entrance. For whatever reason, Jojo preferred to hold Jack's left hand. Knowing this Mini swiftly switched to Jack's right side.

Jack reached into his pocket and took out his two phones. The black phone was from Cooper, his contact in the CIA. Jack hadn't used the phone in months. He turned it off and handed it, along with his iPhone, to the attendant.

As they started down the hallway Jack said, "Mini, Grandpa, go."

The dog immediately turned in the opposite direction and trotted off. All the staff in Zhongnanhai knew Mini and would not be surprised to see him wandering around. Jack thought Wang would enjoy the surprise of seeing Mini show up unannounced, wherever he might be.

There were about forty people already gathered in the small banquet hall. Jack never took much pleasure in these events. He like Jojo would have to mingle which took a lot of energy. "Did you arrange Maotai?" Jack whispered.

Jojo patted his hand. "Yes, Jack. No need to worry."

Jack was relieved. He could at least drink with everyone. It seemed to him that his Chinese was more fluent when he was a little bit inebriated.

Everyone's gaze swiveled toward the entrance when President Wang entered the hall. Dutifully walking on his left side, in perfect sync, was Mini.

Wang walked up to Jojo and took her hands in his. Then he looked to Jack and shook his hand. "I was in a meeting with two ambassadors when Mini walked in and came right up to me. It was a great surprise."

Jack and Jojo began to make their rounds. Jojo grabbed a glass of red wine, the favorite beverage of those attending such functions. Jack asked the waiter, "Can you please get me some Maotai? Three inches, in a wine glass." Jack lifted his hand and showed him how much he wanted with his thumb and index finger.

Jojo grinned. "You really do take advantage of my dad's promise you'll never run out of Maotai."

"I consider it payment for services rendered. People who talk on TV get paid a lot," Jack said, referring to the speech he gave when President

Wang was trying to subdue unrest following the bombing of Taiwan's Presidential Building and Zhongnanhai.

"Let's sit down. I'm a little tired from the day," Jojo said. "We can mingle from our seats."

As they sat down, the waiter arrived with Jack's Maotai. Jack took a sip as he surveyed the crowd of people around Wang. Mini was dutifully still next to him and getting lots attention too. It was clear Wang was delighted with the attention he was getting because of Mini and not because he was the president.

"It was a good idea to bring Mini," Jojo whispered. "When I was a young girl living on our farm we used to have a dog. It was mainly a guard dog and unfriendly. He barked at everyone. We'd feed it whatever was left over after dinner. Mini is completely different. He is a good member of our family now."

People began to take their seats at the banquet tables. President Wang sat facing the door, the place of honor. Jack was on one side of him and Jojo on the other. They were his family. And, Mini was still on his left. Wang gave the dog a pat.

Raising glasses of red wine, toasts ensued as the food was placed on the large tempered glass rotating platform in the middle of the table. There was hot and sour soup, garlic spinach, bok choy, fried fish, fried pigeon, dumplings, braised ribs, and fried rice. All dishes Jojo knew were her father's favorite. Not extravagant food, but exceedingly well cooked.

Using his chopsticks, Wang took some meat and vegetables and put them in his rice bowl. "Mini is such a magnificent dog and has behaved superbly—can I give him a few pieces of meat?"

Jack took a sip of his Maotai. "You can try but he won't eat it."

Wang's fingers were thick and strong from years past working on their farm. He used them to delicately pick up his chopsticks and remove a piece of meat from the beef ribs. Slowly, so Mini could see it, he brought the piece to the dog's mouth, which remained closed. Mini did not move, nor look to Jack for permission.

Jack had long ago trained Mini to refuse food at the table. The last thing he wanted was a dog going around and bothering people while they were eating. It was a simple rule to instill, and Jack wondered why so many others did not do the same.

"I give up." Wang put the meat in his own mouth. "Did you hire someone to train him?"

"I spent lots of time learning how to train him. In fact, I spent much more time learning than training."

"Okay. We should talk later. I want to adopt one. Will you train him for me?"

"It's best if I help you train your dog. If good habits are formed by you, everything is easier. It does take a good amount of time, though."

"I think I'll be able to find the time."

Jack raised his glass of Maotai to his father-in-law, waiting for Jojo and everyone at their table to do the same. "*Yuèfù*, to a long and prosperous life. Happy birthday."

Everyone echoed the sentiment and glasses were clinked and the conversation resumed. It was a festive occasion. There were musicians—a violinist, a cellist, a piano player, plus a singer and a bass player. They were playing rather subdued conservative music that Wang liked but that did not encourage dancing.

Jack stood up and went over to Jojo. "Can you come with me a second?"

She stood. "Sure, what's up?"

"We have to change this music. People should be dancing."

"Jack, these are conservative people. They don't dance."

"Nonsense. Let's tell the band to play some cool dancing music."

"What should they play? I know them well. They're a good group and can play anything."

"Have them play something with more energy. They probably know what dance songs people here would like."

"Jack, give them one recommendation at least."

What type of song he would like to dance to right now? He thought for a moment. "Okay, have them play *Uptown Funk* by Mark Ronson. And have them sing it too."

Jojo raised her eyebrows. "You're crazy, Jack. But, okay."

They went over to the band and Jojo communicated everything. The band members smiled. "You can intersperse slow songs," Jack said. "Maybe try I *don't want to Talk About It* by Rod Stewart. Show us what you got. Pump it out. This place is not a retirement home." Jack knew he was probably a little tipsy, but all the band members nodded approvingly.

Jack stood there as Jojo started to return to her seat. She stopped and walked back over to him. "What now?"

"Will you dance with me? May I have the next dance?"

The atmosphere in the traditional banquet hall instantly changed when the band started to play "Uptown Funk." Jojo and Jack forgot about everything else but the music. They often danced together and when they did it was like they were the only people in the world. They knew how to move their bodies to the somewhat non-traditional beat of the vibrant music and seemingly nonsensical lyrics: "*If you sexy then flaunt it. If you freaky then own it. Don't brag about it, come show me. Come on, dance, jump on it.*"

Jack leaned into Jojo. "Go get your dad to join us." As Jojo walked over to Wang, Jack called for the dog. Instantly Mini left Wang's side and joined Jack on the dance floor. Mini often danced with them and could balance on his two back legs. Jack took advantage of every single opportunity to give the dog exercise and mental stimulation. If Mini danced a few songs, Jack wouldn't have to take him for a walk when they got back tonight.

Jojo and her dad joined them and Wang immediately began moving to the beat. He didn't need to the know what the words meant. Jack knew Jojo was delighted to be dancing with her father and see him enjoying himself, particularly on this special occasion. Once the crowd saw the president dancing others joined in, though Jack could clearly see everyone's dancing experience was primarily formal ballroom dancing.

A few songs later the band sensed the crowd was slowing down and they started playing slower songs, the sound level markedly decreased.

Jojo walked over to the banquet door and stuck her head out to speak to someone, then she signaled to the band. Less than a minute later, a six-layer, white frosted cake with six glowing candles was wheeled into the room. The band started to play *happy birthday* as the waiters circulated with small glasses of Maotai.

Jack looked around. Jojo had arranged orchids, peach, and plum blossoms throughout the room, and they gave the space an elegant and cozy feeling. She raised her glass to her father and everyone else followed suit. "Happy birthday!" she cheered. The crowd echoed her sentiment as Wang took a sip of his Maotai.

A while after the cake was served, everyone relaxed chatting with each other. Wang looked at Jojo and Jack. "We should probably go so the others do not feel compelled to stay. Let's say our goodbyes to everyone."

They circulated the room politely saying their goodbyes. Most were family members and had come in from Suzhou. Wang had spent time with them earlier and a few had visited Jack and Jojo at their home over the past few days.

Jack and Jojo followed Wang down a hallway to his private office. There was a good-sized desk, books, and a delicate looking but comfortable sofa and matching chair.

"Come on in. This won't take long." He poured Jojo and Jack a cup of tea. They both took a seat on the sofa and Wang settled himself on the chair across from them.

Jack was relaxed from the Maotai, but not so much not to recognize Wang was about to tell them something important. Otherwise he would not be serving tea.

"I've been meaning to tell you that an election for president will be held in a few months. You should also know that I'm not going to win."

Jojo frowned and glanced at Jack.

Jack had already absorbed the shock of this after his discussion with Susan. But Jojo was clearly stunned. "And," Jack said, rather reluctantly, "Li Keqiang is going to be the next president."

Wang gave Jack one of his quizzical looks. "How do you know that?"

"Rumors spread. Social media."

Jojo looked from Jack to her dad. "Li Keqiang headed the opposition before and was jailed for illegal things he did. How can he become president?"

Wang sighed. "The National People's Congress votes on who becomes president and there is no law that prevents Li Keqiang from running or being elected. I have to respect China's constitution whether I like it or not."

"Dad, this is going to be horrible. I can't believe the National People's Congress would vote for him."

"The real estate challenges that Chinese companies now face are not small. I feel the market should determine which companies go out of business. This will serve as a warning to all companies not to depend upon the government to bail them out. It'll strengthen the country in the longer run. Li thinks the government should rescue them. But China already has too much debt. This is too much of a risk to the nation. Ultimately, people want money and to be saved, despite the likely consequences."

Jack had studied the situation during the past few weeks and knew Wang was correct. There was no option for a man of true integrity. Wang was not changing what he believed just to get elected. Jack respected and admired that.

Jack took his cup of tea and placed it on the marble floor so that Mini could have a long and overdue drink. Then, he picked up the wineglass he had brought with him that still contained a good amount of Maotai. He poured a portion into to two clean teacups. He handed one each to Wang and Jojo. Jack raised his glass. "Happy birthday. To family and having more time to enjoy life."

The sour mood was broken. Everyone, including Mini, was having a drink. Things would work out. Jojo said, "Dad, I did not know you were such a good dancer."

"*Xiǎo chūn juǎn'er, little spring roll*, thank you for organizing everything tonight. It truly was a wonderful birthday. Jack, thanks for lightening the mood. I could not imagine a better sixty-sixth birthday. Thank you too, Mini."

At the mention of his name, Mini immediately went over to Wang for a scratch behind his ears.

CHAPTER 4

The US Embassy in Beijing was an ugly mass of steel and concrete structures. The construction cost was over $500 million. Jack had never been there despite it being not too far away, located northeast of the Forbidden City. He didn't want to visit but the embassy had conveyed a request for Jack to meet David Pret, the US Ambassador. Jack thought he had nothing to lose. It seemed that Davis, who had been the one to deliver the message, wanted him to go.

As they pulled up, Jack did some quick math. The embassy was 500,000 square feet. Each square foot cost $1,000. Another disappointing example of how the American government could not control expenditures. Besides handing out visas, Jack didn't understand what role the embassy could play. It was simply American wasted taxpayer money.

Jack made his way to a special entrance so that he would not have to wait in the long visa line. He handed his US passport to the marine guard on duty. "What is the purpose of your visit today, Mr. Gold?"

Jack was momentarily flustered. "I'm not sure. I have a meeting with Ambassador David Pret."

After scanning his passport and looking at the screen, the guard handed it back. "Thank you, sir. Please go straight ahead through the metal detector, then an escort will meet you."

His escort was a Chinese woman who spoke perfect American English, "Hello Mr. Gold. It's a pleasure and honor to meet you." They shook hands. "Come this way, Ambassador Pret is waiting for you."

Jack followed her into an elevator and then through another layer of security. As they passed offices and cubicles, he could still not fathom what everyone running around was doing. He had never heard of a single thing any embassy or consulate in China did that was beneficial, other than helping American tourists who had lost their passports. He tried to adjust his attitude and learn something from walking through the long hallways. He noticed the very clear air which he reasoned was a security measure against potential airborne contaminants and a way to get rid of the smog.

David Prat and an assistant were waiting for him in a meeting area within a bigger office. "Hello Jack," the ambassador said. "What a pleasure it is to meet you. We have all read and heard about your exploits. Welcome to the Embassy. You are on American soil now. Relax. Please have a seat."

As Jack shook their hands, he gazed around the opulent office, which was meant to impress foreign dignitaries and Chinese business leaders. There was a large American flag behind an oversized mahogany desk, on which were small American and Chinese flags. The walls were made of dark wood, with photos of major US cities hanging on the walls, probably meant to remind visitors of America's success and wealth. There were good-sized windows looking out over a pool in front of a sturdy looking wall and fence. It struck Jack this would be a good place if there was unrest in China.

The five-chair round table in the office was meant as an intimate meeting area. Jack sat down in the stereotypical boardroom chair across from the two men. Both were wearing dark blue suits and ties. They had a combined China/America flag lapel pin on the left side of their jackets. Jack purposefully wore jeans and a blazer—stereotypical California business attire.

Ambassador Pret said, "We understand that you were at Zhongnanhai the other night. May we ask what the purpose of your visit was?"

Jack was surprised by the audacity of the question. Just because they both had passports from the same country didn't give them the right to ask such a question. "All my visits to Zhongnanhai and discussions with leadership in China are strictly confidential."

"This is a delicate time in China's history and we—your country—would be grateful for any information you might have."

"I'm sorry, you said *your country*. Which country were you referring to?"

"Jack, you are an American citizen holding an American passport. I was referring to America."

"Well, David, I'm also a citizen of China . . ."

"You will address me as Ambassador Pret, please."

"That's fine, Ambassador Pret. Please address me as Mr. Gold."

"Okay. My apologies. We've started off on the wrong footing. Let me explain the situation. There will be an election next month and we need to know if you have any plans?"

"What kind of plans?"

Ambassador Pret looked to his assistant quickly before proceeding. "Plans to try and sway the election away from Li Keqiang to Wang?"

Jack had considered making an announcement in support of Wang and trying to do exactly what they were mentioning—swaying the election. His gut told him to let the country proceed and not interfere. He had already done that and felt enough was enough.

"If I had any plans, you would be the last person I would share them with. If the US government wants information from me then have President Smith give me a call."

Jack had read about Glendon Smith. The president had what some called a globalist philosophy with a progressive attitude and firmly believed in leaving countries alone unless they directly and significantly encroached on America. Jack sorely missed former president Sutton and his forward-thinking beliefs.

Ambassador Pret took a deep breath and exhaled slowly. "It has been years since your actions caused a threat to your life. There is zero noise that a threat to you currently exists. Consequently, it is the view of the State Department that you no longer require a security detail. It will be discontinued starting this coming Monday."

Jack kept his expression neutral. There would still be the Chinese detail. He did not disagree with the ambassador's statement—he too felt things were safe now. He would certainly miss Davis. But it was hard for him to see this situation as anything other than the ambassador asking for information and then, not getting what he wanted, taking something away. Jack had always done good for America in China, at great expense and risk to his life. Broadcasting at the CCTV Building and successfully driving the economic agreement were not small accomplishments. Plus, they hadn't even discussed removing the security detail with him before making the decision. That was bad form.

Jack considered what to say, letting nearly a minute go by. He could see they were both uncomfortable with the silence. Finally, he said, "Ambassador, I would like you to inform your Secretary of State and president that I vehemently protest the removal of my security detail. I am an

American diplomat. I have performed invaluable services in China for the United States of America." Jack reached in his jacket and showed them his American diplomatic passport. "Taking away a security detail from a notable US diplomat, prior to an election, is myopic and puts my family at risk. Moreover, you never discussed this with me beforehand. Your decision and how you made it demonstrates negligence in the performing of your duties. Let me ask you, have you ever visited Zhongnanhai?"

"No, I haven't," Ambassador Pret said after a moment's hesitation, "but that's beside the point. Jack, you must realize that, should Li Keqiang become president, our government's relationship with you will be a liability. You played a big role in putting him under house arrest. We must show the future president Li that we respect him. It's nothing personal."

"Let me be crystal clear: I insist that you notify your president that I strenuously object." Jack paused. "And that you have now deeply offended me. Both you and President Smith."

"Jack, I did not mean to insult you on behalf of the president. Don't be upset with him."

"Ambassador Pret, you represent the Secretary of State and speak for the President of the United States. Your words and actions are an affront to me. This meeting is over."

Jack sat there again without saying anything. His manufactured indignation and anger, he could see, was having an impact on the two men. Good. He wasn't sure what to expect in response from them down the line, if any at all. But at least they would be less likely to seek his help in the future.

Ambassador Pret sluggishly stood up. "Thanks for coming by, Jack."

Jack shook his hand. "It was nothing. Good luck."

He took a last look to see the splendor of the ambassador's office. Like a large law firm lobby, it was meant to impress and intimidate, though Jack felt the exact opposite. It was another waste.

He stepped out of the embassy feeling more comfortable in the smoggy Beijing air. When he got back into the SUV and saw Davis's expression, he knew instantly that Davis had been informed about the security detail.

"When I found out last week, I voiced my disagreement with their decision, but I was overruled," Davis said. "It's ironic since they just augmented security at the embassy."

"Why would they increase security?"

"Not sure. And more tech talent arrived the other day. Something is going on."

Jack didn't like changes. It brought uncertainty and that brought risk. "Can I put you and your colleagues on a contract for services? You could leave the Bureau."

"Jack, I can't leave the Bureau. It's become a part of my life and identity. Plus, I have a pretty good pension coming up in a few years."

"Are you sure that there is nothing I can offer? I'm not as poor as I look."

"It pains me to say so, but . . . no. And don't take it personally. If you would like to hire an external detail, I would suggest that you speak with your friend Ari. He likely has contacts with freelance Mossad groups who take on extended security assignments. They're the best out there."

"How come Mossad and not IDF?"

"Israel's Mossad is responsible for intelligence gathering, covert ops, and counterterrorism. They attract the best and globally kick ass."

They pulled up to the boutique hotel entrance. Davis turned to look at Jack. Jack saw Davis's salt and pepper hair and the fine lines etching his face; he still remembered first seeing Davis at the China World Hotel when he was informed he'd have to leave the country. It was right after he had given the speech to the nation at the Control Center.

"I'll see you later, Davis."

"One more thing, Jack."

He let go of the door handle.

"I'm confirmed for the month of training. The Bureau is granting me my back vacation days and acknowledges the benefit of training before I get shipped back State-side."

Jack smiled. "Excellent news. Best news of the day, in fact. I look forward to it. I understand our instructor from Israel arrives Monday morning. Come by whenever and we can meet him. Where will you be staying during that time? You're more than welcome to take one of our rooms. It'd be great to have you nearby."

Davis grinned. "I've got that taken care of."

"Where? With Rio?"

Davis turned toward the front of the car. "Have a good day, Jack."

"You too."

CHAPTER 5

"It's as if Jojo replicated the fighting area out of the Matrix where Neo fights Morpheus," Jack said, showing Davis the three rooms that had been converted into a dojo, an enormous space with eighteen-foot high, white-painted ceilings. "The Japanese doors, the mirrors, tatami mat floors. Check out the kicking and punching bags. And the weights."

Davis nodded in approval. "Most civilized place to work out in all of Beijing, for sure."

As they walked around to inspect everything in the gym, Jack noticed a series of weapons. Knives, swords, staffs, sticks, fake knives, and guns. "Jojo went all out. How did she get all this stuff? She must have consulted with someone."

"That's my secret," Jojo said, coming into the room. She grinned. "You guys look like little kids checking out their new playground."

There was a firm knock on the door—the instructor from Israel. They all went to greet him. But standing on the doorstep was a tall young lady with long, sandy brown hair. She carried two black duffle bags.

"Hi Jack, I'm Maya," she said. "I was sent here to train you." She reached out and firmly shook Jack's hand.

"Hi, Maya. May I introduce you to my wife, Jojo, and this is Davis, who will be training with me."

"It's nice to meet you all."

"Come on in," Jojo said. "How was your journey?"

"It was a pleasant rest. A thirty-five-hour commute."

Jojo said, "I'll get some tea and then show you to your room."

"That sounds wonderful." They all started to walk in then Maya stopped, looking at Davis and Jack. "I understand that the Palace Museum is not too far from here?"

"That's right. It's about two and a half miles away," Jack said.

"Perfect. Why don't you two jog there and back and we can start training when you return." She looked first at Jack, then Davis, right in the eye. They knew it was an order, not a request. "Except, don't jog—run."

She turned away from them and continued walking with Jojo. "Tea sounds delightful. I really like what you've done with the space and the industrial feel."

*   *   *

They arrived back from the run sweaty, exhausted, and feeling dirty from the pollution. Jojo said nothing but just nodded upstairs, where Maya was presumably waiting for them.

They both were hungry and thirsty, but they rounded the stairs and went up. In the dojo they found Maya, wearing green fatigues, leaning against the wall, reading a book. When she saw them, she closed the book but did not put it down.

"Come here," she said.

They walked over and stood in front of her as she appraised them.

"You, Davis, have the wrong type of muscles. They are too big. You need to lose weight and get more flexible so you can be nimble yet strong." Her gaze fell to Jack. "You need to get much stronger in your legs and upper body. Build up some muscle. Slim down that midsection. So let's begin. Training schedule is that we will start at eight am, six days a week. You get lunch and only one hour per day to use your phone. We'll finish whenever I feel like it. Now, who thinks they can take me on?"

An almost imperceptible smirk came to Davis's lips. Immediately Maya kicked him in the balls, took one step and violently shoved the book she was holding into Davis's throat. She kicked one of his ribs, then kneed him in the stomach, which brought him to the ground. She fell upon him, throwing punches to his face, neck, alternating with elbow strikes everywhere. She even bit his ear.

She stood up. Davis was emotional and angry, but was not really hurt, except for his ego, Jack could tell. He knew that if the hits were full strength, Davis would be unconscious.

Maya brushed off the front of her green fatigues, then looked to Jack. "You think you can take me on with your karate, pretty kicks, and forms?"

As Jack contemplated the question, she kicked him on the side of his head. Then she kneed him in the stomach. He got the same treatment Davis did, as Maya was now on top of him punching everywhere, throwing elbow strikes and thrusting her knee repeatedly into his stomach. Then, it was over, and she was back on her feet.

She let Jack up. He smiled to himself. *Try doing that to me in a month.*
"Okay. Face each other. Fight!"

Jack took a karate stance and Davis defaulted to a boxing stance. Jack waited for a punch so he could counter with a kick. But instead, Davis faked with a punch and then drove a solid front kick forward, sending Jack back several feet.

The kick had hit his stomach but had not caused any harm. Jack drove forward, blocking Davis's punches, getting too close for Davis to kick, and started emulating Maya. Jack used his elbows and fists, then used a swipe kick to get Davis onto the ground and into a Jiujitsu leg and head lock.

Maya approached, yelling at Jack. "What are you doing! Get up! You are never fighting just one person! Never do that again!"

Jack got up. No one was injured but they were breathing hard.

"Listen, you both have some bad habits to get rid of, but at least you're not starting from zero. Krav Maga is all about training, fighting, and survival. It's using anything—in any way needed—to neutralize a threat as quickly and efficiently as possible."

Jack and Davis listened carefully, particularly after the earlier demonstration. "Over the next month, I'll take you through a series of training and exercises. Everything is simple, there are no katas or patters. You'll learn to simultaneously defend and attack with a continuous motion. Conditioning will be very important."

Every evening for the first two weeks, Jack went to bed sore, barely able to help Jojo with the kids or even carry on a conversation. But at the end of the third week, he started to feel different. His reflexes had become faster and he was getting stronger. They had done kicking and punching exercises every day, along with knife and gun techniques. He realized he should have started off learning Krav Maga instead of karate.

He put on some fatigue pants and made has way upstairs. Maya said, "Good morning. Go get the knives and let's do some drills." Davis and Jack jogged over to the weapon area and each picked up a rubber knife. In the time it had taken them to do that, five men had entered the room.

Maya looked at the men. "Kill them."

There was no hesitation by the approaching men. They divided and immediately subdued Davis and Jack.

"You should always expect that you'll be fighting more than one person," Maya said. "The situation here was not ideal so I asked some others to drop by. Starting today, your life will change."

Maya shook hands with each of the men. It was obvious to Davis and Jack that they were old friends. She looked back at them. "Everyone intermix and lie on the ground. Close your eyes. If I drop a knife on your hand, you have to kill everyone. If I don't—the others have to kill you." Maya walked around the room quietly placing three knives down.

"One, two, three. Go!"

They completed many drills like this throughout the day. Jack's favorite was being in the middle of a circle of everyone when numbers were called out and the person with that number would attack. Maya would start calling the numbers faster and faster until the person in the middle was overwhelmed.

Over the next three days, training included the five men. Jack never asked where they were from, what part of the Israeli government they worked for, or how they had gotten there.

Their presence reminded Jack and Davis of how little they knew. When the end of the month arrived, the men entered as before, but this time, Jack and Davis held their own. They didn't defeat their opponents, but they stood their ground with the skills they had learned. Bad habits gone, some new habits acquired.

"This phase of your training is over," Maya said. "I'd go into battle with you any day. But, that does not mean you don't have lots more to learn. There is little that can replace actual in-the-trench experience. You both get a pass."

"Thank you," Jack said as he shook her hand.

"You're welcome, Jack. I always knew you had potential when I saw the pictures of that guy whose eyes you gouged out. That was nice work. I heard he had two long knives."

"Yes. I remember him. Gave me over fifty stitches."

"We were all impressed with that. I hope you get the chance to visit Israel for shooting training. I understand you took out a few people with a handgun, without proper pistol training."

Jack grimaced. "That's one experience I do not fondly remember."

"We all have many of those such experiences. I know exactly how you feel." She patted his shoulder. "You did what you had to do."

CHAPTER 6

Jack punched the long kicking bag and as it swung back at him, he hit it solidly with a spinning back kick, followed by an elbow to the imagined assailant. He had increased the intensity of his workouts, which were always done to the soundtrack of loud 80s music. "Paradise City" blared from the Bluetooth Bose speaker in the corner. Months past the end of his training, he wished Davis was still around to spar.

Ari and Joshua were stopping by tonight and his time was short. After another set of sit-ups and pushups, he was done. Jack wiped his face with a small towel. Then he grabbed his iPhone and stopped the music. Time for a shower. His entire attitude had changed from the consistent workouts—his mind slowed down and he was more observant and relaxed. His nervous energy gone. He was even more patient with Jojo and the kids.

Ari and Joshua had just arrived and were chatting with Jojo when Jack came downstairs. They had been through a lot together; both were with Jack at the Control Center, and they had relied on each other in what was a frightening life or death experience. Though they did not see each other often, they were like brothers.

Hugs were exchanged. Joshua looked Jack up and down. "Jack, look at you! It's remarkable."

Jack grinned. "What happened was I got my ass kicked by a Israeli lady. My manhood was challenged. Now I'm back."

Jojo intertwined her arm with Jack's. "I do not object to the physical change. And I'll never challenge his manhood." She winked.

"I squeezed a bunch of limes earlier," Jack said. "Any objections to fresh margaritas?"

"None here. Do you have any snacks?" Ari asked.

"Jojo made some spicy chicken wings along with carrots, celery, and ranch dressing. Will that be okay?"

"You two should open a restaurant. I can't get an authentic margarita or good wings anywhere in China."

Jack said, "I'll get the margaritas. Make yourself comfortable."

Minutes later Jack came out with a tray holding a pitcher of margaritas and some glasses.

As he poured, Joshua asked, "How is President Wang?"

Technically, former President Wang, as he had indeed lost his re-election bid to Li Keqiang. "He's doing fine. He got a dog that I'm helping him train. The other day he even helped us plant watermelon outside. It was real nice. We see a lot more of him now and he enjoys spending time with the kids. How is Israel?"

Joshua lowered his voice. "Actually, Israel is really worried. President Li Keqiang has rapidly reversed many of Wang's policies. China is now buying oil from Iran and deepening that close relationship. Iran has increased its purchases of both defensive and offensive weapons from Russia, given the extra funds they now have."

Ari also looked worried. "Domestically, things are bad in China. I don't know if you've been keeping track, but China has restarted jailing people in Xinjiang. More severe crackdowns are occurring in Hong Kong, overt threats to Taiwan. Surprisingly, corruption in many areas has returned. Most disturbing is internet access to Western sites has been restricted. The purchase and use of Starlink dishes has been outlawed. They undid our override that we had done in the Control Center."

Jack was surprised to hear this. "I thought the Starlink problems were due to a technical glitch."

"No, it's due to intentional restrictions that haven't been reported yet in the Western media."

Jack topped up all three glasses again as Jojo walked in with two trays, which she placed on the table in front of everyone. Ari's eyes lit up as he reached for the chicken.

Jojo sat down next to Jack and reach for a sip of his margarita as he quickly got her up to speed.

"That doesn't sound good," she said.

"I'm pretty sure President Li doesn't like us."

"That's unfortunately true," Joshua said. "President Li has been moving in on individuals who resist his new policies. We broke the law to help China and got away with it because of broad support by the Chinese people. That's now fading."

Jack asked, "Do you think it is safe for us to stay in China?"

Joshua and Ari exchanged looks. "We are returning next week to Israel. We don't think it's safe anymore, but we could be wrong."

The worst decisions were often made by procrastination or not recognizing a threat. Jack was not taking any chances. He turned to Jojo, "To be safe I think we should spend some time in the States."

"Or Israel," Ari suggested.

"I trust your judgment, Jack," Jojo said, before draining the rest of his drink.

He was relieved she agreed with him. "Okay," he said to Ari. "I want to hire some of your Mossad friends as soon as possible. Let me know how much and where I need to wire funds. Arrange the best. We can afford it."

"I'm on it, Jack."

Joshua said, "Have you been keeping track of American politics?"

Jack couldn't help but smile. "I hear President Sutton is running for a second term. That would be great."

"People blame Smith for high inflation and slow economic growth. Funny, no one fully appreciates that it was *his* approach to China that has emboldened President Li. You just can't make this stuff up."

"I should call Sutton to say hello. We have lots to catch up on."

Ari smirked. "You say it so casually—like he's an old school friend."

Jack leaned forward re-filling everyone's glasses. He looked at his friends' faces knowing that chances were good they would not see each other for a while.

Before leaving, Ari turned to Jack. "WeChat is less secure than before. Do you have a WhatsApp account?"

Jack pulled out his phone, turned on his VPN, and downloaded the app from Apple's App Store in America. Jojo did the same and they made sure they were all connected.

Jack and Jojo walked their guests out. "It's wonderful seeing the two of you," Jack said, giving first Ari, then Joshua, a handshake and a pat on the back. "I hope you both will be safe."

"I'll text you on WhatsApp with details as soon as I get them," Ari said.

"Sounds good."

He smiled at Jojo and thanked her for the food, and then looked at Jack, a more serious expression on his face. "You stay safe, too."

Back inside, Jojo had a frown on her face as she began to clear the dishes. Jack picked up the empty vegetable tray and followed her into the kitchen. "I thought they were just coming over for drinks. Are things really that serious?" she asked.

"I'm afraid they may be. Li Keqiang is the sort of guy who would not like what we did in the Control Center. We should have things ready to go in a moment's notice."

Jojo nodded. "I'll let Sherry know. She has a passport. If she wants to come with us I'd like her to."

"Of course," Jack said.

So much for President Smith removing his security detail. Jack took out his black phone and texted Cooper, his CIA contact: *We're hiring private party for security and plan to leave China soon.*

He hadn't used this phone to text Cooper in so long that he did not expect a quick response. But before he could put the phone back in his pocked it beeped: *Good. Apologies. Resources constrained here. New administration.*

Jack couldn't help but feel let down. All that he had been though and now being left alone in the face of potential dire consequences for his family. New administrations always did things differently, thinking they were right. It was only after actions or inactions that consequences occurred. By then it was too late and inevitably they would be denied or deflected. Jack wished he could change that and make people directly responsible for their actions.

CHAPTER 7

Jack woke the next morning and saw two WhatsApp messages on his iPhone. The first was from Ari, alerting Jack that someone named Daniel Cohen would be contacting him.

The second was from Daniel Cohen: *Hello Mr. Gold. Ari referred me and informed me that you would like some assistance.*

Jack liked the concise message. He responded, *Hi Daniel. Timeline is ASAP. My wife and I plus our nanny and two children. We need to safely relocate from Beijing to United States. Logistical assistance needed including private transport.*

Where in America will you be going?

Not sure yet. Need a few hours.

Okay, I'll have a team there in two days arriving Wednesday around noon. Updated arrival time to follow.

They exchanged a few messages about Jack's location and how the relationship would work. Jack also transferred half a million dollars from his Luxemburg account. Private international travel was more expensive than he'd thought.

When he was done, Jojo was just opening her eyes. "Security will be here in two days," Jack told her.

"Good. I agree with you, Jack. Better to be safe than sorry."

"For the time being, let's not use WeChat or the phone to let anyone know. But maybe we have your dad over for dinner before we leave. Also, I have an important question: Where would you like to move to in the States?"

Jojo stretched and yawned. "Washington DC was nice, but too cold. LA is too spread out. How about near Stanford? I hear Palo Alto is a good area."

Jack agreed with everything she'd just said. "I'll see if I can find a nice place there. We can pack a few things, then have someone come by to send anything else we might want. Does that sound good?"

Jojo nodded but she looked a little skeptical. "I hope we won't be gone long. I guess I can have someone come by and pack up all my sculptures."

"Sure. Remember, we are not resource constrained. If we have to stay a long time, we'll buy something nice."

Jack went into his office and searched the internet. He navigated to Vrbo and found a contemporary house less than a mile from the center of Palo Alto. It had three bedrooms and a small pool he could tell was built just so they could rent it out for a higher price. It was $54,000 a month. He checked AirBnb and found a place a little bit further out but still in Silicon Valley. It had four bedrooms, an open floor plan and was nestled amongst the trees. It was $48,000. Jack knew he could bargain but instead just went ahead and requested a reservation for the entire month. starting in two days. He received a swift reply then placed a deposit with his US credit card.

After receiving confirmation, he forwarded the address to Daniel.

*   *   *

The following evening, they had Wang over for dinner. Jojo had prepared hotpot and put out beef, lamb, all sorts of vegetables, noodles, and rice. People could help themselves by dipping whatever they wanted into the boiling water, then into a sauce she had made.

Jack broke the news after he'd poured some beer for Wang. "Tomorrow we're leaving to spend some time in California. We're unsure how safe it is for us in Beijing."

Wang's chopsticks stopped halfway to his mouth. "What happened to the security that the American Embassy was providing?"

"They removed it prior to the election. They didn't want to offend Li Keqiang by associating with me."

Wang laughed. "That's President's Smith's logic for sure." He shook his head. "It's good then that you are leaving. Li Keqiang controls your security outside and can remove it at any time."

"What do you think will ultimately happen in China?"

Wang did not look as discouraged as Jack felt. "Five years is a long time and China can be transformed during that time. These things have a way of reverberating and Li will eventually make a mistake that galvanizes a force he did not expect. Don't lose hope, Jack. Maybe you can do something you are in the States."

"I don't know what one man can do."

Jojo and Wang exchanged glances, then looked at him grinning. He waited for them to elaborate but they did not, just carried on eating. Of course the implication was that one man—in this case, himself—had indeed done a lot, but Jack wasn't so sure he agreed with them, since he and Jojo were now in the position of fleeing the country that Jack had put his life repeatedly on the line for.

After dinner Jack watched as Mini walked out the front door with Wang. Uncharacteristically, the dog looked back at Jack to check if he was doing the right thing, if Jack really wanted him to go. Jack didn't know what to do but to nod his head. He knew Mini could see the sadness in Jack's eyes—the dog was that smart. Mini would be fine staying with Wang as he had before. But Jack, in that moment, couldn't help but feel regret.

CHAPTER 8

As he settled into bed, Jojo's arms going around him, Jack found he couldn't shake his unsettled feeling. "What's the matter?" Jojo whispered.

"It feels like we're leaving and might not be back."

"It'll be a chance for the kids to get to know America. That's not a bad thing. We need to find a house in a neighborhood with good schools. How is the Chinese food in Palo Alto?"

"The food will never compare to what we get here, but I'm sure you'll be able to buy everything you can here. In America there is an online store called Weee. You can find everything there."

Jack hugged Jojo, momentarily distracted from his own feelings, by her cuteness, and the fact that the kids' future schooling and whether there would be decent food were the things at the forefront of her mind. He wished he could shift his own focus to be more aligned with hers.

* * *

They fell asleep in each other's arms. Some hours later Jack awoke, over-heated, and moved his covers back, gently pulled away from Jojo. He had just settled back onto his pillow when he heard a click from downstairs, as if someone had just locked the door.

They never locked their door as they had so much security they never thought to do so. Jack reasoned someone was trying to get in and locked the door instead of unlocking it.

He shook Jojo awake. "Get into the kids' room and lock the door. Be quiet."

Jack put on his jeans and heard the door again. This time it was the door unlocking. He peered downstairs and saw four people entering.

All seemed to be carrying knives. Jack had done this drill before. *Just another drill*, he told himself.

He turned on the downstairs light and started to walk down the stairs. As he descended, he took stock of what he could use to defend and incapacitate the intruders. "Hi," he said. "How can I help you?"

Two of the men were well-muscled. The other two were large but did not walk as though they were trained. None of them said anything.

"Can I get you some tea? Or are you here to steal things? I can tell you where we keep our money and valuables."

They didn't smile. They were not there to rob the place. As Jack came down the last stair, he was feet away from one of the well-trained ones. The man raised his knife. "We'll help ourselves to that stuff later."

He came forward as Jack stepped toward him, grabbing the man's wrist and using his other hand on the assailant's elbow for leverage. He thrust the knife into his neck. *One down*, Jack thought.

The others were momentarily shocked to see one of their men go down so fast. The second well-muscled man stepped forward, glancing down at blood pooling on the floor. Jack's iPad was right there, within reach on the sofa. In one smooth motion he leaned down and picked it up. He faced the three men and for a moment, no one moved.

Two of them came at the same time. Simultaneously, Jack kicked one in the groin and blocked the other's knife with a swift swing of his iPad. The third man approached, and Jack did a round house kick to his head. The man crashed into their table headfirst. He was unconscious for sure.

One of the men backed up. The one whose hand had gotten swiped by Jack's iPad approached again, this time more cautiously.

Jack lunged at him, blocking the knife with his arm before he shoved the iPad viciously into the man's throat. The last man standing seemed to reverse course and ran toward the door.

His hand had reached the doorknob when Jack got him, kneeing him in the back and then wrapping his arms around his neck, putting the man into a headlock. Finally, he passed out and Jack let him fall to the floor. He dropped his knee hard on the man's neck and instantly heard it snap. He was dead.

Jack circulated the room, checking that each man was dead. Any man who entered his house to kill him deserved to die. *Jack's house rules*, he thought, his heart rate finally starting to slow. He took his iPhone out of his pocket and took a picture of the scene from several different angles.

After, he went upstairs and knocked on the kids' bedroom door. "It's me," he said softly. "Everything is okay."

He waited a moment and then the door opened slowly. "I heard you talking to some people," Jojo said. "What happened?" Her eyes widened. "Is that blood? Are you hurt?"

"I'm not, no. Maya would be proud. But there are four men down there who wanted to kill me. Us. Let me clean up a bit before you come out. I'll be back in a few minutes."

He went back downstairs, wondering what he should do. If he put the bodies out back, they could be seen. The kitchen had a big pantry with a door. Not ideal but it'd have to do.

He dragged each body into the pantry. The last two were the biggest and dragging them was painful. Sweat poured off of him. It was harder to clean up the mess than it had been to create it. Finally done, he took a few more photos of the bodies and then he went back upstairs.

"I put the bodies in the pantry, but downstairs is pretty messed up. We're leaving in a few hours so I think we can manage."

"Bodies," Jojo repeated. "Bodies. Okay. Go get washed up. I'll bring the kids to sleep with us for the rest of the night. If it's even safe to still be here?"

"It is now," Jack said.

He went into their room and got his phone to send a text to Daniel: *Four attackers dead. Stored in kitchen pantry.*

In your house?

Yes.

We'll take care of that. ETA is 12 noon. Don't leave. Gulfstream ready. You and Jojo bring both of your US passports.

Jack put the phone down, took off his pants, and got into the shower. He had no injuries, thankfully. His adrenaline was still pumping. Many times during his training he'd felt it, but not to this magnitude.

Since he couldn't sleep, he packed his suitcase and made sure to place two bottles of Maotai in it. Then, he put another one in his backpack along with his still perfect iPad and MacBook Pro.

* * *

At noon there was a knock at the door. Jack opened it to find four men and one woman—Maya—standing on the other side. "Hi Jack," one of the men said. He was a little shorter than Jack but well-muscled and in excellent shape. "I'm Daniel, it's nice to meet you. Sorry we were late for the action."

Jojo came and stood next to Jack. "Hi Maya," she said. "It's great to see you again."

Maya smiled. "Nice to see you too. I'm glad everything is okay." She nodded to Daniel. "They approached me because of my recent stint here."

"First things first," Daniel said, "Show us where you stored things."

Jack led them into the kitchen and opened the door to the pantry. "I didn't know where to store them and wanted them out of view of the children and if anyone came by."

"Of course. You did exactly the right thing. Someone will take care of them later; you won't be linked. That way you'll avoid any potential fallout, even though you were protecting yourself. They could stop you from leaving the country to first get to the bottom of things."

Jack was relieved to hear that; he hadn't thought something like that might occur. But Daniel was right.

It was time to go.

* * *

Only when the plane started to taxi to take off did Jack feel he could try to begin the process of relaxing. Their security team was on the plane; Maya sat next to Jojo. Jack was grateful that she was with them. Finally, the plane took off and Jack let out a breath.

Daniel took a seat next to him. "Killing four people and storing them is not something easy to handle. Are you okay?"

"No. I'm not." Jack reached into his backpack and took out the Maotai. He took two glasses from the side table next to him and poured a glass for himself and one for Jojo.

"You brought some Maotai? You are crazy," Jojo said as she put the glass to her lips to have a sip.

Jack downed his and then looked at Daniel. "Now I'm okay. In fact I'm perfect."

"That's funny. What are you drinking?"

"Maotai."

"Isn't that stuff expensive?"

"When I helped the Chinese government, my payment was basically all in Maotai."

Daniel nodded. "Yeah, I read about all the stuff you've done in China. Pretty impressive. Hope it doesn't all get undone by Smith and that new Chinese president."

"Yeah. Me too."

"You did good in there," Maya said. "You protected your family against paid killers. You did nothing wrong and they tried to take you out just because you had a voice and could have said something against the government. That's tyranny. You single-handedly defeated it. What you did was honorable."

"It was just like another exercise."

"No Jack, it was real. What's important is that there was zero ambiguity. You should have some sense of satisfaction. You annihilated the enemy. Be proud."

Jack appreciated her words. He'd been angry at first that they had entered his home, then he felt some guilt at the loss of life that he was responsible for. What she was saying made sense. It helped him understand from a logical basis, what had happened and how this might impact his emotions. Hearing this from someone like Maya helped. Their deaths were not his fault—it was a result of their actions.

CHAPTER 9

The plane landed at San Francisco International Airport and taxied to a side area so an immigration official could board the plane and check everyone's passport. After such a long flight, and with little kids in tow, Jack was grateful for this convenience.

Two SUVs waited for them outside, instead of the usual three that Jack had grown accustomed to. Neither Jack nor Jojo had governmental protection anymore. But Jack felt safe being in the Bay Area. He felt relieved to be back on American soil. Daniel and the others immediately put on sunglasses as they encircled them and scanned the perimeter. Jack thought how much cooler they looked than both the Chinese and the FBI.

The drive took about thirty minutes, with the SUVs keeping their speed slightly above that of the other traffic. As they pulled into the driveway of their place Daniel said, "Give use fifteen minutes to do a final scan. We had it checked earlier and all should be fine."

They remained in the car with two of the agents and looked out the window at their new place. There were several large trees out front that provided decent shade. In the side yard, Jack got a glimpse of the swimming pool and outdoor seating area. But the place looked markedly different from the photos, which annoyed Jack. He had the feeling it would be the same inside.

"It's different from the photos."

Jojo shrugged. "It doesn't matter. As long as we're together and safe, any place is fine."

Jack put a hand on Jojo's knee and gave it a squeeze. She was holding up Jack Jr. so he could see his new home. Kai had fallen asleep again in her car seat, but Jack knew when she woke up, she'd be excited about their new temporary home, too.

Daniel motioned for them to come in. Jojo passed the baby to Jack so she could rouse Kai. Everyone exited the SUV and walked through the warm Palo Alto air into the home. They went from one room to the next, noticing the varying colors. One room was brown, another green, and still yet one purple. Some of the windows were square, some were arched. Every room had a different type of ceiling. Some were inlaid, some had wooden beams, others just plain. The kitchen was the one place where Jojo stopped and looked visibly upset. "Electric stove—why?"

Jack went and stood next to her. "Look at the vent system above the stove. It vents back into the room, not to outside."

Jojo frowned. "That's not possible."

"Look closely. The air goes in here and comes out above here." Jack pointed.

Chinese needed high heat to cook with a wok. The vents in homes always vented directly to outside. Otherwise, the kitchen would fill with smoke.

"It might be okay for the time being" Jojo said, "but not forever."

Daniel approached. "We've taken a look around the perimeter and are not excited about this place. There are a few neighboring homes that have line of sight into your rooms. Also, there are no fences or walls, which hinders us deploying electronics to monitor if anyone enters."

"We agree," Jack said. "Is thirty days okay while we find another place?"

"That shouldn't be a problem."

*   *   *

They had nothing. Only one suitcase each. Although the house was furnished, it still looked empty when they unpacked. Jack showed Jojo the Weee app and she went wild ordering food while Sherry looked after the kids. Jack logged onto Whole Foods and ordered everything he needed including coffee, steaks, salsa, tortillas, milk, beer, cereal, and ice cream.

While they waited for the urgent deliveries, Jack pulled up the MLS to see if there were any nice homes for sale in San Jose. He found many homes in the five-to-ten-million-dollar range, but none were modern with the more open style that he and Jojo preferred. He had an unlimited budged yet couldn't find a single home in the area.

Jojo walked by and looked over his shoulder. "Hold on—that one has a nice backyard. What's wrong with it?"

"It was built before you were born. It has great views but needs lots of work. I'm not in the mood for a renovation project."

"But look at that garden. We can plant out there."

"I'll keep the listing for later. There is nothing else on the market."

It was later after they'd put the kids to bed that Daniel knocked and came in. "I just thought you would want to know that Sutton has won the election. The precincts have closed. It's official."

With everything that had happened recently, the election hadn't even been on Jack's radar. But this was great news. He grinned and wrapped Jojo in a hug. "Yes! So there is hope for the world. This calls for a little celebration!"

He was pouring three shots of Maotai when Maya walked in. He grabbed a fourth glass and poured some for her, too. "This is a very special occasion for America, China, and Israel. You must drink."

Everyone raised their glasses. "To Sutton and freedom." No sooner had Jack put the glass to his lips when his black phone started to ring. He had left it on the counter with his iPhone, so he put his glass down and cautiously answered, walking into the other room. "Hello. This is Jack."

"Hi Jack," came the familiar voice. "This is Cooper. It's been a long time. We've missed you greatly. May I transfer the call to President Sutton?"

"Sure, Cooper. Good to hear your voice."

"Same here. Please hold on."

There was a moment's pause and then Sutton's voice came through.

"Hello, Jack. How are you?"

"Happy to have escaped China. We're now in Palo Alto. Congratulations, Mr. President."

"What happened in China?"

"Four guys broke into our home and tried to kill me. I had no security detail. The embassy had removed it."

Silence on the other end of the line. "What happened?" Sutton finally asked.

"I killed all four and put them in the pantry."

Jack could almost see Sutton's smile.

"I hired a private group of Israeli security people, so everything is fine now."

"I want you and your family to fly to Mar-a-Lago and stay with us for a while. The inauguration is in a couple of weeks, but we have lots of planning to do. Jack, this is important. It's about China."

"Sir, I'd love to do that. We now have two kids."

"I know, Jack. Plenty for them to do here. They'll love it. Talk to Jojo. We'll take care of everything once you're here. It'll be fun. We have more than ample room for you. We own the entire area, so you'll get whatever you need."

Spoken like the real estate magnate Sutton was.

"Okay. I'll talk to Jojo, then text Cooper back."

"Thanks, Jack. It's great to hear you voice. We look forward to seeing you soon."

Jack hung up the phone and walked back to the others, grabbing his glass of Maotai he hadn't yet had. He knocked it back in one sip and put the glass down. Maya and Daniel stared at him.

"How did you just do that?" Maya asked. "You drank it like water."

"It doesn't affect him like it does everyone else," Jojo said.

Jack poured himself some more and this time sipped it, enjoying the flavor and the warm feeling that was spreading throughout his body.

Jojo asked, "Who was on the phone?"

"It was President Sutton. He wants us to fly to Mar-a-Lago to see them. He said it's important and in regard to China. He has more than enough room for us. What do you think?"

Jack could see that she was tired of traveling. "What do *you* think?" she asked.

"We have to go find out what Sutton is thinking. We don't want to get entangled like before, but we should help if we can. China is messed up. He's promised to take care of everything when we get there. He knows we have two children."

"Okay, Jack. But we stay here for a few days. I want to visit Stanford. And you have been telling me about Blonde's Pizza right near UC Berkeley. We are not leaving until we visit both those places."

Jack said, "Fair enough. I can't give up on China if there is something we can do. You're right though. The president will just have to wait."

"You are more dedicated to helping China than I am." Jojo poured Jack more Maotai which he threw back in one gulp.

*   *   *

They visited UC Berkeley and grabbed slices of pizza which they took onto the campus to eat. Jack explained the history of Sproul Plaza and the protests during the free speech movement that occurred in the 1960s. Jojo was not particularly interested. Instead, she gazed at the blooming cherry blossoms and magnolia trees.

As they pushed Jack Jr. in his stroller, with Kai slowly tagging along, they made their way past the Life Sciences building. There were people chatting on the large grassy area and three separate groups of people were playing ultimate freebie. Jojo watched them for a moment. "You'd never see that at Tsingtao University. People have to study, but mostly get off campus to eat and visit with friends."

They walked over to the clock tower and took the elevator up. You could see the rolling hills and the bay in the distant. Jack lifted Kai so that she could see the view.

"There's so much diversity here," Jojo said. "I saw lots of Asians as we walked over. But I really can't imagine China ever having such a variety of people."

They passed Doe Library and made their way to the architecture building, Wurster Hall. Jack said, "One night after a few beers my buddy, Jeff Hern, got to the roof and dangled a shoe held by fishing line. It freaked people out because it looked like the shoe was floating in midair."

Jojo smiled. "I'd expect something juvenile like that from you. People in America might find that funny, but not in China."

*   *   *

That night Jack called Jennifer Chun. She had been one America's representatives during the trade negotiations Jack had previously held in DC and Beijing. She had been urging him to visit the Hoover Institution, where she was a fellow. The public policy think tank was located at Stanford University and amassed some of the leading thinkers in promoting economic prosperity.

"Hi, Jennifer."

"Oh my. Hi Jack. How are you?"

"I'm good. I'm in Palo Alto with my family and we're going to have a picnic tomorrow at Stanford. You going to be around? It'd be great to see you."

"Jack, that's great news. Why didn't you give me more notice! Listen, there are a few at the Hoover Institution who would love to meet you and discuss some things, including our director, Condi Stevenson. Can I arrange something?"

"I'm afraid our time is pretty short. My wife wanted to see the campus. We leave the day after tomorrow."

"Jack, behind the director's office is one of the most beautiful private gardens. And the flowers are blooming right now. Maybe we can meet there briefly? What time were you thinking about visiting?"

"We thought we'd wait until it cooled down a bit. Around four, I guess."

"That's perfect. I'll text you a map. Come there and we can have afternoon tea outside."

"Okay, Jennifer. It'll be great to see you."

*   *   *

It was a glorious day and the campus was resplendent with its architecture and large grass areas. Jojo pushed one stroller and Jack carried Kai. They parked the two SUVs at the entrance to the garden and Jack saw one of his men talking to the local parking police.

The four guards flanked them as they moved toward the entrance where Jennifer was waiting for them behind an iron gate. She opened it as they got closer. "Hi Jack."

"Jennifer, I'd like to introduce you to Jojo, my wife. And this is Jack Jr. and Kai."

Greetings were exchanged as they passed through the gate and into the garden. The space had buildings making up three of its borders, but they were not tall, only two stories, and plenty of sunshine poured in, bathing the roses bushes and flowering trees in light.

"It's lovely here, Jennifer," Jojo said.

"Come on in. We arranged for some tea and small sandwiches."

They followed her to a nearby table elegantly set with real teacups and silverware.

"I've arranged for two of our graduate students to join," Jennifer said as everyone took a seat. "They can give you a tour of the campus and Jojo, they are familiar with all the art. So take advantage of them."

Jack was impressed with the forethought. One of the students came up to Jack and Kai, a smile on her face. She held her arms out. "You don't mind do you? I love kids."

"Of course not," Jack said. He looked at Kai. "Can I put you down?"

She nodded and shyly smiled at the student who took her hand and led her to one of the rose bushes. "Aren't they pretty?" Jack heard her ask his daughter.

Jojo poured some tea for Jack, and then some for herself. "Please, help yourselves to the scones too," Jennifer said.

Jojo set her teacup down and gazed at the setup. "This is so elegant."

To Jojo, this was art. Beautiful china and tea in a lovely garden was just as impressive as a statue. It was a painting come to life.

"Jojo, do you mind if I borrow Jack? The director of the Hoover Institution is upstairs and I thought it might be good to introduce them."

Jojo grinned. "Take him. I don't need him."

Jack stood up and followed Jennifer, two of his security detail in tow. Jennifer looked at them quizzically and then to Jack.

"Just a precaution," Jack said. "In case you try to mug me."

They went up one flight of stairs where they were greeted by a secretary seated at a desk. "She is expecting you," she said to Jennifer. "Walk right in."

The first thing Jack saw in the room was a dark wooden desk and the built-in bookshelves overflowing with books. On either side of the shelves were windows letting in an abundance of light. Seated at the desk was a woman with dark-rimmed glasses.

"Jack," Jennifer said, "may I introduce Condi Stevenson, the director of The Hoover Institution."

Condi stood, removing her glasses and placing them on the desk. She held her hand out.

"It's a pleasure to meet you," Jack said as they shook.

"You as well," Condi said, glancing around Jack to the two security guards. "Is it possible that they stay outside?"

"No. It's not. We had an incident in China." The men had moved into the office and were scanning outside the windows.

"Well, please have a seat." Condi gestured to the other side of the room, where there was a sofa and several chairs. "Jack, many of us have been following you and what has transpired over the past several years. Jennifer shared what occurred during the trade agreement negotiations. Fascinating to say the least. What a remarkable journey you have had! The approach you took to the trade agreement has been written up for others as a case study. What are your plans going forward?" She sat on one of the chairs opposite the couch and leaned forward, her gaze intense upon him.

"Actually, I'm not sure," Jack said, wishing he had a better answer. "We're off to Florida tomorrow. That's as far ahead as my planning goes these days."

"The Hoover Institution is where some of the greatest minds come together to share their ideas, research, and so forth. We'd love to have you guest lecture. I could even see you here more permanently."

Before Jack could respond, the door opened and an older man with thinning gray hair and wire-rimmed glasses walked in. Condi smiled.

"Mr. Beckman, I'd like to introduce you to Jack Gold." She turned to Jack. "Dick Beckman is the Hoover Institution head of China. We thought it'd be good to introduce the two of you."

Jack stood up and shook the man's hand, vaguely recalling his name but not anything specific that Beckman had written.

Beckman took a seat on one of the vacant chairs.

"What do you think of China?" Jack asked, intentionally giving him an open-ended question.

Beckman glanced at Condi. "Li Keqiang believes in Common Prosperity. It's necessary to allow the disorderly expansion of capital with a focus on big platform companies, like Didi and Alibaba. The expansion of these platform companies is having a bigger impact on the economy and society compared to the Party.

"A key point is how they treat workers because this relates to the power in society. This is a major factor in balancing the imbalances between urban and rural, inland and coastal regions, ownership and workers. Common Prosperity was achieved after ten years to eliminate extreme prosperity. Up until recently, these platform companies have not been subject to leadership of the party. The National People's Congress of China is most focused on stability. But, there are tensions in society. How to deal with gig workers, about 200 million workers and they do not have new jobs. How to regulate the platforms?"

Jack nodded, impressed with the way Beckman spoke.

"Li Keqiang is pushing his philosophy as the core and guiding doctrine," Beckman continued. "You need Common Prosperity and disorderly expansion of capital is necessary for the effective allocation of resources. They acknowledge entrepreneurs are also needed to continue rejuvenation of the economy by mid-century. China wants to open up. It wants companies to be global in the world, but it wants to control data. A must. Given a choice between market success or security they will always opt for security. Security for party to retain its leadership is number one."

Jack was still impressed by what Beckman said. But if anything at all, it merely described the current situation with zero insight as to what *should* be done.

"Thank you for sharing that," Jack said. "I have a question. Should the United States do anything about the fentanyl flowing into America? Or about Xinjiang Uyghurs, or what's going on now in Hong Kong?"

Beckman pursed his lips. Jack was not surprised that the man could describe the situation but did not seem to have any original, insightful ideas.

"Absolutely. America should work closely with China to form an agreement to address those and other issues."

Jack then knew what type of person Beckman was. If Beckman were allowed to continue to speak, he would no doubt use any number of empty phrases. *We need to get tough. We need to send a message. We need to sanction. We need some measure of reciprocity.*

Jack asked, "Can you name a single agreement that China has signed and adhered to, other than one from the Wang Yang administration?"

Beckman furrowed his brow but said nothing. Jack glanced at Condi and Jennifer who both just shook their heads.

"China did not live up to its promises in the most recently signed trade agreement," Jack said. "They violated their WTO promises. They clearly violated the 1984 Sino-British Joint Declaration. Trying to do another agreement with Li Keqiang would satisfy the definition of insanity."

"Before the two of you get too involved in this," Condi said quickly, "there were a few other things I wanted to discuss with Jack. Beckman, can you please give us some time?"

If Beckman was surprised at his sudden dismissal, he did not let it show as he stood. Jack stood also to shake the man's hand. "It was a pleasure meeting you."

After the door closed Condi looked to Jack, and it seemed she was trying to suppress a smile. "I've been waiting for someone to do that. To shut Beckman down. You belong at the Hoover Institution, Jack. Intellectually, I think you'll find it fascinating and you'll be able to use it as a consulting platform to advise companies and countries around the world. You'll have a real impact and receive very good renumeration."

Jack appreciated the sentiment though he wasn't going to be able to take her up on the offer right now. "Thanks, Director Condi. But right now, my life is unsettled. I hope you'll let me think about it?"

She handed Jack her card. "Jack it was a pleasure to meet you. Give me a call any time when you're ready to discuss this further."

With that, they exited the well-lit office and went downstairs. Like Beckman, Jack had met others who were adept at detailing problems. He'd also met those who were great at concisely breaking down what had already been done wrong and why. What Jack had a hard time finding were people who had good solutions to problems. He would try to develop a good answer to the question he posed to Beckman. "Should America do anything about the fentanyl flowing into America, Xinjiang Uyghurs, or what's going on now in Hong Kong?" There was lots more Jack knew that could be added to that question, but this was certainly enough to start.

CHAPTER 10

They landed at Palm Beach International Airport. Jack had never seen so many palm trees in an airport before. They swiftly exited the terminal into one of the two SUVs. There were thick clouds in the sky and a light rain falling, which Jack guessed that was typical April weather for this tropical climate.

Driving down South Ocean Boulevard they saw all the beautiful homes. Jack could see Mar-a-Lago in the distance. Just then the car turned into a residence on the other side of the street, just a block away.

"This must be where Sutton and Cam live," Jojo said. "The ocean is just on the other side. It's beautiful."

"Looks like it. I see two Secret Service guys over there," Jack said.

As the car came to a stop, the security walked over. Daniel rolled down his window and the smartly dressed man stuck his head in. "Hello Mr. and Mrs. Gold," he said when he saw them. "Please come in."

Jack got out, stretched and waited for Jojo, who was talking with the nanny as she got the kids out of their car seats. "Let's go in and say hello and then I'll come help Sherry with the kids," Jojo said.

Jack took her hand as they went inside. Sutton and Cam greeted them with big smiles. To their right were floor-to-ceiling windows, giving an incredible oceanfront view.

"Hello Jack, hi Jojo!" Sutton said. "Welcome!"

Jojo hugged Cam and Jack shook Sutton's hand. "Mr. President, again."

Sutton laughed. "Yes. They double-checked and it's confirmed. Again."

He could hear Jojo and Cam, speaking rapidly in French as they walked back outside to get the kids.

"This is a nice place you have here," Jack said, his gaze going back to the ocean-facing windows. "Truly extraordinary view. I can barely see the waves crash, the house is so close to the water."

"Jack, we lived here for about seven years until we built another house down the beach that was bigger. This is where you will be staying."

"Mr. President, how thoughtful of you. This will do just fine," Jack said. He loved the downstairs, with its open floor plan and the eat-in kitchen. It was the exact house he had been trying to find online just the other day.

Jojo and Cam came back in, Jack Jr. in Cam's arms, Kai pulling Jojo by the hand. "Sutton just told me we're staying here," Jack said to Jojo in Mandarin.

Her eyes lit up. "The view here must change day to day, and hour to hour. Jack, I may need to get some painting materials."

"Paint away!" Sutton said. "Cam and I would love to see what you come up with. Now, Jack, I know you brought your own security, but I want you to know that this place is very safe. All the guards you saw are Secret Service and the United States takes guarding the ex- and future presidents very seriously."

"That's reassuring to know."

"We want to let you get settled for the next day or two. It takes some time to slow down to the pace of Mar-a-Lago. The refrigerator is stocked with things we thought you might need. You'll figure out how to take care of the rest. Maybe we meet for a chat and dinner—not tomorrow night but the night after. In the meantime, we'll provide assistance to your security detail and whatever else they need. Oh, and feel free to walk across the street to the club to swim or eat. Does that sound good?"

"Yes, it does Mr. President."

After Cam and Sutton departed, Jack and Jojo each took one kid and eagerly headed upstairs to see the rooms. Two were facing the ocean, the other the back courtyard. They entered the larger room and Jack grabbed Jojo's hand. "Baby, I think this is better than Palo Alto, except the sound of the waves might keep us awake."

"I'll take that problem any day," Jojo said, giving his hand a squeeze.

*　*　*

Down on the beach with his family the next day, Jack marveled at the fact that less than a week ago, he had killed four men and then left their home in Beijing, fearing for their safety. Now, he held Kai's hand as the waves washed up over their ankles and the sun sparkled off the surface of the water like crystals. Jojo held Jack Jr. and dipped his toes in the frothy water each time a wave broke. Jack looked at her fondly, appreciating her resolve in dealing with this unexpected upheaval in their lives. Now that they were here, he could see that she was relaxed and had a renewed energy about her.

When they returned, Daniel, who had been shadowing them while they were at the beach, asked Jack if he could have a word.

"I'll be right there," Jack said to Jojo. He turned to Daniel. "What's up?"

"There are a few things I need to share with you. I'm not from an external contractor. We were assigned from Mossad. Mossad is responsible for counter-terrorism activity and covert ops; also intelligence gathering. Our prime minister thought you deserved the best, given what you have done for Israel, and because of the nature of the threat against you. My point is that we are still on active duty with Mossad. I hope you don't mind our lack of transparency. It's really part of our DNA and I hope we can maintain it."

"That's not a problem. I've seen you working to protect me and my family. I'm honored to have you with us."

"There is something else you should know. I can't go into any of our methods, but we have proof that Li Keqiang personally ordered your assassination. The order did not include your family—unless necessary."

Hearing this tore the lid off the desire for vengeance that Jack had been trying to keep clamped on. But now Daniel had said a specific name. The orders did indeed include his family—if necessary.

"I can only imagine what you are feeling, Mr. Gold," Daniel said. "Time has a way of working these things out. I know that from personal experience. Any person who tries to assassinate an Israeli citizen, and American diplomat, will receive retribution. This is our responsibility and specialty, not yours."

"Is there anything else you've learned that you think I might want to know?"

"You are not a target while in America. Wang Yang is fine, so long as he doesn't try to speak out. Otherwise, China's reversion toward a more intense communist state proceeds at a fast pace. They're buying more oil from Iran and supporting the country through other means. Plans to invade Taiwan are being developed."

"Is there a timeline?"

"Invading Taiwan won't be as easy as people think. It's about 100 miles from China. It'd be more like invading Normandy. Six to nine months at a minimum is our guess, though they will get more aggressive beforehand."

"Can I share this information? With Sutton?"

"Please only share with your wife. Israel's prime minister will inform him on their call tomorrow night."

"I appreciate hearing it from you and hope you will let me know if any other important information comes up."

CHAPTER 11

Jack looked at his reflection in the mirror. He was wearing the one suit that he had brought for their evening with Sutton and Cam. The softness and extra weight that he had lamented only a few months ago was gone. Surprisingly, Jojo was still trying to figure out what to wear.

"Do you know where we're going?" she called to Jack from the bathroom.

"We are meeting them across the street at Mar-a-Lago. Wear something on the formal side."

"All my formal dresses are in Beijing. I'll figure something out."

Jack leaned down and picked up one of the two bottles of Maotai remaining in his suitcase. He wasn't sure if the president and Cam would appreciate the Maotai, but it would be bad form to go empty-handed.

Jojo came out of the bathroom. "How is this?"

She wore her form-fitting yellow dress and her hair up in a bun. For jewelry she had on big matching yellow earrings.

"You look perfect!" he exclaimed.

They said goodnight to the kids and Sherry and then headed out. "We're going to a Jean-Georges restaurant," Jack said as they crossed the street. "He's a two-Michelin-star chef. We'll see if it's any good."

With Daniel and Maya trailing them, they crossed the street and walked over to the club, passing by Secret Service agents as they entered through the grand columns underneath high ceilings to the back of the room, where President Sutton and Cam were waiting.

They both rose as Jack and Jojo approached; Cam hugged Jojo, and Jack shook Sutton's hand. Jack waited to be told where to sit at the round table. Long ago he had learned people like the president liked to control such things. Always for a reason.

"Jack, sit here so Cam and Jojo can hold hands," President Sutton said, pulling a chair out for Jack.

"We thought you might enjoy this," Jack said, holding out the bottle of Maotai.

"Thank you," Sutton said, taking the bottle.

"There is a story to that bottle, Mr. President," Jojo said. "When Jack and I broke up, my dad gave him some of that Maotai. The last bottle sold at auction for about $250,000. My dad was the only one who had any left. When Jack helped with the planning project, he wisely took Maotai as payment."

The president looked at the bottle more carefully. "Jack, I thought I would never say this, but this is the most expensive bottle in the restaurant. We should give a glass to chef Jean-Georges. He appreciates this sort of thing."

The president motioned for the waiter to bring some whiskey glasses for the Maotai. Jojo said, "Mr. President, teacups might be more suitable."

"Yes. I remember now being in Beijing years ago when we had some. The stuff tasted like jet fuel, but it was excellent."

Jack said, "Henry Kissinger once said, 'I think if we drink enough Maotai we can solve anything.' I agree with him. Wang Yang said I would never run out of Maotai. Now I'm getting worried."

"Let's have a toast." The president lifted his teacup. "To you and your family being safe."

Jack downed his Maotai in one sip. President Sutton and Cam tried a more modest sip and both ended up coughing. Jojo said, "Usually much smaller glasses are used and even then, only a small sip is taken."

Just then, chef Jean-Georges walked up to the table, wiping his hands on his apron. The president poured the chef a portion into a teacup. "Here Jean-Georges, try this."

Jean-Georges knocked his back, not a single cough. "Magnificent," he said with a strong French accent. "Where did you get that?"

"This man right here," Sutton said, patting Jack on the shoulder.

Jean-Georges turned to Jack, but Jack let Jojo, in perfect French, explain the bottle's origins. While she did so, Jack poured the man another portion of Maotai, knowing it was best to give something nice to the person cooking your dinner. Also, it had been a long time since he had met another who enjoyed Maotai like he did.

Jean-Georges said, "I was going to ask what you want for dinner, but I think you'll be happy with what I come up with tonight." He raised his glass. Jack joined him and then Jean-Georges returned to the kitchen.

The president made another attempt to drink the Maotai and was only partially successful. "Jojo and Jack," he said when he'd finished coughing, "I was going to wait until after dinner to ask you something, but now that we're drinking, I should probably ask sooner since I'm unsure how clear our heads will be. How clear *my* head will be, anyway."

Despite his two shots of Maotai, Jack felt perfectly clear-headed. "What were you going to ask, Mr. President?"

"Jack, this is my second term coming up. I know what I'm doing much better than I did before. We'll hit the ground running and have a faster and bigger impact. Foremost on my agenda are international issues. Jack, I want you serving in my administration. I want you to be secretary of state."

That was not at all what Jack had expected him to say, but he tried to keep a neutral expression. "What does that mean?" he heard Jojo whisper to Cam, who whispered back in her ear. Jojo's eyes widened as Cam spoke.

Jack cleared his throat. "Mr. President, while I may know some about Asia, my grasp of European issues is subpar."

"Jack," Sutton said, looking undeterred, "you're one of the few who actively tries to acknowledge his weaknesses. Ironically, every European country hates Americans who think they know Europe."

"Mr. President, how sure of this are you?"

"Very."

"My views on China have evolved and are rather non-conventional and may end up being extreme. Will I have the freedom and latitude to pursue them?"

"That is the exact question I wanted to hear from you. Jack—yes you will. I give you my word."

A thought came to Jack. "What happened to the artificial intelligence when you left office? Was it left behind?"

"No, it wasn't. That was technology provided by an outside vendor. We now have it."

"What are the chances of my success if I become secretary of state and pursue things as I see fit regarding China?"

"I wish I could tell you that, but I simply don't know. I *will* say that I cannot recall a secretary of state's life ever being at risk. Jack, even without the AI, I'd pick you. There is no one else alive who knows China and America better than you. Plus, many of the European issues we'll be dealing with will be regarding China." Sutton gave him an imploring look. "Jack, will you join my team?"

Secretary of state. Never did Jack envision such a role being offered to him. *The chance of a lifetime.* He could just hear his dad saying that exact phrase right now. "Can Jojo and I excuse ourselves for a minute?"

"Sure. Take your time."

"Thank you. Just give us a moment." Jack stood and took Jojo's hand as they walked out of the restaurant toward the pool area.

"What do you think, Jojo? This would require a move to Washington DC and I'd be busy, but not in danger."

"My Jack being Secretary of State of the United States of America and an advocate for China. My dad would love it. If success for China is what we want, then you are the best person again to benefit the Chinese people."

In Chinese there was no clear word for *yes* or *no.* So when Jojo spoke in English, she almost never used these words. Sometimes it frustrated Jack, but not in this instance—he knew the answer was *yes.*

They returned to their table and Jack took his seat, after holding Jojo's for her to sit down. He looked at Sutton. "I'm in."

Sutton clapped his hands together once and nodded briskly, the grin on his face expanding. "Excellent news! This calls for another toast." Jojo reached for the bottle and poured everyone more Maotai.

Sutton raised his glass. "America is the leader of the world and as such, must be the leader of peace. Jack, soon to be Mr. Secretary, together we can live up to this imperative." Jack downed his third shot and now his face was feeling a little flushed. He didn't quite feel giddy but there was certainly an upbeat atmosphere in the air now that he had agreed to Sutton's offer.

Which made the meal all the more delightful. There was honey encrusted wagyu steak and tangy fresh crab, with eggs, others with tasty truffle. Jack could see Jojo was enjoying all the various flavors. Usually, she did not care for most American food but this was global cuisine made by a Frenchman with intentionally subtle flavors.

When the meal was complete, everyone sat around the table pleasantly satiated. "Here Jack, you better take the rest of the Maotai with you. I'm certain that Jean-Georges will try to track it down and drink the remainder of it. It was a remarkable meal and a pleasure to see the both of you. The transition team will be in touch with you on next steps. We still have a few weeks before the swearing in, but just because I'm not in office doesn't mean we cannot get started with planning. Think about China and what you want to do. Let's see you in a few days for dinner again someplace."

Jack took the Maotai bottle and then shook Sutton's hand firmly. "That sounds great. Thank you for dinner tonight."

As they were leaving Jean-Georges came out from the kitchen and intercepted them.

"I saw that bottle of Maotai online," he said. "Thank you for sharing it with me. Truly extraordinary."

Jojo said something to him in French. When she was done, Jack shook his hand and thanked him for the meal. "We're staying across the street and hope to see you again."

"Yes. Yes. Please come visit again. I will make you something special!"

"Jack, I think he found out how much that Maotai costs," Jojo said after Jean-Georges left. "Did you forget we have a few cases in Dali? Maybe we should try and have them shipped out."

Jack kissed her. "That's a great idea! I bet Secretary Bo can help us with that."

"You have a few *cases*?" Sutton asked. "Each case is worth $1.5 million—way more than my entire wine collection!"

"That's how Jack got paid," Jojo told him.

Sutton pointed at her. "Ah yes, you mentioned that!"

"It's true," Jack said. "I didn't report it to the IRS. I hope you'll keep our secret safe."

"No worries, Jack. Maybe I should let you know the US government is not as generous when paying salaries."

"I'm not terribly worried about that, sir."

"Well, please feel free to take Jean-Georges up on his offer. Anytime you use the club the expenses will be paid under transition costs or by donors."

"That's very generous, Mr. President. Thank you."

As they walked back across the street, Jack saw Daniel and remembered the information about Li Keqiang. Mossad had told Jack that Li ordered him killed, but Jack did not share this news with the president. He could have told him, but it would have been impolite to the president of Israel, who was talking with Sutton tomorrow night.

Later, in bed, Jojo said, "*Monsieur le secretaire*. I like the way that sounds better than Mr. Secretary."

"You can call me whatever you want," Jack said, hugging her tight, listening to the waves coming in from the open window.

As Jack sometimes did, he instructed himself to think while he was asleep. To address the China question. He repeated what he asked Beckman just a few days ago: *Should the United States do anything about Taiwan, the fentanyl flowing into America, Xinjiang Uyghurs, or what's going on now in Hong Kong? If yes, then what?*

*   *   *

A few days later, two individuals from Sutton's transition committee stopped by to visit Jack and Jojo.

Jack opened the door to find a tall, attractive brunette who introduced herself as Samantha and a gentleman, Arthur, who wore spectacles and a slightly disheveled looking suit.

They came in and everyone took a seat at the dining room table; Jojo served tea. "It's an honor to meet the both of you," Samantha said. "Our role is to assist you in your relocation to Washington DC. Our experience tells us that unless you are comfortably settled early on, this may disrupt your important upcoming duties. The biggest issue is usually housing. Is it okay if we start there?"

Jack said, "Sure."

"As a cabinet member, you will earn about $220,000. Do you know whether you'd like to rent or buy a residence?"

Jack looked at Jojo, who shrugged, her non-committal signal.

"We'd like to buy a house."

"Okay, we can arrange a very good broker to give you a call. What is your price range?"

"I really don't know. We need a good amount of space. Anywhere from ten to thirty million."

Samantha did not bat an eyelash. "Oh, you'll find some beautiful places for that amount. You may want to look into Georgetown. That's at most a twenty-minute drive to the White House. Also, you know that the government pays certain transition costs. Arthur here will be your point person for keeping track of your reimbursable expenses. He can also provide everything to your accountant so it's no hassle to you."

"That'll be a big help," Jack said. "Thank you."

"Will you be moving things from a different residence?"

"No, we won't."

"Okay, you'll need to furnish the entire home. Let us know when you get to that point, and we can be of assistance. Same goes for schools. We can help ensure you get in where you want."

Jojo nodded; education was important to her. When the kids were ready for school, she'd want them to go to a good one.

"One more small but tedious thing. Mrs. Gold, I understand that you just moved from China, but already have an American passport."

"Yes, that is correct."

"Getting a bank account open for you is another thing and requires a social security card, along with copies of utility bills. It's rather a pain, I'm sorry to say. Anyway, we'll get you a social security card. When you want to open a bank account, just let us know and we'll make sure there are no problems. Best to do that after the inauguration, if it can wait that long."

There were lots of details. Jack hated bureaucracy and he was glad there were people available to help.

* * *

That night the realtor, Becky, called on Jack's iPhone. Jack took the call downstairs and put it on speaker. "Becky, I have you on speaker. My wife Jojo is here."

Becky immediately started speaking fluent northern Chinese. "Hi, Jojo. We should connect via WeChat so it's easier to communicate."

Jojo smiled as she began to converse; it was the first comfortable smile Jack had seen on her in a while.

"Do you have a computer nearby?" Becky asked. "We can connect via Zoom and I can show you a few homes."

Jack grabbed his MacBook Pro and entered the Zoom ID and PIN she gave to him. Becky appeared on the screen. "Hi!" she said. "Nice to meet you, Jojo. I hear you have two kids and want a place with some room, in a good area."

"That's right," Jojo said. "But you know, there is so much more we need. Like food."

"Haha. Yes. Chinatown is not too far away but there are no nice places there. Here, let me share my screen; I found a few places that I can show you."

She showed them several homes, all large, a few were quite contemporary, with lots of glass, clean lines, and high ceilings. The other two Becky showed them were also bespoke homes but more classic looking. One had a front porch with a swing; the other a brick Georgian colonial.

"I like a lot about all of these houses," Jojo said.

"Okay," Becky said. "I have a better sense of what you want. I'll send what I find via WeChat and you can tell me if there is anything else you like. When will you visit DC to see some places?"

"Whenever you have a few that look suitable," Jack said.

"Sounds good. By the way, will you be getting a loan for this purchase?"

"No. We'll pay in cash."

"That helps a lot. This market moves fast. When you find something you like, it'll be best to put down a sizable non-refundable deposit. My guess is that you'd like to avoid making lots of offers for different properties."

Jack nodded. "You are correct. Let's find the right one."

After they got off the call, Jojo turned to Jack, "I've got the house covered. I'm looking forward to it, actually. Focus on what you should be dealing with."

"Okay. Just tell me where to wire the money, when you are ready."

CHAPTER 12

Three days later, Jojo left for Washington DC to visit some homes, leaving Jack with the nanny and the children.

He spent some time with the kids in the first part of the day and then, when Sherry put them down for naps, Jack finally had a chance to put his thoughts to paper. He sat at the desk in their second-floor bedroom, MacBook Pro open as he began to outline thoughts on China and how he wanted to approach Li Keqiang.

He stopped typing and looked out the window at the unobstructed view of the ocean. The water was perfectly flat. About half a mile out there was a small-cabined boat; Jack thought he could make out two people moving about on it. While Palm Beach was not the Gulf of Mexico he was sure the warmer waters were full of all sorts of fish. It reminded him of Cabo and his dad, and that his dad had no idea the new path his life had taken. He'd give him a call when Jojo got back.

The boat came closer to shore. Jack could easily see one of the people on deck reel in a fish. It was nice to see life and leisure, to witness someone doing something natural like fishing in the beautiful ocean.

As the fisherman landed the fish, he lifted it as a trophy and then looked directly up to Jack, or so it seemed. Then, the man raised his right hand and clearly gave Jack the finger. Jack blinked in disbelief. Surely that did not just happen. But then the fisherman put down the fish and gave Jack the finger with both hands.

Perhaps it was because Jack had spent too much time in China, but someone there giving you the finger was offensive to the point of prompting a physical confrontation. Jack stood up, went downstairs and made his way outside onto the beach.

Daniel and Maya intercepted him as he made his way down toward the boat.

"Jack, stand down," Maya said. "We saw everything. We got this."

The boat got close enough that one of the men could jump out and make his way onto the beach. He wore a baseball cap and walked directly to Daniel and Maya. "Sir," Daniel said, holding a hand up, "this is a restricted beach under the jurisdiction of the United States government. You'll have to get back in your boat and leave immediately."

The man kept walking as though he hadn't heard a thing Daniel just said. Jack waited for the explosive and violent subduing of him, but the only thing Daniel and Maya did was step aside, opening a direct path straight to Jack.

There was no time for him to question this. Jack readied himself as Maya had taught, adrenaline starting to flow through him. But when the man was only a few feet away, he lifted his head and grinned at Jack from underneath his baseball cap.

It was Davis.

Jack's jaw dropped in surprise. "Davis!" The two men embraced.

"Good to see you, Jack." Davis said, still grinning.

It had been a long time and so much had happened since Davis was pulled from his security detail in Beijing—Jack was thrilled to see him.

"I heard what happened in Beijing, in your home. I'm sorry, Jack. That idiot President Smith and incompetent Ambassador Pret."

"I'm looking forward to dealing with Pret later, personally. He'll now report to me."

"That's right. I heard you've been named Sutton's secretary of state. Congratulations. And I hope you'll involve me in any retribution."

"Look at you," Jack said. "You're in great shape, mean and lean. How come you didn't look like that before?"

"I altered my training regime and diet, and . . . I'm engaged."

Jack's eyebrows shot up. "To Rio?"

Davis couldn't hide his smile. "Yes. As you and Jojo always suspected. She resigned from the Chinese military so that we could be together legally. And—I have an important question for you."

"Let's hear it."

"Will you be my best man?"

Jack grinned. "It'd be my honor, Davis."

"That's great, Jack. In the meantime, since Jojo took part of your security to DC, I've been assigned to your detail."

"I hope that's permanent."

"Yes, it will be."

Daniel and Maya came up and shook Davis's hand and the three of them laughingly congratulated each other on pulling off a successful ruse. "We wanted it to be a surprise," Davis said.

"Well, the surprise worked," Jack said, laughing.

"Glad to hear it," Davis said. "Now, come on Jack. Show me the pictures I know you took in Beijing."

They all gathered around as Jack reluctantly brought the photos up on his phone. The pictures were from various angles of the four men sprawled on Jack's first floor in his Beijing home. Then, Jack swiped to the final two pictures of the bodies piled in his pantry.

Davis studied the photos. "The Chinese government clearly ordered the killing since these guys were let in the front gate. If they were in America, the assailants would have had guns and you would have been dead. They were trying to make it look like a robbery or something."

Jack looked at Daniel, wondering if he could tell Davis that confirmation was received that Li Keqiang ordered Jack killed, but Daniel said nothing. "Ultimately, it had to have been Li Keqiang who ordered it. He didn't want me trying to sway the election toward Wang. Even the American Embassy was wondering if I'd get involved."

"I probably would have wondered the same thing, considering everything you've found yourself involved in," Davis said. "You'd think Li Keqiang would know better than to try to take you out."

"You would," Jack said, "but I expect he's certainly not going to admit defeat yet."

*   *   *

Sutton and Cam lived in a huge Mediterranean-style home, open, airy, with big windows and spectacular ocean views. It was grand, comfortable, and Jack could tell everything was the best, with gold being the dominant color.

"Hi Jack," Cam said. She wore a sleeveless tan silk dress with a tie around her waist. "*Comment ça va?*"

"Jojo warned me that my French is so bad that I should stick with Chinese. I'm great. How about you?"

"We're enjoying our final few weeks before moving back to DC. I'd rather stay here, but I have to support my husband."

Sutton handed him a flute of champagne. "Let's go to my office and chat for a few minutes before dinner."

They walked down the hall to Sutton's office. Jack took a seat on the sofa as Sutton sat down across from him in a leather armchair. "Any initial thoughts on what you want to do?"

Jack set his champagne down on the coffee table in front of him. "Yes. I've started to drafting a document that outlines China's atrocities to the world and its people. It's loosely fashioned after the Declaration of Independence except meant for all the leaders of democratic countries to sign. This is step one."

"What's next?"

"The purpose of the document is threefold: first to educate and unify the world. Second, to prepare Congress to act or at least not resist action against China. Third, to help to start educating the Chinese public."

Sutton raised his eyebrows and rubbed his palms together. "That sounds like a tall order."

"The step after that will be to take some rather extreme actions—hopefully in concert with other nationals—to attack China financially and economically. I'll share these with you later, if that's okay. All of this will need to be reviewed by lawyers. We'll need to have some groups, including the Pentagon, do some scenario analysis. Either way, we should start as soon as possible to develop a way for all Chinese to see outside news. Starlink satellite dishes have been outlawed and our uploaded software that enables unfettered internet access has been undone. We need to develop and plan for a free VPN that can be aggressively and broadly distributed in China. We must reach the Chinese people directly in order to bring pressure to the government."

"I agree."

"The ultimate purpose is not to change how the government behaves. It's to remove Li Keqiang and his standing committee. Pressuring them to change their behavior will not produce meaningful results. Their atrocities make them good candidates for war crimes prosecution at the Hague. We must go step-by-step. I'd like to hire three people from China who used to work for President Wang Yang. I worked with them before, and they know how the president's office works and can help with all sorts of things, including messaging to the Chinese people. They may be branded as traitors, so we might need to offer them citizenship."

"Jack, I like what I hear and am reassured you know a bunch of people who need to review things at each stage to see if you've missed anything. Bring those Chinese in ASAP. They can stay at Mar-a-Lago. We'll reimburse you for any expenses you incur. Who will sign the document?"

"My initial thinking is England first, then France and Italy, followed by Germany. Asia will be easy after that. You'll sign last."

"Germany won't sign," Sutton said, shaking his head. "They get oil from Russia—China's best friend—and would not want to upset them."

"That's why you will be providing me a signed order to the Pentagon to immediately remove the thirty-five thousand American troops based in Germany. If Germany doesn't sign, I'll email the order it right there in front of them."

A slow grin spread across Sutton's face. "Jesus, Jack. Finally—someone thinks like me. Damn right Germany will sign, or we will recall the troops. Good work. Keep going. We'll start planning those meetings with the other countries a few days after inauguration."

*   *   *

Even though he had plenty to keep him busy while Jojo was in DC, he found himself missing her greatly, despite speaking every night and most mornings via WeChat. Seeing her face on a screen just wasn't enough.

"I have good news!" she said from his iPad screen.

"Do you? You look excited."

"They accepted the offer! We are going to get it!"

Jack loved seeing her so happy. "That's great! I assume you are referring to a house."

"Jack, you'll like it. Anyway, we beat out the other bidders, fortunately. Tomorrow I'm having two inspection companies go out."

"Two?"

"I want to know everything that needs to be fixed, if anything at all. They can take care of any repairs too, if need be."

"That's pretty smart," Jack said. Getting an inspection was relatively inexpensive. Finding the right people to fix stuff was a pain.

"When will it close? When can we move in?"

"It'll close in about ten days. I'm doing a little remodeling that'll take at least a few weeks. This stuff can be done much faster in China, and cheaper. It's amazing how slow things are here. Becky will be super helpful with buying beds, sofas, and rugs. I don't know what I'd do without her. And you'll like Georgetown. It's not too big but it's very international and there are some pretty good restaurants. We're fourteen minutes away from Founding Farmers, which looks like an incredible restaurant."

"I'm looking forward to taking you out there. The inauguration is January 20th so we need to move in a few days earlier."

"That's not a big problem."

"Can I call Secretary Bo and have him ship the Maotai?"

"Absolutely. Send for your precious Maotai." Jojo grinned. "I'll send over the address."

"I miss you," Jack said. "I love you."

"I love and miss you too."

CHAPTER 13

Jack put in his earbuds and connected to Spotify on his phone, turning the music up high to block out any distractions. He hoped this document he was working on would be simple and compelling. That leaders would sign, while at the same time it would heighten the attention to China and the CCP.

Jack knew that there were so many documents about China, what it had done, and the problems. Yet, no single document clearly articulated the facts and situation. Jack recalled the beauty of the Declaration of Independence. The elegance of the language and arguments put forward. Nearly everyone knew its first words: "We hold these truths to be self-evident, that all men are created equal, that they are endowed by their Creator with certain unalienable Rights ..." It did seem to Jack that most people had not read the rest of the powerful document, the written justification for America declaring independence from England. Maybe, Jack wondered, it was because it was signed only by representatives from American states and not world leaders.

After two days he had a draft, but he knew it was best to let it sit for a while. His completion of this draft coincided with Jojo's return from DC. He closed his laptop when he heard her voice call out from downstairs.

Jack wrapped his arms around Jojo and gave her a kiss. "I'm glad you're back. You look beautiful. New clothes?"

"Yes. Becky showed me some nearby shops while we were looking at sofas. The place should be ready in time."

"When do I get to see pictures of it?"

"I was thinking about that and decided that it's best if you arrive without any expectations." Her voice had a teasing note in it but Jack also knew that she was serious—he would arrive at his new home in DC, sight unseen. "Have you eaten?"

"I ordered a pizza and Caesar salad. It'll be here in a few minutes. By the way, the Suttons want us to join them for dinner tomorrow night. Maybe you'll show them pictures of our new house."

"Jack. The place is nice. You'll be okay with it. The neighborhood is great and the nearby schools are excellent. Georgetown is lovely and has a good energy with lots of students and charming places to eat and get coffee. Now, where are the kids?"

*   *   *

The next evening they made their way over to the president's house along with the SUVs and three of their security. Jack felt safe in Palm Beach. Maybe because they were back in America or because of the constant presence of Sutton's security surrounding Mar-a-Lago, which evidently Sutton often used as an office.

Like the last time Jack was here for dinner, he and Sutton went into his office before the meal. They sat and Jack took the declaration document out of its sleeve and handed it to Sutton.

Jack sat there patiently as the president carefully read the document.

When Sutton was done, he looked up at Jack. "Who has reviewed this?"

"No one, sir."

"No one needs to. I love the title, and the fact you did not use the word *democracy*. The paper and font need to be adjusted. But you hit it out of the park. This is not a legal document and compels no one to do anything except acknowledge what they already know. Beautiful. Any nation that does not sign it will be in support of tyranny. You've created a tool that will embarrass them into signing, thereby heightening the awareness of China's transgressions. It'll be unifying in a way we have not managed to achieve before."

"Yes sir, then we can take further action with a solid foundation and support."

The president wrote on top of the paper: *To: KC, DR, & LM. Pls comment to Jack.* "I'll get this to my secretary Madeline and she'll tidy it up and circulate it for comments; then we'll get it back to you. Jack, tonight you are drinking the best champagne in my wine cellar. Excellent job."

Jack followed Sutton into his cellar again, to the champagne section, passing by racks of wine that went nearly to the ceiling. Further ahead were two cigar humidors; Jack wished he could see what type of cigars Sutton had. Sutton started looking at various bottles of champagne, pulling out a few before putting them back. Finally, he reached to the top shelf and pulled out a bottle, which he handed to Jack. "That's Louis Roederer, Cristal Brut. That'll do. We need to let that chill for a while, but you and Jojo will enjoy that."

They found Jojo and Cam in the kitchen, enthusiastically talking in French while Cam sauteed shrimp and Jojo sat on a tall stool at the counter, drinking white wine.

"Jojo, Jack was busy while you were gone!" Sutton said. "He did some rather amazing work."

"What did he do now?"

Sutton turned from the refrigerator where he had just placed the champagne. "He put together a document for major countries to sign to help address the problems existing in China. My prediction is that it will end up being a historic document."

Jojo raised her eyebrows. "Mr. President, you sound so impressed. I'm rather accustomed to Jack doing those sorts of things."

"Doesn't sound like you get a lot of respect at home, Jack," Sutton said jokingly.

Jack rolled his eyes. "Mr. President, if I wanted respect, I'd buy a dog."

"It was Harry Truman who said that about the dog," Sutton said.

"Yes. I like the corollary mentioned by a secretary of defense that goes something like, *Make sure it's a small dog, it might bite you.*"

The president laughed out loud. "Leave it to a secretary of defense to say that."

*   *   *

"I'd like to read that paper you wrote," Jojo said when they'd returned home for the evening. They had just gone in and kissed the kids goodnight and were now in their bedroom; Jack was getting ready to take a shower. "If you don't mind."

"No, I don't mind. I'll print out a copy for you."

He left the copy on the bed while he took a shower. When he came out of the bathroom, Jojo was reclining on the bed, reading the document. She set it down, a pensive expression on her face.

"Jack, you wrote this all by yourself?"

"Yes. The president has sent it around to get input from others."

"You know not everyone who is a member of the communist party is bad, right? I had lots of friends at university who were members. My own dad is still a party member."

"I know, Jojo. But the Party now is doing some really bad things, like it did before your father arrived. And the lives of hundreds of millions of Chinese are being impacted because of the Party. Other countries are, too."

"You laid out the evidence so well that it's challenging how I've felt. But I still have mixed feelings. Not all Party members are bad."

"I agree with that, for sure. And no one is saying so. However, the group they *belong* to is definitely bad and there certainly should be some guilt by association. I have no idea what that might be and hope I'll never have to figure that out."

Jack could tell Jojo still felt uncomfortable. He took what she said seriously and would have to deeply consider not just her feelings but their origin so as to make sure he did not make a misstep. "I hear you, Jojo. Thank you for sharing your thoughts with me. I will be careful."

"I'm tired; I think I'm going to skip the shower."

"You're perfect the way you are."

Jack got into bed next to her and held her as they listened to the waves.

CHAPTER 14

At six am Jack woke up and went downstairs to make coffee. As he waited for the water to boil, he opened WeChat on his iPhone and sent Susan a message. *Please use VPN to download WhatsApp from U.S. Apple Store then video call me.*

Susan had his U.S. phone number ever since they had worked together on the provincial planning project. She also understood security, given her tenure at President Wang's office.

When the coffee was ready, Jack went to the sofa and opened his MacBook Pro. Seconds later the call came in and Susan's face appeared.

"Jack, hi," she said. "Where are you?"

"I'm in Florida with Jojo and the kids. How about you?"

"Still in Beijing. Just glad I'm out of government service. I can't believe what's happening."

"Yeah. Regarding that—Let me get to the point. There is a company in the States that would like to hire you, Jason, and David. You'd be media and cultural advisors and paid at least seven thousand US dollars per month. You'd have to come to Florida but then move to DC in about two weeks."

Jack knew he could set up a Delaware-based LLC in about one hour, give it a high-tech name, then use that to hire them.

"Jack, rumors are flying around in China about you working in the Sutton Administration. Would we be working for you? This line is not being overheard by the Chinese government."

"Yes you would. I thought it would be best if you did not appear to work directly for me in case there might be repercussions to your families."

"That's very smart. Thank you for thinking about that."

"There is an added bonus in that I have assurances the three of you would be on a fast track to get US passports if you wanted one. Do you all have active visas?"

"Yes. We all have five or six years left on our ten-year visas. When were you thinking of having us come out?"

"Get on the next flight you can to Palm Beach. There's a nice hotel across the street from where we're staying."

"I'll talk to Jason and David and keep you posted."

Jack thanked her and they ended the call. He felt relieved that his three former assistants were going to be working with him again.

Ten minutes later, he received a WhatsApp message from Susan, informing him that they would be there soon.

Jack responded with his address, thrilled that they would be on their way. All three were experts on China, the running of China's presidential office, and in media management within China. Compared to everything else he had done in China so far, he felt certain he could get some countries to sign a piece of paper—especially now that he had others who could help him. The key for everything would be in the details.

*   *   *

The next morning Davis came by, requesting a word with Jack.

"Sure, come on in," Jack said, stepping back, noticing that Davis seemed a little down.

"Hi Davis," Jojo called from the kitchen. "Coffee or tea?"

"Hi Jojo," Davis said, seeming to force a smile. "A cup of coffee would be great."

"Oh, Jojo," Jack said, hitting his forehead. "I completely forgot to tell you—Davis is engaged—to Rio."

"I knew it!" Jojo set the cup of coffee down and held her arms out for a hug but Davis just stood there, looking as if he were in some measure of pain. Jack swallowed. Had Rio backed out?

"Okay, Davis," Jack said. "Out with it. What's going on?"

Davis took a sip of the coffee Jojo handed him. "We booked a hotel for the wedding and reception several months ago, but they just backed out. It was all set for the day before the inauguration, as I told you. They used a clause in the contract which says they can cancel if the US government needs the hotel. And we can't have it outside in January, it's too cold. Rio's family is flying in from China. What a mess."

"How many people are attending?" Jojo asked.

"I don't know. Not more than seventy-five."

Jojo gave Jack a meaningful look, like she was urging him to do something. Uncharacteristically he had no idea what she was trying to communicate. Jojo said, "*Jack.*"

He realized what she wanted him to say. "Oh. Shit. Have it at our place. I haven't seen it, but from what I hear, there's plenty of room."

Davis shook his head. "Oh, I couldn't—"

"Davis, it's settled," Jojo said. "There is more than enough room at our new home. I can give you the address and you can see some pictures online."

Expecting pushback from Davis, Jack said, "That'll be our wedding present and we'll take care of all the food and drinks. And the taxi rides home for people who drink too much."

Davis opened his mouth but didn't say anything for several seconds. "I had no idea you would offer that. I hadn't even thought of it. But . . . I think that could work." He grinned. "I accept."

"Now, Davis," Jojo said. "I still haven't met Rio and we're both from China. I need a friend. Can we get formally introduced?"

"Actually . . ." Davis said, looking uncharacteristically shy, "this is my day off and we were going to go for a drive . . . She's in the car waiting for me. We didn't want to interrupt your morning but I just wanted to tell Jack, since he's my best man and all."

Jojo's eyes widened. "She's in the car? Bring her in now! We can make breakfast together while you and Jack chat."

Davis's smile returned. "Yes, ma'am," he said. A moment later he returned, with Rio by his side. She was nearly as tall as Davis, dressed in jeans and an oversized white shirt that looked like she may have borrowed from him

"I remember you are from Hangzhou," Jojo said in Mandarin. "We went hiking together in Dali. I miss Dali. Do you?"

It was obvious to Jack that Jojo and Rio were going to be like old friends and for that, he was thankful. He and Davis sat on the sofa with their coffee.

"Thanks for saving my wedding," Davis said. "I didn't know what we were going to do."

"What's are best men for?" Jack said. "Glad we could help."

Davis peered into his coffee cup and then glanced at Jack. "So, Mr. Secretary, any idea what you're going to do in your new position?"

"Come on upstairs and I'll show you." They went up to Jack's office and he handed Davis a copy of the China Declaration. "This is the first step."

"You'll be a good secretary of state," Davis said after he finished reading the document. "I could never do that. What comes afterward?"

"For now, I'm going one step at a time. We'll need to travel to various countries to get everyone's signature. Some will resist."

Just then, Jack heard the doorbell downstairs. "Please no sharing with others. It gets formally announced after the inauguration."

"Of course," Davis said as they headed downstairs.

Susan, Jason, and David were just coming in. "Hello everyone," Jack said. "Welcome!" He gave them each a hug, excited that his trusted assistants had arrived. They put their things down and said hello to Jojo, Davis, Rio and were introduced to the kids.

"You're just in time for breakfast," Jack said. "Can I get you coffee or tea?"

The three of them exchanged quizzical glances with each other, clearly reluctant to speak. It reminded Jack of the times when they first started working together and would go to a restaurant. They would all hesitate at ordering a drink beyond water.

"Jojo, how about if Davis and I make breakfast," Jack said. "You all can relax and chat."

In the kitchen, Jack made more bacon while Davis sliced onions, bell peppers, and mushrooms for two large omelets. When the bacon was done, Jack put bagels in for toasting and set cream cheese and salmon on the table. Davis followed with bowls of fresh fruit, and in twenty minutes, everything was ready and every seat was taken around the large dining table.

Jack raised his orange juice glass. "Welcome to America."

Everyone raised their glasses, then the feast began. They ate as though they loved the food. Jack knew better; they were as yet unaccustomed to Western food. That would take time.

When the meal was finished, Davis and Rio said their goodbyes.

"Thanks for stopping by," Jack said as he and Jojo walked them out. "It was great to finally meet Rio for real. I bet Rio and Jojo can plan everything. You and I can sit around and drink beers."

"You think so?"

"I don't know. As best man, what other things should I plan on doing? Get some cigars?"

"That sounds good, actually. Otherwise, just show up."

"That I can do."

They waved as Davis and Rio drove off. Back inside, they found Susan, David, and Jason clearing the table.

"Let's hold off on that," Jack said. "I'd rather have a chat then get you to your hotel so you can relax."

Jack was happy to have his old team back together. "I'm glad to see all of you and I'm excited to work together again. How was getting out of China? How was the flight?"

"There were no problems at all," Susan said.

"Good." Jack had not expected any difficulties. "We can chat tomorrow morning after you've had time to freshen up. Let me walk you over to your hotel."

While they went to fetch their bags, Jack went to the corner and picked up two bags, one large and one small.

"I got each of you a new MacBook Pro and the latest iPhone." Jack winked. "For security purposes. Probably best to set up a new U.S.-based iCloud account for both. You all have been given phone numbers, so it'll be easy to activate things."

Jason looked into the bag. "Sweet. That's the latest iPhone Max Pro. Perfect."

They walked across the street and Jack waited to make sure there were no issues with checking in. "You'll have jet lag and probably wake up early tomorrow morning. Let's meet in the dining room at nine am for breakfast. I can give you more information then."

He could see the tiredness on their faces and knew how much better they'd feel after a good night's sleep.

* * *

The next morning, while waiting for the expresso machine to heat up, Jack used his iPhone to call Gérard in Geneve. Gérard was the founder of Gérard Pere Et Fils, the most renowned cigar establishment in the world. "Hello, *bonjour*," a woman's voice said.

"*Bonjour*. This is Jack Gold calling from America."

"Hold on," she said with a strong French accent. "Let me transfer you to Paul in the store." Jack waited a few seconds and then Paul's voice came over the line.

"Hello. This is Paul."

"Hi Paul. This is Jack Gold, in America."

"Jack. It's been a long time since we have heard from you. How may I help you today?"

"Just a few things. I need three boxes of Montecristo #2s, and one box of Cohiba Esplendidos."

"Certainly. Just so you know, we'll have to send those individually."

"No problem." They would repackage the cigars in a Dominican Republic box and send them. The U.S. was cracking down on cigar imports.

"Do you need the cigar bands sent separately?"

"No need." Lots of people liked to show off what type of cigar they were smoking. Jack thought for a moment. "Can you also send me a high-quality humidor suitable for about five boxes?"

"We can, but honestly, you can find one locally that's just as good and save shipping costs."

"That's okay," Jack said. "Please send the humidor."

"Not a problem. Should we send all of this to your address on file?"

"Actually, the billing address is the same, but let me give you two different shipping addresses."

Jack looked at the house sales documents that Jojo had left on the counter and gave him the address.

"Thanks, Mr. Gold. We'll get those out to you tomorrow and they'll be there in a few days."

"Perfect. Thank you, Paul."

Jack hung up, appreciating the swiftness of the transaction. Usually he would call and discuss which cigars were particularly good right now and they would candidly tell him. In a sense, cigars were more complicated than wine. Each year differed and even each shipment of cigars varied—knowing this was the secret to getting great cigars.

Jack understood it was illegal for Americans to buy Cuban products. The strict trade embargo ban was still in place. It was good that buying Dominican Republic products was not illegal.

*   *   *

Jack walked over to the hotel and went to the same room where he and Jojo had dinner with the president just a week ago. He was surprised there were so few people sitting at the tables, but that meant he was able to get a spot for four easily.

He'd brought four copies of the China Declaration. He wondered how his assistants would view the document and he knew he could expect their candid feedback.

When they arrived, Jack stood up as they made their way over, all three looking refreshed and well-rested in their formal navy-blue suits.

"Good morning," he said.

"This place is amazing," Susan said in Mandarin. "Everything is so nice. Look at this room! Incredible."

David nodded as he looked around, taking in the opulence of the décor, while Jason had his new phone out and was taking a video. Of the three, Jack knew that he would be most thrilled with the latest Apple technology.

After their waitress came over with menus and took their drink order, Jack was about to get started when he saw Sutton enter the room and head right their way. Jack introduced him to his three assistants.

"Nice to meet you all," Sutton said. "You have a big job and I'm glad to see you moving so swiftly, Jack. Or, should I say, Mr. Secretary. Anyway, I'm not here to bother you. I'll let you get to your meeting. Though we do need to see you and Jojo soon for another dinner in a few days, okay?"

"Sure, sir, we look forward to it."

"Oh my gosh, that was President Sutton," Susan said in a low voice once he was out of earshot. She looked at Jack. "But . . . Why did he call you Mr. Secretary?"

"It won't officially be announced until after the president's inauguration, but he will be appointing me secretary of state. I'll be the president's advisor when it comes to foreign affairs. China will be very important after the inauguration on January 20th and he thought I could help. In fact, it's so important to him that he wanted me to get started early with preparing to take office. That's why you all are here. You see, since Li Keqiang was elected, things have taken a turn for the worse with China selling fentanyl, cracking down in Xinjiang, threatening Taiwan, attacking everyday freedoms of Chinese . . . I don't need to tell you."

The three of them nodded vigorously. Jack continued. "As a first step in addressing these severe issues, I wrote a document we call the China Declaration to summarize the situation and get agreement from other Western countries. Let me give you this and you can take a look at what it says in both English and Chinese." Jack handed each of them a copy of the document.

When the waitress arrived with their drinks, Jack ordered Eggs Benedict, French toast, corned beef and hash with poached eggs, with fruit and yogurt for all of them.

Susan finished reading first and waited quietly for the other two.

"What do you think?" Jack asked, when everyone was done.

"It's a powerful document if esteemed countries sign it," Susan said. "It shows what China has done, that the world sees it and will not tolerate it. One thing I noticed is the Chinese translation is not great. To be more precise, younger people will not really understand it since it uses older language that is too formal. People just don't talk that way."

"I agree with everything Susan said," Jason said, and David nodded as well.

Jack took a sip of his coffee. "What will the average person think?"

"The average person in China never thinks about these sort of things," David said. "They are not reading articles about what's going on."

"Yeah," Jason said. "They're not even reading what the government says about things unless it's related to them or their hometown. Moreover, even if they *do* read or think about something, they know there is nothing they can do."

The discussion continued in that manner until the waitress returned with their food.

"I appreciate everyone's feedback so far," Jack said. "But now, let's eat. Enjoy." Everyone dug in. But the focus on the food did not last long.

Jack helped himself to one of the Eggs Benedicts and took a big bite. Breakfast was the only white people meal Chinese liked and it was clear that Susan, David, and Jason enjoyed everything that was ordered.

"I have an assignment for the three of you," Jack said after the waitress had come to clear their plates.

They reached for their notepads and pens, pens that Jack had gifted them for their diligent work on the province planning project. "Nice pens," Jack said. "Over the next three days I'd like you to visit a bunch of places—

for example, The Domain, the Botanical Gardens, the university. Shop and interview people. Then, just for fun, I'd like each of you to make some very short videos on the misconceptions Chinese have of Americans. Florida is not representative of America but being here is like having one hand on an elephant. Have fun with it, like you're going to post on your WeChat newsfeed. But for now, please don't. Make it personal. Tell a brief story or make a clip of someone and narrate it. Include them if you can."

Jack took the two thousand dollars out of his pocket that he had gotten at the ATM before he came to the hotel this morning. He handed it to Susan. "This is for all expenses you incur. Get some casual clothes so that you fit in with the local scene. Additionally, for a few days, please only view Western media like FOX News, BBC and MSNBC. Try to only speak English. Then, on the third night, I'd like you to go shopping at 99 Ranch Market. They have everything you'll want to eat from China. Buy some stuff and cook yourselves a huge dinner at my house. You'll need a good Chinese meal by then."

"Will you be there when we cook?" Susan asked.

"If you invite us, sure."

"You're invited!" all three of them said together.

"Then it's set. Tell us when to be there and we will. Oh, one more thing—Within three days can you please send me a revised translation of the China Declaration."

"No problem," Jason said, making a final note in his notepad.

"The goal is to relax, get over your jet lag, and get a few things done. I promised myself I would never relive the visits to the provinces and the toll that it took on us."

Jack waved to the waitress when he saw her, indicating that he wanted the bill. She came over with a smile on her face. "Your bill has been taken care of, sir. As are all of the bills for your guests who are staying at the hotel."

"Sutton owns the club and agreed personally to host you," Jack told his assistants. "It's good that you get spoiled before we go to Washington DC."

*   *   *

Three days later, Jack invited Sutton and Cam over to enjoy the authentic Chinese meal that Susan, Jason, and David were going to cook with everything they procured at the 99 Ranch Market. When they arrived, carrying multiple overflowing grocery bags, Jojo was waiting for them with Kai, ready to offer any assistance they might need.

They were enthusiastic and had clearly allocated tasks amongst each other. Jack tried not to look, but saw prawns, fish, chicken, and an array of vegetables.

"Did you like that 99 Ranch Market?" Jojo asked.

"I never thought I'd see such a market in America!" Susan said. "And, seeing it in Florida, full of Chinese. We all were really surprised."

An hour later, Sutton and Cam arrived, carrying two bottles of champagne and two bottles of red wine, which they handed to Jack. "Nice! I bet you get invited to lots of dinner parties," he joked, taking the bottles. "Come in!"

"Never mind that, something smells delicious!" Cam exclaimed as she made her way to the kitchen. Jack opened the wine and poured glasses for everyone. Then, he and Sutton went and sat outside.

A box of cigars sat on the wooden table in between the two deck chairs. "I got these for you."

Sutton looked at the box skeptically. "From the Dominican Republic?"

"Take one out."

He opened the box and picked up one of the cigars, inspecting it closely. "These are not from the Dominican Republic."

Jack handed him a cutter and lighter. "Cohiba Esplendidos," Sutton said after he exhaled a plume of smoke. "Jack, this is one of my favorite cigars. How did you get them?"

"Gérard in Geneve."

"How did you know I liked cigars? I try to keep it on the low down since everyone is so sensitive these days about smoking."

"I saw the humidors in your cellar."

"Well, we all have our vices."

"That's true," Jack said as he selected a cigar of his own.

"John F. Kennedy secured 1200 cigars just before he signed the Cuban embargo," Sutton said. "Hours before. Timing is everything."

"From what I understand, he had a few vices."

"That's one way of putting it," Sutton said. "How are your Chinese friends doing?"

"They've spent the past three days immersing themselves in America and producing some videos about the largest misconceptions that Chinese have about Americas. And they redid the translation of the China Declaration."

"The translation wasn't good?"

"No. My written Chinese is not great, but theirs is remarkable. They translated all the briefs for the province overviews from English into Chinese for China's Standing Committee. For the Declaration, they changed a lot so that everyday Chinese could read it and understand. What they said is that most Chinese will never know or care when it's signed because it doesn't directly impact their own lives."

"That's a good thing to know beforehand. What'll you do?"

"We need to reach all the citizens. Have them share their own stories. But China is now blocking the internet. We need our own platform that can't be touched by the government, that everyone can use."

"After the inauguration you'll have more resources to address those issues."

"About that. I was thinking a chief of staff will be critical and is something that should be considered now, particularly when it comes to non-China related issues."

"Did you have anyone in mind?"

"I met Ron Timmons in Taipei. What do you think about the former secretary? I know it sounds odd, but I'll be fighting the battles and he might enjoy a front row seat."

"Jack, I never would have thought of Timmons. He wouldn't even have thought of himself for the position. He's retired. No secretary in history has been rehired for a more junior position. But I think you have a good chance of getting him—and he'd be great. He'll know most of the people in the administration and certainly will steer you clear of any landmines."

"May I contact Madeline and have her put me in touch with him?"

"Sure. No need to ask. I like the unconventional thinking, Jack. After getting countries to sign the Declaration, then what?"

"My thinking currently is that we develop a more aggressive policy toward fentanyl. Then we become more aggressive and close all our embassies in China—and blame China. With modern technology, visas can be done online. We'll be able to save money and do things more efficiently. CIA agents will need to find other homes. Our move after that will be to increase awareness globally of China's atrocities. After that, sanction all Chinese Communist Party members."

Sutton raised his eyebrows. "That's the big move, I know," Jack said. "No one is ready for it now. We'll need to involve some Republicans in Congress to properly message on TV. I suspect I'll have to hold Zoom meetings with leaders, maybe involve you, to get them on board before we pull the CCP member trigger. There will need to be some caveats when something like that applies to all CCP members and their families. We'll need to plan ahead. Like prepare an appeal process. Such drastic action is necessary to help all Chinese become aware of the brutalities of the CCP. That communication platform will be critical. Maybe I'll give Ari, my Israeli friend, a call. He may have an idea. None of this is set in stone. We need to go step-by-step starting with the Declaration. We'll need a strategy for Chinese leaders, one for the Chinese people, one for other nations, and of course one politically for the US that also includes the American public."

Sutton tapped his cigar into the ashtray on the table. "That all sounds good. I did not expect you to take all those constituents into consideration, but it's good that you do so. You'll need to present to the cabinet so things are well-coordinated. I'm certain there will be some constructive feedback."

"Evidently, I don't have a problem talking in front of people, at least in Chinese."

The president laughed. "And they say most people fear public speaking more than even death. When you go to England you'll probably meet the Queen. Let's see how you do then."

Jack hadn't thought of that. He thought he would only be meeting with Andrew Jones, the prime minister of the United Kingdom.

Jojo popped her head out. "Dinner is ready!"

They placed their cigars carefully in the ashtray, leaving them for later. It wasn't because each cigar cost over sixty dollars. It was out of respect for the cigar.

Inside, the long rectangular table was laden with different plates of food. There was steamed fish, onion cake, rice, watercress, roasted duck, spicy pork, eggplant, fried fish, and a beef dish.

"We each cooked our favorite dish from our hometown," Susan said.

"This looks remarkable," Cam said, her eyes wide. "Let me take a photo."

"Mr. President," Jack said, "please sit at the head of the table. Everyone else, please sit wherever you'd like." Jack went to the other end of the table and took a seat as everyone began serving themselves.

Jack looked at all the food as he tried a bite. It was authentic and satisfying. He had not realized how much he missed good Chinese food. Jojo's plate was full and she was clearly thrilled at the meal.

"Mr. President, can you get Chinese food like this in the White House?" Jack asked.

"No, you can't," Cam said. "The Vietnamese food is not bad, though. Maybe things will be different this time around." She looked at Sutton.

"Don't look at me—You control the kitchen."

Jack raised his glass. "We're all very happy to have you here in America," he said, looking first at Susan, then David and Jason. "Jojo and I are your family here for anything you may need. Thank you for this heartfelt meal."

Everyone raised their glasses. "Thank you," Susan said, her cheeks flushing a little.

"How did the past three days go?" Jack asked. He nodded to Susan's shirt, which was from the University of Miami. "I see you got some new clothes. Did you make any progress on the misconceptions Chinese have?"

"We did. We went to the university and pretended to be students doing a project. I interviewed a friendly couple. The man was African-American. Wait—He was from Nigeria. That's West Africa. Yes. Anyway, his girlfriend was from Japan. They looked so different. When I asked them what they liked about America they were quick to say *freedom and diversity*. Those themes came up repeatedly as we interviewed more people."

"I did one interview in the Chinese market," David said. "No one in China expects to have such a place in Florida. The prices of things were very reasonable, too. The Chinese were not willing to be interviewed, unlike the white people."

Jason nodded vigorously. "I interviewed a Chinese girl in a bar. She didn't speak Chinese. Not a word. She was adopted by an American family and they have a big network of friends who were also adopted from China. She sounded white but looked Chinese. All these white families adopted girls from China. I didn't expect that."

Susan said, "We can share others with you later. We'd like to post them on our WeChat newsfeed for others to see, if you think that's okay."

As Jack listened to Susan, he was impressed with how she spoke in English. Previously, they had nearly always spoken in Mandarin, but her English now was more confident and her attitude was positive and factual. She spoke in a way that Jack knew others would listen to and enjoy hearing. "I'd love to see them, but please do not post them yet," he said.

"Why wouldn't you want them to post those in China so others can learn more about America?" Sutton asked.

"It's hard to get authentic content. If we start using another platform, that's good stuff to seed it with. WeChat is heavily censored. We can't use it to communicate what we want. The government even censors or modifies messages put out by the U.S. Embassy. It's not the right time yet."

"That makes sense. I'm glad you're in charge of this, Jack."

For the rest of the meal, the conversation centered on Susan, David, and Jason, as they shared stories about their hometowns and the contrast that they had encountered in America.

When it was time for Sutton and Cam to leave, Jack slipped back outside to get the box of cigars he had for Sutton. He also grabbed the cigar that Sutton had been smoking previously. "You forgot these," he said, handing over the box.

"Almost the biggest mistake of my life." Sutton grinned. "The Siglo 6s are good too. If you happen to find a box of those in the Dominican Republic, feel free to drop them off anonymously to Madeline."

"Certainly," Jack said, returning his grin. "The cigars produced in the Caribbean are getting better and better these days."

"So it would seem," Sutton said. "Thanks again for a great evening."

By the time Jojo and Jack had returned, everything in the kitchen was spotless.

*   *   *

Susan, David, and Jason left not long after Sutton and Cam. Sherry had put the kids to bed, but after everyone had left Jack and Jojo went in to check on them, both sound asleep. They made their way back downstairs.

"I'm going to give Ari a call," Jack said.

"Maybe Mary will be around," Jojo said. "Let me get a glass of that red wine first. You want some more champagne?"

"Yes, that'd be great."

Jack called Ari on his iPad Pro, via WeChat. After a few rings, Ari answered.

"Jack. Great to see you buddy!" Jojo sat down next to Jack, handing him his glass of champagne. "And, Jojo," Ari said. "Hey, we heard that you are in Florida. Partying on the beach? I hear the Cuban food there is great."

"Some Chinese friends just came over and cooked us a huge dinner," Jojo said. "It was amazing. Mary would have loved it. Jack enjoyed smoking cigars more, I think. How are you and Mary?"

"All is good. Glad we left China and moved away to Israel. Life here is always good. By the way, Jack, that internet project we discussed has made some progress. Do you remember the one aimed at communicating into outer space with lasers?"

"I do. I actually have a question for you. Not about that exactly but something similar. What if I wanted a separate WeChat platform that any Chinese in China could access. No censorship. How could I do that?"

"Hmm." Ari leaned back into the sofa he was sitting on. "I have an idea. Let me ask a few friends some questions, then we can talk."

"Is Mary around?" Jojo asked.

"No. She took the kids out and left me all alone. What are you guys up to in Florida?"

"Sutton gets inaugurated next week," Jack said.

"Israel is very happy about that. I mean everyone. There will be parties in the street."

"Sutton has asked me to be his Secretary of State."

Ari sat up straight and leaned in close, his face taking up nearly the entirety of Jack's iPad. "What did you say?"

"I said, 'Sutton has asked me to be his Secretary of State.'"

"Jack! What was your answer?"

"I said yes, of course."

"Is this public information?"

"No, but it's not top secret. I wouldn't go telling the press or anything like that. Best to keep it to yourself."

Ari grinned and settled back into the couch. "Great news! I'll have a drink with my sandwich to celebrate." He paused. "Now I think I'm understanding a little more why you asked about a separate WeChat platform."

"I'm developing some ideas."

"You're smart. I'm eager to hear about them."

"Confidentially, please look into the WeChat democracy thing for me."

"Yes. I understand. I will."

"And give our love to Mary!" Jojo said.

"Certainly! She'll be disappointed she missed the call. And Jack, I'll call you again soon. Congratulations again. I can't believe you'll be the next Secretary of State. It totally makes sense, though, with China as it is now. You two have a wonderful day—I mean night."

"You too, Ari."

They got off the call. Jojo took the last sip of wine from her glass and set it down on the coffee table. "Ari seemed pretty excited. You think he'll keep it to himself?"

"No. I think he's calling the top of Israeli's government right now."

"But you told him anyway, knowing that."

"We need help on that separate WeChat platform. Israel is our best bet to help with that and telling him about my new position will place more seriousness and urgency on their side. We need that."

"Oh my heavens, you are not even in the position and you are already planning all this stuff. Jack, even for you this seems like grandmaster chess or something."

"We'll see about that," Jack said.

"Well, since we're calling people, how about my dad next? It's been so long since I've spoken with him."

"I'll let you go ahead. I think it's best if I can say that I haven't spoken to him. That way China cannot get mad at him for interfering. And please do not mention my new job. The conversation you have with him will definitely be monitored."

A look of disappointment crossed Jojo's face, but she nodded. "What you said makes sense."

"But call him. Ask him how Mini is too."

Jack got up and left the room so Jojo could make the call. He wanted to speak with Wang but knew it was fraught with potential problems. Wang would understand.

CHAPTER 15

The transition team asked Jack if he wanted to meet with the other living secretaries of state. He had declined. He wanted to develop his own perspectives devoid from other leaders and felt he should speak with the president of Taiwan, and hopefully she'd have some staff with insights as to any new developments in China. Jack didn't trust America to have any good sources. But at the same time, it would not surprise him if the NSA had all senior leaders bugged. He'd find out in a few days when his briefings began.

*   *   *

Moving to their new house in DC was relatively easy. They didn't have much to bring from Florida, just a few suitcases. The house had an oversize three-car garage and both were constructed with a stone façade and tiled roof. The surrounding trees gave a sense of privacy. The home had seven bedrooms, a few of which had been converted into an office and a gym. It also had an astounding ten bathrooms. Jojo had redone the kitchen, den, and formal dining area so that it was a single wide-open space, as they liked. It had a counter and stools in front of a gas stove, a table for eating and a cozy sitting area near a fireplace. Their bathroom had a Japanese feel to it with one wall made of bamboo, a huge stone tub, and a glass shower. The house had large windows which brought in a nice amount of natural light.

"The spare bedrooms we can deal with later," Jojo said. "It was just too much to furnish everything before we moved in." What furniture she had purchased was tasteful, high-quality, and comfortable. "Did you look in the garage yet?"

Jack had been looking and had found the Maotai that Bo had sent, along with the humidor. Two cases of Maotai. He put them in their wine cellar but would wait until later to place the bottles in the wine rack. Jack felt vulnerable. Twenty-four bottles might not be enough. He had been reading about diplomatic bags and pouches. Evidently, a crate could have diplomatic markings and get through customs without a problem. Maybe one day Wang would be able to honor his promise that Jack would have Maotai for life.

"I'll go right now. Want to come?"

"Sure."

They walked out the front door to the oversize garage. Jojo had the controller to open the door and when she pressed the button, the door rolled up to reveal two vehicles. There was a yellow Range Rover with tinted glass, and a sleek Flying Spur Bentley.

"Beautiful," Jack said. "This looks awesome."

Jojo nodded to the Range Rover. "Maya made sure it was customized with bullet-proof glass and some other things."

"Nice. Great family car."

"I figure you'll enjoy driving that to work, and it'll be nice to be driven in too," Jojo said, pointing to the Bentley. "Maya also had some features added like the glass, but it's pretty standard. I understand the engine is quite big."

"Jojo, I don't know what to say. It's beautiful. I knew you had great taste but this is really wonderful."

Jojo smiled. "There's one more thing."

She led Jack out to a second garage that he hadn't even realized was there. It was empty except for a motorcycle, a Bonneville Triumph, a classic, definitely a British motorbike. All black with a little bit of dark gray.

"I just thought the Ducati was a little much for a man with two kids and a wife. There are no enhancements to the Triumph. It's a good date vehicle for you and me."

Jack pulled Jojo to him and gave her a kiss. "Everything looks amazing."

"It's a Manor-style home, in case anyone asks."

They were walking back to the house when a car drove up, having just been waved through by security. It was Davis and Rio.

"This is really quite the place," Davis said, gazing around. "Luxurious."

Jojo went up to Rio and gave her a hug. "Let me show you around. We just got here yesterday ourselves."

Jack gave Davis his own tour. First of the garages and the vehicles inside, then they stood outside looking at the house.

"It's much bigger than I was expecting," Davis said. "We could have a guest list of a thousand! Which we don't," he added quickly.

"It's over 11,000 square feet," Jack said. "I had no say about the matter. I wasn't even allowed to see pictures before I got here. Come in. I'll show you around."

They went through the rooms on the first floor, then down to the wine cellar. "Here you go," Jack said. "Two boxes for tomorrow night. Montecristo number 2s. Authentic, despite the Dominican Republic label."

Davis looked at the boxes appreciatively. "Thanks, Jack. Where did you get them?"

"Géneve. One phone call. Hey, aren't you going on your honeymoon right after the wedding?"

"Yes, why?"

"Because you really don't know what will happen to those cigars tomorrow night. So I got an extra box for you." Jack handed him a third box.

Davis laughed. "Perfect. And hey, I have something for you." He dug into his pocket and handed Jack a velvet ring box. "I trust you'll keep this safe."

"Absolutely," Jack said. "I'm not sure where you and Rio want to hold the wedding. Outside would be ideal but the weather will be cold."

"I'm fine letting Rio and Jojo figure that out. It seems like a lot, Jack, you just getting up here yourself to host a wedding the next day."

Jack waved him off. "It's the least we can do. I'm happy for you, man."

*　*　*

Jack woke up the next morning to the sound of furniture being moved around. A half-foot high platform was brought in on which a long table was placed. Smaller tables were arrayed in front of it for all the guests.

Outside the chairs were set up in neat rows next to the pool and an awning decorated with an assortment of white flowers. Flowers were everywhere. Outside and inside, they came alive in a matter of hours.

"Rio decided it was worth it to have the wedding outside because it is so beautiful," Jojo said. "People can stay inside, go out for the ceremony, then go back in. The pictures will be nice."

Jack recalled his own wedding and the formal reception in front of thousands of people that was broadcast all over China. He was a little jealous of Davis having a small, intimate gathering. The caterers began to arrive. Jack decided to go upstairs and do a little bit of work.

*   *   *

Later, Jack showered and changed into the one suit that he had. He went downstairs and found Davis, who had changed into a white tuxedo.

"How are you doing?" Jack asked.

Upon closer look, Davis was nervous, but in a good way. Jack could see the excitement on his face but like many men before getting married, there were lots of emotions traversing through him. "How about a cigar." Jack handed him one of the Montecristos.

"Is it okay to smoke inside?"

"What are homes for, Davis." Jack took the cigar back, cut and lit it, then handed it back to him. "We'll go stand by the window."

"Much better. Thanks, Jack."

The wedding got going with Davis outside near the end of the pool under the trellis decorated with yellow and white rose petals, waiting for his bride. The sun was out and the temperature was near forty-five degrees. There was no breeze so things were relatively comfortable, even outside. All the guests were seated. Most were in dark suits and were FBI agents. Jack saw Rio's family, sitting together near the front.

Jack took his place next to Davis and the priest while they waited for Rio. When she appeared, on the arm of her father, Jack glanced at Davis and saw sincere happiness in his face. Rio looked stunning in her gown which was ivory and form-fitting with a long train. Her hair was styled in an elegant updo and she wore a simple diamond necklace. Jack caught Jojo's eye from where she sat in the front row, Jack Jr in her arms. He gave her a wink and she smiled back, wiping at her eyes as Rio passed by.

Jack had Rio's ring in his hand in his pocket, at the ready. He listened as the priest spoke and then Davis and Rio said their vows. When the moment arrived he was ready and handed Davis the ring. Afterwards, Davis kissed her and the crowd erupted in applause and happy shouts.

Once the ceremony was over, everyone went inside and got a drink. The DJ began to play music as Davis and Rio wandered through the crowd and mingled.

When the food started coming out, Rio and Davis made their way to their table. Jack said to Jojo, "Come join me at the head table."

She waved him off. "You are his best man. I'm not his best woman."

Jack sat next to Davis with a full glass of champagne. After a few minutes, Davis stood up, holding his glass. Everyone quieted down.

"As many of you know," Davis started, "my parents passed away when I was young. Though they are not here, they will always be my family and in my soul. Please join me in a toast to them." Jack raised his glass with everyone else.

"I also want to thank Rio's family for coming all this way," Davis continued. "To Rio's family who have enriched my life." He raised his glass to them. Davis looked out to everyone in the audience. "You all are my family. The FBI is my family. Thank you for being here. I love you." Loud claps erupted.

Jack could tell he meant it, and he could see the looks everyone was giving Davis. They were a close-knit group of people who truly cared for one another.

Davis turned to Jack. "Jack, you are my best man. I consider you, Jojo, and your father as family. Over the years you have enriched my life in many ways—and we have been through so much together. I love you, brother."

Jack stood, wiping at his eyes, and hugged Davis. "I feel the same," he said.

Jack sat down. Davis turned to Rio and started speaking to her. It was only after the first sentence that Jack realized Davis was speaking in Mandarin to her. It was not the type of Mandarin spoken by a student, or an adult who had learned the language later in life. It was spoken with the fluency of a mature man speaking to his wife. Davis spoke with native fluency.

Jack saw Jojo's jaw drop. Davis continued. "You are the center of my life and heart. I adore you. Your parents are my parents, your brother is my brother, my family is yours. We are lucky to have a big family, my wife. Please share a glass of wine with me."

Rio picked up her glass with her left hand as she stood up. She put her right hand under the bottom of the glass, slightly lowering her head and the glass to Davis, then to the crowd. Then, she placed it to her mouth taking a good-sized sip.

Jack almost lost it. What Davis had said in Chinese was so delicate and beautiful. For some reason Jack remembered a beautiful garden in Suzhou where a man had made an extraordinarily beautiful garden for his wife, as a representation of his love for her. Jack could see Davis making such a garden for Rio.

Davis looked to Jack. "Your turn."

"What?" Jack said.

"It's your turn to say something, best man."

Jack stood, realizing that he hadn't considered what he might say. "Hi, I'm Jack." He looked around the large, open space of his new home, at everyone seated at their tables. He smiled. "I've known Davis for many years and it's only now I realize he knows Mandarin and has been eaves-dropping on all my conversations."

Everyone laughed.

"I've known Davis in different parts of the world. One early morning, we went jogging on the Great Wall. Someone tried to kill us with a drone, the blades of which were laced with deadly tetrodotoxin, we later found out. Davis jumped in front of us and successfully shot the drone down, with his taser gun. Yes, a taser gun. He nailed it."

Everyone clapped. A few people let out enthusiastic cheers. "So, it's fair to say, he is the only FBI agent I would jump in front of to take a bullet for!"

Jack looked at Davis. "But Davis, am I really your brother? You see, one time we were in a Mexican restaurant in China. After my staff walked out, Davis sat down next to me at the table. He leaned over and said, 'Jack, do you see those two guys at the bar? We think they are here to knife you when you go into bathroom.'" Jack paused. "That's when I ordered two shots of Patrón." There was laughter throughout the room. Davis shook his head slowly, chuckling. "Then I turned to Davis and asked, 'Why don't you just take them down?' Davis said, 'We are not sure and have nothing against them. We think it's best if you go first to the bathroom and I'll follow you. I'll take the second one and be there if you need help.'"

As he spoke, Jack realized just how much he and Davis had been through together, how many life-threatening situations. And they'd made it through each one.

"The tequila arrived and we both took a shot, of course. I thought to myself—but never said it to Davis—*Why do I have to go into the bathroom first and not you?*" Jack paused. "Sometimes Davis is just unfair. I then said to Davis, 'I'm tired of this stuff. If these guys do come after me that's it, I'm taking mine out.' To which Davis said, 'No. You can't. We need them alive.' So, he puts me in danger *and* won't let me get any satisfaction. What kind of brother does that?" Then Jack looked out at the guests. "It's a friend who lets his buddy have some fun but is smart enough to see the big picture and knows when to get him to stop. That balance in a man is rare to find. It may not sound like it, but it is." He raised his glass and said, "To Mr. and Mrs. Davis." He was about to look for Jojo but his gaze seemed to zoom in on a gun. The barrel of which was pointed right at them. He instinctively moved in front of Davis. The explosion of the shot reverberated throughout the whole room.

Jack crumpled to the ground.

CHAPTER 16

Jack opened his eyes to an unfamiliar ceiling and an antiseptic smell. There was a moment of confusion before his mind catapulted back to what had happened and he realized he was in the hospital.

"Hey, you awake?" came Jojo's voice. She appeared in Jack's line of vision, her dark eyes looking at him intently. Her mouth a tight line of worry.

He tried his voice. "Yeah."

"Oh, Jack. I'm so sorry. But I'm glad you're awake. What can I do?"

He didn't know what to say. He wasn't angry; he was sad. "Tell my staff to interview the FBI agents and to get all the pictures and film from the event. Get presidential approval if necessary."

"Are you sure?"

"Yes. I want to know what happened. We need the stories from people."

"I'll do it. My dad heard about what happened and called. He's very upset. I mean really upset. He thinks this is all his fault."

"It's not. I'd like to speak to a doctor."

"I'll go find him."

Jack closed his eyes after she left the room but his mind raced: *Was he okay? Who did it? How did they get through security? When could he leave?*

Jojo returned with the doctor. "Hello Mr. Gold," he said. "I'm Dr. Demesh Shih. You're at the Inova Fairfax Hospital. You were shot in the shoulder. It was a clean shot and no blood vessels or organs were injured. You should be fine."

"How long will I need to be here?"

"We'd like to keep you tonight for observation and if nothing else comes up you should be clear to leave tomorrow."

Jack thanked the doctor before he left the room. Everything the doctor had just said was good, all things considered. No major organs damaged, a full recovery. Out of here by tomorrow.

"There are a lot of people outside," Jojo said. "The president announced your appointment after the inauguration. It's all over the news."

"Is Davis out there?"

"He is."

"Please send him in."

A minute later Davis entered looking stricken, his eyes red. He stood by the side of Jack's bed.

"I brought my family into your home and one of them shot you."

"Davis, it wasn't them. Someone got to them. Now, I have an important question. Did you cancel your honeymoon?"

"Of course. How could we go with you in the hospital?"

"Davis, I got shot in the shoulder. I'll be fine. You owe Rio a honeymoon. Go. I'll be there when you get back."

Davis shook his head. "Jack, the shooter was aiming for you. But you stepped in front of me." Tears came to Davis's eyes. "It should have been me protecting you."

"Go on the honeymoon. Smoke cigars, and make Rio drink a little bit too much. Use me as an excuse if needed."

Davis said nothing for several long seconds and Jack could almost hear the inner battle he was having. Finally, he exhaled. "Okay, Jack, we will. Just so you know—everyone at the Bureau is embarrassed. They're still looking into why the guy shot you and who was behind it. You have their full attention, I assure you."

After Davis left, Jojo came back in. He was starting to feel a hint of pain through the cloud of pain medication they had him on. "I got a call from the president and updated him on what the doctor said. He'll make sure the FBI agents can be interviewed by your friends and will have access to all the media. He also said he's going to stop by and have you sworn in."

"We can talk about that later," Jack said. "The only thing I'd like right now is a kiss."

Jojo took a step closer, bent down, and kissed Jack on his dry lips.

He smiled. "I'm glad you're maintaining a positive attitude over all this," Jojo said.

"How could I not? I'm alive. I have you as my wife and apparently it's going to be fun being Sutton's secretary of state."

*   *   *

Later that day Sutton showed up, his expression solemn with concern in his eyes. "Jack," he said. "How are you doing?"

He was in more pain now than he had been when he'd first woken up, but he also felt like he was as ready as he'd ever be to leave the hospital. "The food here isn't too bad. I've had worse." He used the button on the side of the bed to raise himself to almost sitting.

"We hear that you can leave tomorrow, but I thought you'd want to be sworn in now. Is it okay if I bring in the vice president, Jojo and some of the press?"

"Sure."

The president hesitated. "Do you think . . . Will you be able to raise your right hand, and put your left hand on the flag?"

"Just glad it's not the other way around."

Sutton stuck his head out of the room and called everyone in. First came Jojo, then Vice President Valentina Rodrigo, along with a few press and TV cameras. There was a bit of shuffling as everyone tried to arrange themselves in the room. Jojo stood on Jack's left while the vice president was on the right. Sutton and the photographers were at the foot of the bed. He was surrounded.

The vice president began. "Will you please raise your right hand and place your left hand on the flag." Jack did as she said and she continued to speak. When it came time for him to affirm his commitment to the country as secretary of state, he nodded.

"I do," he said.

Photographs were taken and there was some subdued clapping.

"Congratulations, Mr. Secretary!" Sutton said.

One of the news outlets respectfully asked, "Do you have anything to share with us?"

Jack thought for a moment. "My being here is factual proof of the many threats that exist to the United States and other countries. Threats to liberty, prosperity, and democracy."

"Well said, Jack," Sutton said. He clapped his hands together. "All right everyone I think we let the secretary rest now."

After everyone left, Jojo pulled a chair over close to the side of the bed. She touched his good arm and smiled. "My Jack, the secretary of state." Her smile wavered a little and tears filled her eyes. "I'm sorry," she said, wiping at her eyes with the back of her hand. "This has all been so stressful. Even though I know you're going to be fine. I just thought . . . that we were finally at a place where your life wasn't going to be in danger all the time."

"Come here," he said, raising his good arm. Jojo leaned in and he gave her the best hug he could. "I don't want you to be stressed. I'm confident I will not be in further danger."

She lifted her head. "How do you know that?"

"It's a gut instinct. Also, I'm pretty sure every leader of every country just saw me being sworn in as secretary of state. Anyone harms me they'd receive the indignation of the world. And the FBI is hunting down whoever tried to kill me. They won't give up."

"I'm just worried that the people who want you dead won't give up, either."

"Well, I've got you as my bodyguard."

That got him a little smile.

"I do need one thing as soon as possible," Jack said.

"What is that?"

"A tailor."

"Oh, that's right. Your only suit got a little bloody. I'll call Cam and have one stop by tomorrow."

CHAPTER 17

Jack was glad to be home. The downstairs had been cleaned and restored to the comfortable area it was before. Jojo had added Persian carpets, which gave the room a warmer feeling. It was late afternoon and the tailor just left. He had brought some suits with him and modified them on the spot for Jack. He also took measurements, carefully avoiding Jack's left arm in its sling. Suits, shirts, and ties would be sent over based on the material Jack had selected. He liked Zegna and Armani. Jojo had picked up two pairs of shoes he liked.

When his iPhone rang with a call from Ari, Jack put in his earbuds and answered the call.

"Hi Ari."

"Jack, hey buddy, I heard the news. I also saw you getting sworn in. Congratulations."

"Yes. It's been a crazy few days. I'm just sitting here wanting to do lots but knowing I should rest."

"Any word on who did it?"

"They're just getting going and will keep me informed. I'll let you know when I find anything out."

"We're looking into it too. We have confirmation it was Li Keqiang who ordered those guys to take you out in Beijing. In your home."

"Can you get me some proof on that or send it to our guys in the US? I'd like to be able to use that information."

"It's not going to happen, and you didn't hear it from me or us. That information would reveal sources and methods and it's just not worth it. But I do have some other good news."

Jack propped himself up on the cushions. "Give it to me. I need some good news."

"You wanted a WeChat for democracy type app so people could communicate. Well, our guys reversed engineered—okay, literally copied the entire WeChat app. The main functions, not the payment features and other services. They then overlayed a supercharged VPN on it."

"They stole WeChat's IP?"

"Yes."

"I don't know, Ari."

"This is the only way to get something the Chinese are comfortable with. If the real WeChat in the US gets an injunction to stop it, then the app's VPN will just use an IP address from another country. The data will be simultaneously co-hosted in a bunch of countries. This is how people will be safe using it in China."

"I need approval before unleashing it."

"What do you want to call it? We can easily brand it. That'll help."

"Let's call it 'LibertyChat.' That should help with branding and create some ambiguity when comparing it to WeChat."

Ari wrote something down. "Also, we can moderate the postings. The Chinese government can have its army of people start posting all over the place. We can remove them if you want."

"No. As long as people get validated with a code sent to their phone, I agree with Elon Musk. I too am a 'free speech absolutist'. We just want to avoid computers setting up accounts."

"That's exactly how we set it up. I'll send it over to you after we finish the branding. Also, there will be a link where people can download it. Both ways should ensure anyone who wants the app can get and use it. And it'll automatically update. We are able to do this since we are not distributing it through the Apple Store, which China could restrict."

"Sounds like you've thought this through." Jack was pleased. "Send it over and we'll take a look. Who will own the app and maintain it?"

"Good question. It's basically open-sourced software that's being distributed without a license. No one will own it, which is along the anti-commercial lines of people who develop this type of code. Any enhancements to the code can be made but must be approved by unknown individuals before integration. We don't expect that to happen but are prepared for the eventuality."

"There must have been a lot of people involved in this. Anything else I need to know?"

"You can tell them you had the assistance of a group in Israel, if you must. That's all. The only risk is that if we want to download something malicious to someone's computer we could do so since automatic updates occur. Phone security protects against this already, though."

"Okay, send it to me. I bet I'll need that piece of information. I'll let you know how it goes."

Ari leaned closer to the screen. "Jack, enough with getting shot and stabbed. Everyone was concerned. Me especially."

"Like I told Jojo, my gut instinct is that now I'll be safe." The paternal tone in Ari's voice reminded Jack that he should call his father.

Jack and Ari ended the call. Ten minutes later Jack received an email from Ari that contained the app and a link to it. Jack considered opening the app and checking it out, but hesitated. When he shared it with Sutton, the legality of using the platform would then become an issue. He'd rightly insist on having a group of people evaluate it. Was it IP theft? What would be the recourse on the United States government? What would happen if Israel *did* do something malicious by downloading some nefarious software? There were too many risks.

*   *   *

The next morning Jack slowly got dressed. If he moved the wrong way his shoulder still caused pain. With patience he got everything on except for his tie.

"I need your help, babe," he called to Jojo.

"This is the first time I have had to do this for you," she said, coming over. She delicately tied a lopsided knot. "Hey, this is kind of fun. Does that look okay?"

Jack looked at his reflection in the full-length mirror. "Yes, perfect."

He said goodbye to the kids and Jojo walked him out to the SUV. "Be a good boy today," she said. "Play nice with everyone."

"I'll be good. I love you, baby."

"I love you, too."

He gingerly got in the back saying hello to the driver, and took out his iPhone. Once again he looked at the email from Ari. He selected it and forwarded it to Susan, Jason, and David and including a note: *Why don't you try this and let me know what you think when I see you later today. Feel free to post your stories here.*

He put the phone back in his pocket and tried to relax. It was his first day at work—A meeting with the president then a visit to his office. Jack tried to enjoy the ride despite forgetting to bring a cup of coffee.

As if he could hear his thoughts, the driver reached back and handed Jack a to-go cup. It was Davis. They both burst out laughing, which made Jack grimace because it hurt his shoulder.

"You think I'm missing today?" Davis said. "No way!"

"I wouldn't want anyone else with me right now. How was the honeymoon?"

"It was great. We spent a few days in Florida; Rio loved it. She insisted we come back early though. She's smart."

"Except for the last speech, your wedding was really nice."

"You didn't see it but after that shot there were ten people on top of the guy."

"Did they find anything else about him?"

"Not so far, except they don't think it has anything to do with China."

Jack's eyebrows shot up. "Really?"

"I know. That surprised me too. The guy has had zero relations with China or anyone Chinese. But it makes sense. He seemed fanatical. Who'd shoot someone knowing you'd get caught? That would suggest Middle East. Though nothing definitively."

"That's out of my hands. I've got other things to do."

"Yes, about that. Did you know that the White House is fifteen minutes away, just like Zhongnanhai was from your place in Beijing? Did you plan that?"

"Coincidental. Jojo got the house without me. It's nice that it's so close."

"They augmented all your security. Expect more people on the road and in the air."

"I've sort of given up."

"Jack, that feeling is temporary. You'll bounce back. You always do."

They arrived at the White House, Davis stopping the vehicle to show his credentials then driving forward. Jack got out and Davis led the way. It seemed that everyone had stopped to watch. A few people started to clap, then everyone was. Jack smiled though he wasn't exactly sure why people would be clapping. In fact, they were lined up nearly the entire way to the Oval Office. Madeline, the president's secretary, was there and waved Jack in.

President Sutton stood up and walked toward Jack. "Hello, Jack. You look a lot better than you did in the hospital. How do you feel?"

"It's good to be back on my feet. Just have to take things slower than normal for a little while."

"Well, just in case we are having a doctor accompanying you."

"Sir, I can see a doctor in whatever country we're in if something comes up."

"Jack, I insist. This is a security issue. Too many promises have been made to you that were not lived up to. Now, have you read the briefs for each country?"

"Yes, I did. The only one I suspect we'll have a problem with is Germany. Even with threatening them to withdraw troops, my guess is they still won't sign the Declaration. They'll think it's a bluff. We would be almost setting up a trap for ourselves by threatening that."

"Do you have a suggestion?"

"Honestly, if they don't want to sign, I think we should say we'll leave NATO. We can use their lack of contribution to NATO as part of our excuse. Anyway, I'll have them call you. As long as you reinforce our anger at their lack of moral rectitude, if you reinforce that we will remove troops *and* leave NATO, then they'll sign. There'll be no repercussions."

"I can go along with that," Sutton said. "But you are never getting invited over to the White House for poker night."

Jack lifted his eyebrows. "I didn't know there was a poker night."

Sutton grinned. "Okay, Jack. Let's get some pictures, then you can go over to the Truman Building. The China Declaration—the revised one— has been sent from my office to the leaders of all the countries. There will be a nice copy on the plane for you to get signatures."

After pictures were taken, Jack and Davis returned to the SUV and made their way to the Harry S. Truman Building, home to the United States Department of State. The building had a floor area of 1.4 million square feet; over eight thousand people worked there. There were forty-four elevators, which reminded Jack of China's Control Center. Also, forty-four was an unlucky number since *four* "sì" sounded like *death* "sǐ" in Chinese.

Jack got out at the East Entrance and went inside. Ron Timmons was waiting. Jack stopped and shook his hand.

"The president contacted me and sent over the China Declaration. He mentioned there might be a chief of staff position open." Ron smiled broadly. "I'm here to apply."

"That's great," Jack said. "You're hired. Last night I was reviewing the layout of the building. I understand your new office was originally designated for the secretary of war and chief of staff."

"Things change. Any space will do."

"Great. You can show me to my office, if you don't mind."

They went through security and were escorted to the seventh floor. All the staff had come out. Evidently they had received word he had arrived. As Jack passed them, they smiled or nodded and said, "Hello, Mr. Secretary."

When he got to his office, Jack met his secretary, a woman named Jessie Parker. She was tall and had excellent posture. Her slightly graying hair was pulled back in a sensible ponytail that went slightly past her shoulders.

"It's a pleasure to meet you, Mrs. Parker," Jack said, shaking her hand. "Could you please urgently send for Ambassador David Pret in Beijing? I'd like to meet him tomorrow morning in my office before I leave for Europe."

Mrs. Parker wrote something in shorthand on a notepad. "Certainly. And we have your three assistants on the third floor. We had space down there."

"Kindly have them come up immediately, with all their things. They are highly valued guests. Please, let's try to spoil them any way we can."

Mrs. Parker smiled. "I like to spoil people."

Jack started to enter his office but stopped and turned, surveying his surroundings. Then he turned back so he was looking out from his office and his eyes landed on a huge conference room. It could easily seat thirty to forty. He walked over and went inside. "Perfect." There was a large white board at the front of the room. Jack took a seat.

Ron followed him and took a seat further back. Mrs. Parker came into the room. "They are on their way."

"Mrs. Parker, could you please summon all the under secretaries and above, and the East Asian Pacific Affairs Assistant Secretary, to join us in here? And any legal staff we have."

"Certainly."

"Also, arrange for lunch in about ninety minutes. Maybe an assortment of sandwiches, salads, fruit, and drinks."

"Certainly."

"Could you also have three Chinese meals delivered from the best restaurant you can find? How about three soups, a vegetable dish, and meat fried rice to share. For my Chinese friends, please."

"Certainly," Mrs. Parker said, scribbling on her notepad.

There was movement at the door and Susan, David, and Jason walked in. Jack felt his spirits lift. He stood up, wanting to hug each of them but refraining, as it would be inappropriate. "Hi. I've missed you all."

"How are you?" Susan asked. "We all saw too much of the video and pictures of what happened. It looked awful."

"It *was* awful. But, no lasting damage, and no one else was hurt. So we can continue with our work. How are you guys? How is the place you're staying at?"

"It's nice . . ." Susan said slowly. "We each have our own unit in the same building."

Jack could tell they were not happy with it. They worked hard. They needed a nice comfortable place to live.

"Let me see pictures, please."

They took out their phones and showed Jack photos of three separate small kitchens, main sitting area, and a small bedroom.

"How about the three of you share one bigger and nicer place with a much better kitchen? The kitchens look way too small."

"We won't say no to that." Susan said.

"Okay." He gestured to Ron. "I would like to introduce you to Ron Timmons, my chief of staff. He served as secretary of state during Sutton's previous term. You should address him as Mr. Secretary, even though I am the acting secretary. Mr. Timmons, I would like to intro-duce Susan, David, and Jason. I worked with them in China. They're orig-inally from President Wang Yang's office and they'll be taking a leading role when it comes to China. Please, if they need anything—help them. I trust their judgment. I don't know who to call, but can we get them into a much nicer single apartment? The company they work for will pay for any excess rental charge."

"They don't work for you?"

"No, they do not work for the government. They work as consultants. I hired the company they work for. Best to keep their assistance informal and out of public for now since the Chinese government might take retribution against their families."

"Oh." Ron nodded. "I see. Sure, I can make a call and take care of that."

"Thank you, sir."

People began walking in. The seats were filling up. Jack looked to his three assistants. "The secretary will help you out. We're lucky to have him, given his deep knowledge and experience. Feel free to ask him if there is anything you need if I'm not around. But try asking me first. You report directly to me and only me. Please have a seat close to the white board, near me." Jack knew he had to clarify things, particularly to Chinese who were most accustomed to working in very hierarchical organizations.

There were about twenty-five people now seated around the conference table. Jack stood up. "Hello. Welcome. It's a pleasure to meet you. I'm Jack Gold; I think everyone knows me. Please, let's go around so that I can start to learn a little bit more about you."

Each person stood and introduced themselves. All were friendly and seemed happy to be there. When it came to Ron, Jack stood to introduce him, though he suspected everyone in the room already knew who he was. Jack then introduced Susan, Jason, and David.

He was getting tired and his mouth was dry. This first day at work was taking more out of him than he anticipated. "We have a few things I'd like to get started on right now. But let's take a five-minute break."

Jack sat down next to his team. "What'd you think of the platform?"

"You haven't seen it?" Susan asked.

"No."

She took her phone out and showed Jack. She clicked an orange app icon. As it started to open, "LibertyChat" appeared, in vibrant colors. Susan opened the drop-down menu, and Jack saw in Chinese it said, "Chats, Contacts, Uncover, Scan." Similar to WeChat but not exactly the same.

"So, what did you think?" he asked.

"It's amazing. The interface is very comfortable. We invited a few friends and then posted stories. It says that a VPN is built into it. Anyone can use it. Many of our friends have already joined. It's growing."

"You invited other people?"

Susan looked at him in confusion. "I thought that's what you wanted us to do."

Jack winked, making sure Ron didn't see. "No. I absolutely did not expect you to invite others. Which type of devices are using the app?"

"Just our cell phones."

"Under no circumstance are you to download that app to your computer. There may be security issues associated with it."

Jack looked over to Ron and others at the table. "The app is a way for us to communicate and share stories directly with people. The Chinese can use it to share theirs too. The app has been built with a VPN so it can use any number of IP addresses in different countries. The software automatically updates so it can constantly update the VPN to ensure it does not get blocked by the Chinese government. It's a double-edged sword, though, since that presents a potential risk that malicious software could be downloaded. Apple is really good at phone security, but the app company could download something to a less secure computer. I don't think they will, but they could. At least we finally have a good platform that the Chinese government cannot turn off or control, like they do with WeChat."

After the break, everyone returned to their seats. Jack helped himself to one of the Diet Cokes that had been brought in.

"Since we are all here," he said, "I would like to share with you how I like to work. I have an open-door policy. You can come in whenever you want, or you can arrange a meeting limited to thirty minutes. This will force us to be organized and efficient. If you want something from me, please come in with a clear-cut recommendation, supported by arguments that have facts as their foundation. Then, I'll give you an answer. Or, if you have a problem, feel free to share it for potential ideas on how we might solve it. I'm excited to get to know all of you, and to make the Department of State a place we are exceedingly proud of. There is one thing in particular that I would like to emphasize. Everyone is an expert at looking at the past and being brilliantly critical. Any pundit can do that. I want solutions for the future, not a retrospect." He paused and took a sip of his soda.

"Although I must visit other countries and their leaders, and address a looming China situation, there will certainly be more than enough time to address the issues you feel are important to the United States. Tomorrow I am off to England to meet with prime minister Andrew Jones. The intent is to get him to sign the China Declaration. After the document is signed by world leaders, there will be the next steps. I'd like to start detailing those now."

Jack stood up and walked to the white board. He picked up one of the markers. "Our overarching goal is to address the issues outlined within the Declaration document. The intent is to make them go away so that the Chinese population has a more peaceful and prosperous existence. This in turn will help grow the global economy and save lives. It's both a humanitarian and economic mission. The question is—what can be done to change things, to make the Chinese aware of the horrible situation that exists within their country—that is thrust upon them by the Communist Party—that will then lead to pressure on the government for actual change?" He paused though he did not expect anyone to respond.

"In my experience with China, we cannot do things predictably like previous administrations. There will be no typical sanctions and then a waiting game to see if China capitulates. They will not. We will develop a plan for rapid action to surprise and overwhelm them. China has not been the recipient of a series of swift actions. Our plan will have consequences. We must anticipate these and pre-empt them before they occur."

Jack began to write and fill in a big matrix on the white board.

INITIATIVE	HOW	DURATION
1. Heighten Awareness Globally		
Write China Declaration	*Jack to Write*	
Get Leaders' Signatures	*Jack to Make Visits*	
Publicize Globally	*Press Conference*	
Risks & Response	*China to impose sanctions*	
2. Close all China Embassies/Consulates		
Prepare online visa processing	*Ron Tillerson*	
Prepare facilities in US	*Ron Tillerson*	
Prepare staff relocation	*Ron Tillerson*	
Execute security measures for secret materials	*Ron Tillerson*	
Lease facilities	*Ron Tillerson*	
3. Find, Test, Adopt WeChat Alternative		
Find WeChat Alternative	*Jack*	
Test	*Susan, David, Jason*	
Security Check	*Gov Cyber Security*	
Launch Platform	*Susan, David, Jason*	
Populate with Content	*Susan, David, Jason*	
4. Modify Taiwan Policy		
5. Fentanyl Initiative		
6. Blacklist CCP		
7. Open China Immigration		

Someone in the back of the room spoke up. "I can't believe you are going to blacklist all CCP members and their families."

Jack stopped writing and turned. "Why?"

"What if the family members had nothing to do with their father? You'd be punishing innocent people."

"You bring up a good point and we need to discuss these items. That's what this exercise is for. What if the family is living off the ill-gotten gains of their CCP father? Then what? We'll discuss all of these; your objection is duly noted. We might end up recommending that only National Committee CCP members are sanctioned. But please remember we must take into consideration what the Chinese think about when it is explained to them. You see, this initiative may make you uncomfortable, but it might play a huge role in escalating awareness in China. Once this is done, maybe we intentionally scale it back due to severe disagreement. Please everyone, do not think single-dimensionally about these issues. You must think three to five moves ahead and how emotions are impacted."

Everyone except for his assistants was copying down the matrix Jack had written on the white board. "We have to not just detail all sub-tasks, but the timeline and who owns every task and what they need. Again, this is the very beginning, to give you a sense of what is required. We need to think ahead. For example, if taking action on fentanyl we need to prepare well beforehand through stories and so forth to massively heighten global awareness. In particular—awareness amongst Chinese. We'll need to also, down the line, look at this plan with a pure Chinese perspective. We have several different stakeholders that we must have a separate plan for and consider overall. I think you get the idea. A key overarching theme should be speed. Remember—everything attempted before did not work. None of it. It was a failure. No agreement was ever lived up to. Things must be done differently. That is why I am here. And why all of you are here."

"Jack," Ron said, "could you please humor me and go through the logic of closing all the embassies and consulates in China?"

"They are almost a complete waste of taxpayer's money. I cannot think of a single useful thing they have done because of a presence there. They process visas. This can be done online with documents sent by the person applying, with interviews being done by Zoom. The real issue is the inefficiency of visa processing. Businesses don't need the State Department for assistance when entering China. You might say they're supposed to protect US citizens. That never happens. When it is done the State Department should call a local attorney. They can do that from anywhere. They're supposed to coordinate official visits for other US agencies. Anyone can book a hotel and conference room over the internet. And lastly, China assumes everyone working at the embassies and consulates is a spy and they track them. I guess the one thing that might be useful is the registering of diplomatic vehicles. My sense right now is that a handful of staff based in the ambassador's residence will be more than sufficient. We're talking about a huge amount of money saved. The embassy in Beijing cost $500 million to build. That's $1,000 per square foot."

"You make a compelling argument," Ron said.

"This is my thinking for the time being. We won't be telling China that we are closing the embassies to save costs. We will be sending a serious message about our displeasure. The small businesses around the embassies like restaurants, will be devastated by the closures. It may surprise you that this concerns me. The bottom line is that we need to plan for the closures and how visa processing will be moved online. Where will the additional people in the United States be placed to process visas? These issues must be detailed, and preparatory action taken very early."

Ron cupped his chin and nodded thoughtfully. "The internet has fundamentally changed things, but the State Department has not fundamentally changed."

"Exactly. Well said."

The food arrived. Jack called for a thirty-minute break so everyone could eat. His shoulder was aching but the pain was nothing he couldn't work through.

When everyone was done eating, Jack stood up again. "We've got a few important documents to discuss. The first that I just started to discuss is a spreadsheet called the *Appeasement Plan*. In other words, how can we and the Chinese people be appeased? The second document will be essential too. I call it our *Cheat Sheet*. This sheet will summarize other things we can leverage over China." Jack wrote out the following headings on the white board: *Country, Dealings with China, Pivot Point, State Contact, Action, Note*.

"We need to fill this in for every country and person that might have some sort of leverage or pivotal leverage over China. I think you all understand what I am getting at. We need a strategy when it comes to other countries. It will help us make sure others put leverage on China if they do not want to follow all of our initiatives. We can easily suggest something else. Does this make sense?" Everyone nodded.

"Good." Jack sat down. His shoulder was hurting more. Standing so long had not helped. "I think that's enough for today. Let's all work on this while I am gone. Thank you all for your dedication to making our mission a success."

CHAPTER 18

The next morning, after a long goodbye to Jojo and the kids, Jack sat in the SUV with Davis. "I'll be meeting with Ambassador Pret at nine this morning," Jack told him.

"You going to fire him?"

"Yes. You want to watch? Maybe bring Tim with you to make sure I don't kill him."

"That'd be my pleasure. Keeping you out of trouble is a responsibility your dad would want me to do."

Shit, Jack thought. He still hadn't called his dad.

"Do me a favor and confiscate his government-issued phone and his diplomatic passport before he enters my office. Then, both of you stay in the office."

"Want me to take his wallet too?"

"If you can get away with it, yes."

They arrived in no time. Jack, Davis, and Tim walked in and took the elevator up to the seventh floor. It was 8:45am and the Beijing ambassador had not arrived; there was time for a cup of coffee.

Jack pulled out his iPad Pro and opened it. Just then, his desk phone buzzed. He picked it up and heard Mrs. Parker's voice. "Ambassador Pret is here. May I show him in?"

"Sure," Jack said. "Show him in."

Davis set his coffee cup down and got up from the chair he'd been sitting in. He went to the door and opened it. "Good morning, Mr. Ambassador. May I please have your phone? I need to keep it outside for security. I also need your passport. Those GPS chips inside, you know."

Ambassador Pret handed both to Davis, who exited the room briefly and then returned to his chair. The ambassador looked to the two FBI agents then to Jack, confusion etched across his face. "The president has augmented my security detail," Jack said.

"Ah yes," Pret said. His demeanor instantly changed and he smiled a wide, charming smile. "Mr. Secretary," he said. "Congratulations. It's great to see you."

"Thank you. I had some pictures I thought you might want to see." Jack turned his iPad toward Pret. "Come around so you can see."

The ambassador moved around Davis to get closer to Jack's desk.

"These are the four guys who attacked me in Beijing after you removed my security detail. My wife and kids were upstairs."

Pret squinted at the screen but said nothing. Jack went to the next picture, showing one of the dead men. He swiped to the next photo of a different dead man. "You can see I killed each one of them, despite me not having a knife. Here's another picture—I dragged them and put them in our kitchen pantry."

Pret swallowed and then cleared his throat. "Jack, I'm so sorry that happened. We never knew."

Jack put his iPad down. "You knew Li Keqiang was worried about me saying something prior to the election. You told me so."

"Yes Jack, but I never thought something like this would occur."

"Did you know President Li would attack me?"

A muscle under Pret's eye quivered. "How could I have known?"

"Did you talk to anyone in the Li administration about the removal of my security?"

He hesitated long enough for Jack to know that he indeed had. "No," Pret said.

"Did anyone tell you there might be an attack on us?"

The ambassador hesitated again. "No, of course not. We would have notified you."

Jack knew for sure Pret was lying. He had informed the Li administration and knew there was going to be an attack. He looked at Davis, who remained in his seat and did not make a move to arrest him. Jack knew Cooper was recording everything.

Jack turned his attention back to Pret. "It is my belief that you have negligently performed your duties as the ambassador of China, in particular when it comes to your obligation to provide security to United States diplomats in China. I hereby officially notify you that you are relieved of your duties effective immediately."

Pret paled. "Jack, this is really just a misunderstanding. Please. This can all be explained."

"You are excused."

"Can I at least get my passport back?"

"That is a diplomatic passport. You are no longer a diplomat."

"How will I get back to China?"

"Apply to the State Department for a passport, just like everyone else."

"Then I need to get a China visa from the Chinese consulate. Doing both will take forever."

Jack leaned back in his chair. "I haven't the slightest idea why you are still in my office."

Now Davis and Tim stood up. "Sir," Davis said. "We'd like to escort you out of the building please."

Pret's eyes were wide. "Jack, please," he pleaded. Davis and Tim stepped toward him and escorted him out. Jack got up and went out to Mrs. Parker.

"Ambassador Pret was just fired from his post. Can you please draft something and inform whoever needs to be notified? Let's please make sure access to all information and places is immediately suspended."

"Certainly, Mr. Secretary."

When Davis returned, he came into the office and closed the door. "How come you didn't arrest him? He was guilty as sin."

"You know why. We need proof. Between the three of us and what you said, along with the pictures, we have enough information and collaboration to open a case. I'll file it today while we're on the plane and we can then look into all the records; even those from the embassy in Beijing."

"If you open a case, are you sure you want to let him get a passport and leave the country?"

"That's a good point. I'll bring up that issue internally."

While swift justice would be nice, Jack knew it seldom worked out that way.

Davis said, "I was impressed with your questioning and calmness upon hearing the responses. Your dad would be proud."

"I still haven't called him. We should get to the airport. I can call him from the plane."

*   *   *

The plane Jack was flying in was Air Force Two, a C-32A recently remodeled. It was a larger plane than what he was used to, meant for carrying more people. It was like a newer van, instead of a nice Bentley.

Once Jack was settled in his seat, he started a FaceTime call with his dad.

"Sorry for not calling sooner," he said when his dad picked up.

"I've been waiting to hear from you, Jack. How are you? I saw that you got shot. Wish I was there to take a look at it." Jack's father had retired from his successful obgyn practice years ago. Now he lived down in Cabo, where he had a place right on the beach and preferred to spend his time out on the water on his boat.

"I can take off my shirt if you'd like to see it."

"No. No need. I just can't believe with all those FBI agents nearby someone would be able to get a shot off. I'm glad you're okay and I have been thinking about you. I thought about calling but figured you've got plenty on your plate now. Didn't want to be a bother."

"Dad, you can call me whenever. But yes, there's a lot going on. We just moved to a new place in DC. Then I got shot. And yesterday I started a new job."

"I think everyone in the United States saw your inauguration. All my buddies did. I got calls from patients I haven't seen for years. We are all extraordinarily proud of you, Jack. I can only guess that you have lots to do, particularly with regard to China. Go get 'em. You'll do great."

"I hope so."

"Are you on a plane right now?"

"I'm on Air Force Two, about to leave for England."

A smile spread across his dad's face. "Are you trying to impress me?"

"No. Actually, the name of the plane is nice but I prefer something smaller."

"Feel free to drop by. I'd love to see you and Jojo and the grandkids. The sun is coming up now and all the boats are making their way out with tourists aboard. They are over-fishing the area."

"I hope to see you soon, Dad. If you ever want to come out this way . . . we've got plenty of room. You should see this house Jojo picked out."

"When things settle down for you, Jack. We'll see. Take care."

Jack smiled. "You too, Dad."

CHAPTER 19

Jack's meeting with Andrew Jones at 10 Downing Street was to be delayed. "The Queen would like you to drop by to say hello," Jones said. "A quick courtesy visit," he added. "We can go to Downing Street afterwards."

Jack was not entirely shocked. Sutton had mentioned this might happen and he found himself eager to meet the Queen. If there was one person in England he would like to have a chat with, it would be her.

The castle rose above immaculate lawns and beautifully landscaped flower gardens. It was the oldest inhabited castle in the world, and Jack could feel the history that the place was steeped in. He followed Jones through rooms that were grand and opulent, passing by large oil paintings of ancestors hung in gold frames. The crown molding in each room was intricate and beautiful.

To Jack's surprise, he was escorted into the Queen's sitting room. Everything in the room was well appointed but gave off a much more comfortable feel. "Your Majesty, may I introduce you to the United States Secretary of State, Jack Gold. Mr. Secretary, Your Majesty."

Jack tilted his head forward slightly before looking back up, as Jones stepped out of the room.

"Nice to meet you, Mr. Secretary," the Queen said. "Did you know that your tie is crocked?"

Jack spoke carefully. "Yes, Your Majesty. I was shot in my shoulder last week which makes tying it a challenge. An insufficient excuse, of course."

"Yes, right, I saw the file about you. You have had your share of escapades over the past few years. You've been on the job just a few days. How have you found things?"

"I brought in four people so we can hit the ground running. I'm reassured since the State Department offices occupy the Harry S. Truman Building."

"That *is* interesting."

"How is that, Ma'am?"

"Would you like to join me for a cup of tea, Mr. Secretary? May I call you Jack?"

"Certainly, Ma'am."

The Queen walked over to a nearby sofa that was facing away from the window, in front of which was a mahogany oval table and a china teapot with matching teacups. After the Queen sat, she motioned for Jack to join her. One of her attendants appeared and poured tea for both of them before disappearing again.

"In 1951, when I was a princess, I visited Truman. In fact, we stayed with him and his family for two days at the Blair House. At the time, the White House was being renovated."

"I'm happy for you that you got to meet such a great man. He's my favorite president."

"I'm curious as to why that is?"

"He was straightforward, decisive, simple, and entirely honest. Those traits are hard to find these days."

"I was only twenty-five when I met him. He was all those qualities you mentioned but the one that sticks out is 'genuine.' To this day, I still hold such an affectionate memory of him."

"Your assessment of him was excellent. Your Churchill underestimated him."

"Ha. That he did. By a great deal, in fact."

Jack took a tiny sip of his tea. "I find it ironic that Truman never went to college, but he received an honorary degree from Oxford."

"He proved that the ordinary American is capable of grandeur." The Queen looked at him for a moment without saying anything. "I inquired and understand that you wrote the China Declaration. Is that true or was it a group effort?"

Jack had the Declaration in a leather folder that he had placed next to him on the sofa. He glanced at it. "I wrote it, Ma'am."

"May I?"

Jack handed the folder to her. He watched as she opened the folder and began to read. After a moment, she paused, and then began reading aloud. "*Wherefore today we make amends in the annals of history for the ills brought upon the noble Chinese people and by China on the world.*" She looked at Jack. "You wrote that?"

"Yes, I did, Ma'am."

"I didn't know Americans knew how to write."

They both laughed.

"Ma'am," Jack said. "I have a question I'd like to ask but I know it's impertinent."

The Queen closed the leather folder. "Then don't ask it."

"But as the United States Secretary of State, I have a duty to the world."

"Very well, for the world. Ask. I promise not to be too cross with you."

"Ma'am, I know the vital separation between the Crown and politics. But, if your husband were here now, how do you think he might counsel you?" Jack looked to the China Declaration.

"You are impertinent, indeed, Mr. Secretary." The Queen opened the folder again and extracted the pen from its holder. She signed her name on the bottom.

She closed the folder and handed it back to Jack. A grin came to her face. "I'd love to get you and your wife out here to visit. I hear she is a talented sculpturer and she speaks French. Do you know when this China *play*, shall we call it, will be over?"

"Yes, Ma'am. It'll be over by the end of Chinese New Year. We'll be able to watch things from afar near the end of December."

"Splendid. We shall spend New Year's together."

"We'd be honored."

"Thank you for dropping by, Mr. Secretary. I wish you godspeed in your undertaking."

Jack stood. "It was a pleasure, Your Majesty."

* * *

The prime minister was not happy. He had barely looked at Jack and they hadn't even exchanged words since getting into the car. When the PM finally did speak, it surprised Jack. "I really must insist that you print out another copy of the Declaration for my signature. It is not befitting to have the Queen's signature on that document."

Jack knew the politics. Some in England wanted the Crown dismantled or at least entirely separate from the government. "I have no authority to destroy the Queen of England's signature on an official document. I did not request her signature. The Queen decided on her own."

The car pulled up to 10 Downing, and Jack followed Jones through the famous blue door. He'd been looking forward to visiting but now the mood was ruined, and Jack could tell that the PM's mind was elsewhere.

Jones showed Jack to a sitting area and was introduced to the others already in the room. Tea was brought in. Jack tried it, again taking just a small sip.

"Americans aren't accustomed to good English tea," Jones quipped.

The snobbery was uncalled for. "Actually," Jack said, "I'm used to having the best tea in the world with the presidents of China. Some of it they age for hundreds of years. I wouldn't expect you'd be accustomed to that, though."

"Touché Mr. Secretary. I do have my mind elsewhere. My apologies. Let's sign this and take some pictures."

Jack handed him the document. "Please sign smaller below, to allow room for others." The PM dutifully signed, much smaller and well below the Queen.

"After I make my rounds to other countries, let's have a Zoom call," Jack said. "We're now preparing a plan for next steps. I'd like to share that with you."

"Of course. That'll be better timing."

*   *   *

On the way to the airport, Jack called Sutton. "Hello, Mr. President."

"I heard," Sutton said.

"What did you hear?"

"The Queen called me. Jack, she said wonderful things about you. Excellent job."

"That's not why I called, Mr. President."

"What were you going to say?"

"Her Majesty signed the Declaration. Her signature was the first one. It's a bold signature."

"Like John Handcock's signature?"

"Exactly, sir."

"I never thought the Queen would sign the document, Jack. I didn't even know you were going to ask her."

"I wasn't but the opportunity came up. I hope that's okay."

"That's tremendous news. No one gets the support of the Queen, particularly on what can be perceived as a political issue. I don't know how you did it. Everyone else will see her support and that will incline them to give theirs."

"Maybe it would be a good idea if we made sure to leave some room near her signature for yours."

"That's an excellent idea. Now, try to enjoy the rest of your visits."

"Thank you, sir."

As the car continued its way to the airport, Jack marveled at his visit with the Queen. They both shared an affinity for Harry Truman. The State Department had provided him a briefing document before the meetings; it had been of little use. What *did* strike Jack as remarkable was the little-known fact that the Queen was the closest living relative of George Washington.

*   *   *

His next stop was France where Jack had an exquisite lunch with the president, prior to him signing the Declaration. He then flew to Italy and had an equally extraordinary dinner and spent a quiet night at the Hotel Artemide, the nicest hotel in Rome.

The following morning, he was in Berlin. He was met at the airport by Larry Goldstein, the United States Ambassador to the European Union. Jack did not understand why America also had individual ambassadors in each of the countries.

"Good morning, Mr. Secretary," Goldstein said. "It's a pleasure to meet you."

Jack shook his offered hand. "Same here, Mr. Goldstein."

There was a car waiting right outside for them. "Any more information about Emma Kohler and whether she will sign or not?" Jack asked as the driver began to navigate out of the airport.

"Same story. Going against China will offend China's best friend, Russia. And Germany is at the mercy of Russian oil. I should say gas."

"Okay. We'll see how it goes. I'll have to twist her arm, I guess."

"They're pretty adamant and expect you to apply pressure."

"I feel like I'm about to go into battle when they should just sign and celebrate the importance of our union."

Goldstein smiled and shook his head. "We'll stop by the Ritz for a while. You can relax and we'll leave at two pm. You might want to get a bite to eat beforehand since lunch or dinner will not be provided."

"Gosh, they won't even feed me. I only had tea in England. Did you hear about the visit?"

"No, I did not."

Jack handed him the leather folder. The ambassador opened it. "Mr. Secretary," he said. "You got the Queen to sign? Congratulations. But that will have no impact on the German chancellor, unfortunately."

*   *   *

"Nice to meet you Mr. Secretary," Emma Kohler said. "Thank you for visiting us, and congratulations on your appointment." After they shook hands, everyone took a seat at the u-shaped wooden table, the German chancellor directly opposite him while the others in her administration sat to her left.

"Thank you for having me," Jack said. "It's nice to meet you and a pleasure to visit Berlin for the first time. Did you have a chance to read the China Declaration?"

She glanced down at the papers in front of her. "We did. We would so much like to support you and hate to bring bad news, especially since this is our first visit. We find ourselves at a disadvantage here, with no solution."

"That is unfortunate. We have the support of France, Italy, England, and even the Queen. What is preventing you from signing, if I may ask."

"Russia has threatened to cut off all our oil if we support you. This will impact all of Europe, but Germany in particular. We get forty percent of our gas from Russia."

"The United States repeatedly warned you in the past that your reliance on Russian oil made you vulnerable. Now your mistake is preventing you from signing a document that factually outlines broad-scale injustices of a nation."

Jack looked at the four other people opposite him before continuing. "A country with your history should be the very first to stand up to injustice. I reject your response to not sign. It is an affront to humanity."

The German chancellor's expression did not change. "Don't you think that is a bit extreme, Mr. Secretary? There is a great deal at stake for Germany."

Jack was not going to budge. "No, I do not. If Germany decides not to sign the China Declaration, then the United States will remove it's 35,000 troops."

He took a piece of paper from his leather folder and stood up and presented it to her. "President Sutton has signed the order, as you can see. It is up to me to deliver it to the Pentagon—or not."

She barely even glanced at the document. "President Sutton would never remove those troops. Europe has a long-standing agreement with the United States. Those troops are part of the NATO contingent. Plus, the world will know that I signed this document under duress and threat of troop removal."

"The world already knows the nature of you and Germany, the support of Russia in buying their oil while Ukrainian children were being executed. Your reputation will simply go down from here." There was much more he wanted to say, none of which would be productive, so he refrained, though it was difficult.

"We simply disagree with your argument, Mr. Gold. We do not believe America will remove its troops from such a strategic position. We discussed this at length prior to your arrival, suspecting this might be the only card you have."

"I'll be staying here until tomorrow morning. I suspected you might need some time to consider America's reasonable request," Jack replied, echoing her language. "We are asking simply that you acknowledge what is going on in China. We are not twisting your arm to have you install sanctions against China. Do you understand?"

"Yes. I hope you understand the delicate position we are in, economically."

"I do understand that you're letting economic issues trump human rights. You are kowtowing to Russia, a nation just recently guilty of war crimes. There is another ramification of your refusal to sign the Declaration. If you do not sign, President Sutton will discontinue America's NATO membership and stop all associated funding. The United States contributes over $800 million a year, four percent of its GDP. Germany contributes about $65 million. You don't even contribute two percent.

You're not committed to NATO. Americans are being killed by China through the shipment of fentanyl. Under Article 5, if a country attacks one of us, they are attacking all of NATO collectively. If the situation were in reverse and in Europe, then America would have to come to your aid. But this is in Asia. If you won't stand with America in Asia, then America will not stand with you in Europe. We'll move our troops to Japan and take our funds with us. Feel free to call President Sutton. You know my schedule."

Jack stood up, unable to hide his disgust. He could understand how Germany could create a monster like Hitler. They had a twisted mindset. Maybe it was just them negotiating, but Jack felt they had crossed a line. Sutton was willing to pull out of NATO. So was Jack. Without America in NATO there was a definite increase in the likelihood that Russia would invade Germany down the line. Jack had hoped the negotiation would not come to this.

Driving back, Goldstein said nothing for a while but then glanced at Jack, a smile on his face. "That was very good indignation, Mr. Secretary," the EU Ambassador said.

"Part of the job description, I'm learning."

* * *

Davis knocked on Jack's door early the next morning. "Emma Kohler's office called. She'll be coming by in thirty minutes and would like to see you. There are some photographers that have already started to enter the hotel."

Jack thought about handing the document to Davis to pass along to the president for her signature. That way he could go back to bed and then order breakfast. It was too early to call Jojo but he could catch up on some of the paperwork next to his bed. As tempting as it was, he begrudgingly decided against it.

"Okay, I'll get ready. Thanks. Can you please make sure that Larry Goldstein is there, along with our photographers?"

"Sure."

Once Davis was gone, Jack got ready. The German chancellor was here to sign the Declaration. He was pleased that Germany had come to its senses.

*   *   *

In India, Jack expected a similar fight as had occurred in Germany. India exported a lot to America, things like metals, precious stones, machinery, and pharmaceutical products. They then used that money to purchase oil from Russia. If need be, all those goods could be sanctioned.

But President Ram heard how things had gone in Germany and he was eager to show Jack that had no interest in taking things that direction. He had both his arms stretched out in welcome when Jack entered his office and he wasted no time by asking to sign the Declaration right away.

Then, it was off to Singapore where the friendly leaders of Malaysia, Indonesia, Thailand, Japan, and Australia agreed to meet. There was no problem with all signing the Declaration, despite them all having direct commerce with China. Jack ensured everyone left space near the Queen's signature and he informed them that this was just the start of plans and that he looked forward to speaking with them soon.

*   *   *

On the plane back to DC, Jack let Davis see the Declaration. He carefully opened the folder and whistled softly upon seeing all the signatures. Jack looked at the document from afar and realized, with all the signatures, it took on a different look. It looked legitimate. It looked like a formal and important document signed by the leaders of democratic nations.

"The Canadian and Israeli presidents will be signing this afternoon," Jack said, "then tonight, President Sutton will have a news conference and sign it." He was looking forward to that. Once Sutton signed, the document would be formally released to news agencies around the world.

Jack rested on the long flight back, then took a shower, shaved, and ate. When they landed at Andrews Airforce Base, he felt refreshed. There was a helicopter to take them directly to the White House. The ride was about fifteen miles and over more quickly than Jack would have liked.

He walked directly to the Oval Office, holding the folder, feeling like the whole thing was rather surreal. He was now actually comfortable in the White House.

He dutifully stopped in front of Madeline, again noting the slight angle of the door, given the oval shape of the office inside. "Welcome back," Madeline said. "Did you have a good trip?"

"It was many trips. Truthfully, it was an experience I hope not to repeat."

"Yes. Well," she said with a smile, "the meals you had in Italy and France didn't look all that tortuous. At least in the pictures we saw. You can go right in, Jack."

Jack opened the door and saw Sutton sitting at the Resolute Desk. "Come on in Jack," he said, "take a seat. I just got word that China has commenced a full force invasion of Taiwan."

Shit, Jack thought.

"What are we going to do, Jack."

"Nothing. There is nothing we can do but proceed with the plan we have developed. Direct military confrontation with China cannot yield any positive results in this instance. What happened with Taiwan makes the Declaration that much more relevant and imperative. But China has taken the Taiwan piece off the table. If we had only moved faster, that could have been prevented."

"When can you present your plan to everyone?"

"Any time tomorrow morning. I must meet with my team and get fully up to speed. If we execute the plan properly, with the world's support, I'd place a bet we can get Taiwan back."

"Everyone will take this a lot more seriously now."

"In a way, China has just helped us increase the visibility of their misdeeds."

"Okay. We'll go ahead with me signing the agreement in front of the press. I will preface it with some words about Taiwan. See you at eight pm tonight. Oh, one more thing—We'll have a cabinet meeting tomorrow morning at seven. You can share your plan then. Later tomorrow morning, you should be prepared for a press briefing about the Declaration."

Jack placed the folder on the president's desk and started to leave. Sutton picked up the leather folder and opened it.

"Good job, Jack," he said after he'd look at all the signatures. "Good job."

"Thank you, Mr. President," Jack said before he stepped out.

But instead of heading home, Jack told Davis to take him to the office.

"China just invaded Taiwan," Jack told him. He called Jessie Parker. "Please assemble the team. I'm on my way over."

*   *   *

The elevator opened on the seventh floor and Jack walked directly to the war room. The mood was tense. Everyone took their seat and Jack walked past Ron, nodding hello, and sat next to his three assistants.

"Susan, do you want to give me an update on the plan?"

She leaned closer to him. "The communication platform is operating just like WeChat. Membership in China is increasing steadily. We have not posted any more stories on the platform. Stories about Taiwan with video are being posted regularly. Regarding the plan, we added issues and tasks under each key initiative and a great deal of additional action items."

The spreadsheet was now projected up on a large white screen in front of the white board. Susan had her laptop open in front of her. She selected the first initiative, *Heighten Global Awareness* and a bunch of sub-tasks appeared. Many were grayed out, indicating that they had been completed. She selected one of the subtasks, and more action items appeared underneath.

"We adjusted the order of the initiatives after the Taiwan invaision," she said. "For a host of reasons, we feel one of the first initiatives should be to close all US embassies and consulates. The reason for this is that it sends a clear message to China. It also seems like something the past administration might do, but more extreme. The likely repercussions are listed. The key for us will be to ramp up the communication component by getting stories in Chinese on the platform, including you speaking in an official capacity. The topic will be the China Declaration and the rationale for the closing of the embassies. We need to drive traffic up, leveraging your profile in a way of interest to Chinese. We'll make the stories. This will go on for about one week, then the next initiative will be restrictions on National Congress members. We think this is better than all party members, which would be controversial and potentially diminish our credibility. That's 2,300 members and their family members with an appeal process already being worked out internally. I believe that if we did all CCP members there could be an irreversible backlash toward the United States."

Jack looked around the room, caught Ron's eye. He nodded. No one else said anything.

"I can go on," Susan said, "but it may be best if you took some time to look through everything on your own. We have tried to make everything self-explanatory, knowing this document, along with the Cheat Sheet, will be circulated to others. Also, we have begun to gain some useful fentanyl stories that can be used on LibertyChat and American platforms. In order to make sure there is good communication to Chinese, upon our request, we have informed the president's press secretary that you would like Chinese subtitles on all press briefings dealing with China. They have also agreed to arrange for the press to be given a translation device if you decide to use Chinese when addressing them or China."

Jack was pleased with everything she had said so far. He was also impressed with the work they'd been doing in his absence. Susan continued, "The key over the next seven days is to get content posted on the platform. Unless there are more people there, it will not be useful. At the same time, we'll start to share real stories. This, we feel, will help create an environment that people believe is safe and where they too can share their stories. Also, just to let you know—When someone in China has LibertyChat open, it allows the user to access any external site, evading government controls. This feature is helping to attract other users."

"How long do you think it will take to get through all the initiatives that will result in us achieving the desired outcome?" Jack asked.

"Five to seven months. There are a lot of variables, though. We cannot predict every potential response by China."

"Internally we should plan on executing everything faster. In the document we circulate let's please extend the execution period of everything so that completion is done by January, after Chinese New Year. Unexpected things will happen. Plus, I'd hate for everyone to have expectations that we don't meet."

Susan frowned. "You are right. If it hasn't happened before then, it will on Chinese New Year. Everyone will be home for the holiday. They will just stay at home in protest by then as momentum gets going. We didn't think of that."

Jack took out his iPhone and dialed Madeline. "I'm presenting tomorrow morning at the cabinet meeting. I need a big screen to project from my computer."

"We'll arrange it."

"Also, I'll be bringing one person. Is that okay?"

"I'm sure it's not a problem. It is your presentation, after all."

"Okay. Thank you so much."

When Jack put his phone away, he looked at Susan. "You're coming with me tomorrow. It's at seven am."

Jack then turned his attention to the rest of his team. "I want to thank everyone for all your efforts. I hope I can do us justice tomorrow. In case you didn't know, the Queen of England signed the China Declaration. So has Germany and India. We are now ready to go to the next step of the 'China Play', to use the Queen's terminology."

"Jack, congratulations," Ron said. "That is a major achievement and a good start to the China Play."

It was a catchy name. "Things are going to speed up. I need the three of you at the president's signing tonight," he said to Susan, David, and Jason. "I want you filming and creating stories. I'll be there too. Anytime there is anything going on regarding China, let's get some stories. Real, honest stories that you think citizens in China would want to see. Review each other's stories before you post. Let's also think about how we can turbo charge interest, like posting references on WeChat itself. And Weibo. After you make any last minute changes to the Appeasement Plan, can you make sure Mrs. Parker sends a copy or link of the document tomorrow to all cabinet members at seven am?"

"We will," Susan said.

Jack went into his office and closed the door behind him. He went over and lay down on the sofa. It was time to rest, at least for a little bit.

*　*　*

Jack stood next to the president. The gaggle of press stood in front of Jack and President Sutton, holding their phones, pens, pads of paper, and TV cameras. Sutton stepped up to the lectern. "At approximately two am today, The People's Republic of China invaded Taiwan. Roughly thousand paratroopers landed, surrounding the Presidential Building. Other troopers landed throughout the city, and in the city of Taichung, Taiwan's second largest city. There are no reported deaths. We expect the island country will be overrun with Chinese forces in a matter of days. China has invaded Taiwan. The United States vehemently opposes this unprovoked invasion."

Sutton paused and cleared his throat. "This is but one more example of China's egregious behavior. China has contempt for the rule of law.

They have contempt for democracy. They have contempt for the rights and liberties of people. China has contempt for the world." Flashbulbs went off all over the room.

"This is no surprise to us," Sutton continued. "Spearheaded by Jack Gold, my secretary of state, we have developed a document called the China Declaration. It outlines the atrocities China has been responsible for, the attempts Western countries have made to try to remedy them, and the summation of the need for China to change. After a marathon effort, the China Declaration has been signed by the leaders of every major democracy, uniting with America in this common understanding toward China. This is the first time such a document has been created and gained such signatures."

There was a small desk next to the lectern, on which the Declaration sat. Sutton looked at it. "Before I sign this historic document, I think it is only proper that its architect also sign it." He turned toward Jack. "Jack."

The president went over and pulled out the chair from the desk, motioned for Jack to sit down. The room was alight with flashbulbs as photographers snapped photos; Jack was certain they'd show the confusion on his face. He sat down and Sutton handed him a pen. The cameras were still flashing. Was this really happening? It was hard for Jack to believe.

Sutton leaned down and said, "Sign next to the Queen. I insist."

He did as Sutton requested. This was not the time to protest or ask questions. He put the pen down and looked out at the press. "China's government has made a historic mistake. I fear for all Chinese who have to live under such tyranny."

Jack stood up and President Sutton took a seat, carefully signing his name in the remaining space. "This is a historical day," he said. "This is a historical document. China and all Chinese take notice."

Sutton did not take any questions, despite the reporters shouting a litany of them. He and Jack went back to the Oval Office.

"You speak well, Jack. I forgot to mention that the German chancellor did call me, just as you thought. And she caved. I have to be honest, I doubted that would happen. I suspect it might not be bad if you avoided visiting Germany for a while."

"There are a few other places I'd rather visit."

"Like where?"

Jack stifled a yawn. "Like my bed."

"Of course. Okay, rest up because tomorrow you share your plan at seven am. I was going to offer you a drink, but I totally understand."

"Thank you, Mr. President. It was a rather tedious trip."

"Before you go, though, I have to ask: Did you enjoy meeting the Queen?"

Jack nodded slowly, recalling his time in the Queen's sitting room. "It was remarkable. We talked about Truman; she visited him in 1951. She wants me and Jojo to visit for New Year's."

Sutton let out a low whistle. "What an invitation!"

"After what she called the 'China Play' is over."

"I thought inviting you to Mar-A-Lago was cool."

Jack was eager to get home; exhaustion was starting to set in and his shoulder was aching. He got into the backseat of his car, for the first time greatly appreciating being driven. He was that tired.

CHAPTER 20

Early the next morning, after a restorative night's sleep Jack returned to the White House, going directly to the Cabinet Room that overlooked the Rose Garden. A big screen had been brought in as he requested, and a technician was there to make sure he could connect his laptop. Jack put his computer on the long wooden table. A tent card with his name on it sat in front of him. Around the entire table were similar cards with the names of twenty-four others, the heads of all the executive branch departments. Jack was reminded that he was the head of only one branch.

Susan walked in timidly, her eyes widening at the sight of the table with all its name cards. "Jack . . . are you really sure I should be here?"

"Susan, you'll be fine. You used to work for the president in China. Just remember to speak English and talk like you normally talk to me. Pull up that chair and sit next to me."

"Okay," she said, the uncertainty still saturating her voice. "Oh and here." She handed him printouts of the plan on large B4 pieces of paper that Jack could distribute to everyone at the right time.

People began filtering in, finding their seats. When Sutton arrived, everyone stood.

The president walked over and sat down in the seat dictated by tradition, in the middle of the table. "Good morning, everyone. It is early, isn't it? Welcome to our first cabinet meeting. I only wish it were under better circumstances. China has continued to land paratroopers throughout Taiwan. The government building is in complete control of China. We understand Chinese troops are now actively changing uniforms and taking positions in Taiwan's military. Citizens are at a loss as to what to do. The Chinese military has cracked down on protests. Other than that, the occupation has gone smoothly with businesses and society continuing as normal. The Pentagon was taken off-guard by such a simple air invasion and expected more of a Normandy-type assault. We need to discuss America's response. Today, Secretary of State Jack Gold will share his plan, which incorporates recommendations related to Taiwan. The beginning of that plan was the writing and signing of the China Declaration, as you may have been briefed on and seen on the news. Jack, why don't you take it from here."

Vice President Valentina Rodrigo looked to the president. "May I first ask Mr. Gold a question or two?"

"Of course."

The vice president tucked a strand of dark brown hair behind her ear before she began to speak. "I heard from Ambassador Pret in Beijing that you fired him because he was Hispanic. Was this because you do not like Hispanics, or think less of them?"

Jack was not surprised to hear this line of questioning. He had become immune to such assaults. Though in all honesty, he had a feeling she was picked for the role to get the Hispanic vote.

Jack looked at her calmly. "I dismissed him because he was negligent in his duties to provide security to US diplomats."

"And how exactly was he negligent?"

"The ambassador was concerned that providing security to a diplomat, who was not in support of Li Keqiang, might offend the Chinese president. This was before the election and Li Keqiang was worried that diplomat might say something that could influence the election."

"Who was that diplomat?" the vice president asked with an expression that could be easily construed as a smirk. She knew the answer.

"Me," Jack said. "And Pret took away my security detail, knowing Li Keqiang could attack me for political reasons."

"And did they attack?"

"Yes, ma'am."

"I never heard there was an attack on a diplomat in Beijing. Are we just to take your word on it?"

"That should be sufficient, I would think."

"You'll have to excuse me, but I am not accustomed to just taking someone's word on an issue of such magnitude."

Jack nodded. "Fair enough. Give me a second."

He opened his computer to the pictures he had and then plugged in the cable. An image appeared on the big screen of his large open living room. "This is a picture of where I lived in Beijing just after the election. Ambassador Pret removed my security detail and what remained was security solely responsible and under the control of the president, the forces of which are charged with protecting the families of leadership. About two weeks after my security detail was lifted, four armed men entered our compound, without any resistance from the Chinese guards. They were let in and entered this room while I was upstairs with my wife and kids."

Jack flipped to the next slide, showing a wide picture of all the men on the ground in pools of blood. Then, Jack flipped to close-up pictures of each individual assailant. "I disarmed them all and killed them. Since I knew my kids would be coming down in the morning, I dragged the bodies into our kitchen pantry." He flipped to the pictures of the piled up bodies.

There were a few gasps. Some people averted their eyes.

"The next day," Jack continued, "a private security team that I hired arrived. Later, I learned from a reliable source that the order came directly from Li Keqiang."

"Who was the source?" the vice president asked.

"That's confidential."

"We all have clearance. I instruct you to share your source."

Jack held her gaze. "No. You are asking me to do something that could have national security implications."

"I'll tell you what has national security implications—having that Chinese person next to you when we are talking about China." The vice president glared at Susan. "She should leave. Mr. President, I don't think Mr. Gold is the right person for this job. His father-in-law could benefit from any plan he comes up with and he has a vendetta against Li Keqiang. He has a substantial conflict of interest."

"I have another idea, Mr. President," Jack said, his eyes still on Valentina Rodrigo.

"Yes, Jack?"

Jack leaned forward and in a clear voice said, "The vice president has called me a racist against Hispanics. She questioned my integrity, my objectivity, and then *she* was a racist, in stating a Chinese should not be in this room. And she wants me to release confidential information, risking national security. I hereby resign from the administration. I cannot be associated with someone so offensive, unqualified, and dangerous."

Jack looked to Susan, who looked crestfallen. He unplugged his laptop. She picked up copies of the plan and they walked out.

They went to the front of the White House and his car was called up. While they were waiting Jack said, "Call David and Jason. Have them meet us at my home. We can cook something and relax. I'd love some dumplings."

Susan texted them and then looked at Jack. "You don't seem terribly disappointed about losing your job."

"The vice president was just too offensive to both you and me. She questioned my integrity. She fell on her own sword. I don't know how anyone in that room could ever trust her or want to work with her. I know I can't. And we're the ones with the plan to address China, not her."

They got in when Davis pulled up. "What happened?" he asked. "That was a quick cabinet meeting."

"I resigned."

"You did *what*? Why?"

"The vice president was offensive to both Susan and me."

"What about the China plan that you put together?"

"Ron Timmons will have to do it. I'm pretty sure he wouldn't be able to execute it, unfortunately."

"Damn," Davis said. "That's pretty serious news. Did you say anything to the press?"

"No. Out of respect to Sutton I'll let him position my resignation however he wants."

"All those leaders you met will be shocked."

"Not my problem. Hey, is Rio around?"

"Yes, she's at home."

"We're going to make dumplings. Jojo doesn't know yet. It'd be great if you both could join. I insist."

Davis chuckled. "You really know how to celebrate career changes."

"I better let the wife know." Jack pulled his phone out and texted Jojo.

When he got home, Jojo came right over and wrapped her arms around him. He held her and whispered, "I need to spend more time with you."

She looked up at him. "Did you really resign? Why?"

He wanted to tell her everything, but it was just too much to relive right now. "Because you never visited me at the office."

Jojo wrinkled her nose. "I know that's not the reason why."

Jack let Susan explain, which she did in rapid fire Chinese. Jason and David arrived and Jack motioned for them and Davis to follow him down to the wine cellar.

"Come with me gentlemen. We have something important to do."

He pulled out a bottle of Maotai. "We need a drink."

"It's eight in the morning, Jack," Davis said, eyeing the bottle warily as they made their way back upstairs.

"Well that means it's eight pm in China." Jack went into the kitchen and got some teacups.

"That's true," Davis said as Jack poured the clear liquid into the cups. Davis was the first to pick his up and raise it.

"Congratulations to resigning." Jack, David, and Jason raised their cups as well.

After a couple shots of Maotai, Jack finally felt himself start to relax. Rio arrived and she, Susan and Jojo started to make dumplings; the aroma of the fragrant spices soon filled the air.

Jack was so happy to see everyone, and that they were able to relax, chat, and enjoy each other's company, as was so common in China but less so in America. He had missed this.

Jojo had just announced the dumplings were about to be put into boiling water when there was a knock on the door.

Jack took another sip of his Maotai and got up.

"Are we expecting anyone else?" Jojo asked.

Jack opened the door. Sutton stood there, a rather tense expression on his face.

"Hi Jack. Sorry to drop by unannounced. But may I have a word?"

"Sure," Jack said, stepping back. "Come on in."

"Oh," Sutton said as Jack closed the door behind him. "Hello, everyone." He turned to Jack. "I'm sorry, I didn't realize you had company. Sorry for the intrusion, everyone, I just need to borrow Jack for a minute. Jack, is there somewhere we could go for a quick chat?"

"How about the wine cellar? Would you like something to drink?"

"As much as I feel I need one, no. Thank you."

They made their way down to the wine cellar and over to the small table and two chairs that were down there. "Jack, this is an absolutely lovely house," Sutton said as they sat down. "I didn't know you were so settled. It's marvelous."

"I look forward to spending more time here."

"Yes. About that." Sutton cleared his throat. "After you left I had some words with the vice president in front of the cabinet, I might add. Then I obtained the input from cabinet members, still there in the room. It seems that the vice president has lost the confidence of all the cabinet members. While we were in the room, her resignation was typed up and signed. She'll be leaving for personal family reasons."

Jack raised his eyebrows. "Congratulations—that's great news."

"Those pictures were pivotal. If only she had stopped after we saw them. I'm sure you surmise why I selected her and the problems I was expecting in the next four years. Anyway, I called Ron Timmons and he says the plans you and your team put together are truly remarkable. I came here because I do not want you in the role of secretary of state anymore. I'd like you to be my vice president. Americans and global leaders respect you. You can still oversee the China plan. It'll help make sure you get all the support that is needed. Jack, it would be great for the nation if you could serve in the VP role. You can focus your attention where you like and help me. It'd be perfect."

Jack kept his expression neutral though he was thrilled to hear the offer. But it wasn't going to be up to just him to decide. "Let me get Jojo. I want to hear her thoughts."

He said nothing about Sutton's offer as he and Jojo made their way back downstairs.

"Again, Jojo, I'm sorry for just barging in like this," Sutton said. "But my vice president resigned. I'd like Jack to take the position."

If Jojo were surprised at the offer, she did not let it show. "Will he have to travel less?"

"How much he travels will be solely up to the both of you."

"Do we get access to the presidential dining room?"

Jack and the president laughed. Jack said, "She's a good negotiator."

"You can have access to anything you want." Jojo looked at Jack, the tiniest of smiles on her face.

Sutton held out his hand.

Jack shook it.

"We can have the signing in ceremony tomorrow when you are sober and rested," Sutton said, grinning. "And now, I'll see myself out."

They walked upstairs and Sutton said goodbye to everyone. Jack closed the door behind him and turned. All eyes were on him.

"It seems a new job opportunity has come up," he said. He paused. "Sutton just asked me to be his vice president." Jack looked to Susan. "Valentina Rodrigo has resigned."

"Did you know this might happen?" Susan asked.

"As much as I'd like to take credit for some real 3-d chess here, I can't." He let his gaze settle on Susan, then David, then Jason. "I hope you don't mind working for the vice president. Tell me when you want a passport. I think I can swear you in personally."

"We want one," the three of them said in unison.

"Great," Jack said. He wanted them to get to know America better, especially now that they were working for him in his role as Vice President of the United States.

CHAPTER 21

The weather was cold the following day, so the swearing in ceremony was shifted to the East Room in the White House. In attendance were ambassadors from other countries, department heads, press, Democratic and Republican congressmen, and select other individuals of distinction. He had made sure that Susan, David, and Jason were there as well.

Jack was up on stage with Jojo, along with President Sutton and Cam. Duncan Weber, Chief Justice of the Supreme Court, stood in front Jack, who had his right hand raised, his left hand on an American flag. The chief justice read, "*Do you solemnly swear that you will support and defend the Constitution of the United States against all enemies, foreign and domestic, that you will bear true faith and allegiance to the same: that you take this obligation freely, without any mental reservation or purpose of evasion, and you will well and faithfully discharge the duties of vice president on which you are about to enter. So help you God.*"

"I do."

The president was the first to shake Jack's hand. Then Jojo kissed him and Cam gave him a hug. They posed for a series of photos, after which Jack circulated the room and took pictures with a host of individuals, most of whom he didn't know.

"I understand you are stealing some of my staff," Ron Timmons said. "Congratulations, Jack." They shook hands.

After introducing Jojo to the new secretary of state, Jack said, "I don't think we'll have any problem working together."

"I heard what happened. Good job. That was a big gift you gave to President Sutton."

Ron handed Jack an envelope. "Thank you," Jack said. "Perfect timing. We should do this now." He went and found Susan, David, and Jason. "Which is your favorite color, green or blue."

"Blue," they said, without hesitation.

"Okay. Follow me." They walked just nearby to the oval-shaped Blue Room. "The three of you stand over there. Now, repeat after me, "I hereby declare, on oath . . .""

When they had repeated the words back to him, Jack opened the envelope and took out their US passports. He handed one to each. "Congratulations. Thank for your service to America so far."

"Okay, the four of you stand together and let me take a picture!" Jojo insisted. She took a few and then asked Ron to get in the picture too.

Before they left, Susan, David, and Jason gave their old passports to Ron. "We need to follow the rules, like everyone else," Susan said.

"Thank you," Ron said. "I appreciate that."

"Do you mind if I hold on to those?" Jack asked.

"Not at all," Ron said, handing them to Jack. He slipped them into the inside pocket of his jacket.

Jack took Jojo's hand. "Let's see if the president has left yet."

"Yes, Mr. Vice President."

"Stop that."

"Certainly, Mr. Vice President."

"I see you're enjoying this."

Jojo grinned. "*Lái shàng chúang*, Mr. Vice President."

Susan, David, and Jason were just a few steps behind them and immediately dissolved into giggles, knowing that Jojo had just asked Jack to "get on the bed" which really meant to have sex.

Jojo clapped a hand over her mouth. "*Bù hǎo yìse*, Mr. Vice President." *I didn't mean to say that.*

The giggling continued.

It did not appear that anyone had left when they returned. Jack started to look for Sutton but instead found himself face to face with the ambassador from China, Qin Gang. He held his hand out but Jack made no move to return the gesture. Qin's hand hung out there in the empty air for a little while before he lowered it. Jack gripped Jojo's hand tighter, aware of Jason and Susan, holding their phones up. Jason was most likely recording video; Susan was taking photos.

There was plenty he could say to the man, but now was not the time. He spied Sutton across the room, talking with the secretary of defense. "Let's go over here," he said to Jojo, still holding her hand as they walked past the ambassador without saying a word to him.

"Jack!" Sutton said. "Just the man I was looking for. Where did you go? You need a glass of champagne. There are some people you need to meet."

"I just ran into China's Ambassador, Qin Gang."

"And how did that go?"

"I avoided shaking his hand."

Sutton laughed. "Excellent Jack. I'd like to introduce you to Rex Matheus, secretary of defense. Rex, this is Jack's wife, Jojo."

"Nice to meet you," Jack said.

"Are you coming to poker night at the White House this week?" Matheus asked.

"He's pulling your leg," Sutton said. "There is no poker night. We say the same thing to everyone when we know for sure they'll fit in. Now you know our secret code."

Jack loved it. "You'll hear more about that plan tomorrow," he told Matheus.

"I look forward to it, Jack. I liked what I saw. Don't think about taking my position at the Department of Defense, though."

"You have the presentation tomorrow at eight am, then a pretty serious press conference the following morning," Sutton said. He looked at Secretary Matheus. "I feel like I get to sit back and relax while Jack does all the work."

"Secretary Matheus, do you have an expert in cyber security?" Jack asked. "I'd like to run something by them."

"Sure do. We had a meeting earlier. He's around here somewhere. Let me introduce you. Oh, there he is. Jeff! Come over here."

Jack turned and was shocked to see he recognized the man Matheus had just called over. It was his old friend Jeff Hern, from UC Berkeley. "Jeff," Jack said. "Great to see you. I didn't even realize you were here! What a coincidence."

Jeff grinned as he shook Jack's hand. "Congratulations, Mr. Vice President."

"Do you have a few minutes for a quick chat?"

"No problem."

Jack returned to the Blue Room, this time with Jeff and Susan.

"Jeff, are you familiar with LibertyChat? It's a new platform we want to encourage Chinese to use. We want to use it too. It's just like WeChat, without the bells and whistles."

"I'm not familiar with it."

"Susan, will you show it to Jeff?"

She tapped at the screen of her phone and then took a step closer to Jeff, showing him what was on the screen.

"What we know is that it has a built-in VPN and pretty much uses the WeChat look and feel. I think it's okay to use, but updates are automatic, which I fear can expose the user to malicious intrusion, especially if you use it on a computer."

"I can look into that," Jeff said. "When do you need an answer?"

"By tomorrow at seven-thirty am. Sorry for the rush. Also, if you can join the cabinet meeting at eight, that'd really be useful."

"Is that okay with my boss that I attend the meeting?"

"Last time I checked, I was the Vice President of the United States."

"Well, when you put it that way . . ."

"It'd be a big help and give everyone reassurance."

"Gotcha. I'm looking forward to checking it out."

"I'll email you the link to the app right now," Susan said.

Back in the East Room, Jack mingled a little more, but his shoulder was getting sore and he was ready to go home. He said goodbye to Sutton and Matheus, then found Jojo having a conversation with Cam, in French.

"Okay, Jack," Jojo said. "I can see the look on your face."

She kissed Cam on both cheeks and then hand in hand, she and Jack made their way through the crowd to the exit.

CHAPTER 22

At the cabinet meeting the next morning, Jack tried to sit still without fidgeting as people filed in. It wasn't nerves, exactly, but he felt as though he'd had multiple cups of coffee that morning despite the fact he'd only had one. Perhaps it was the fact that he was here at his first meeting in his new position. But really he knew his energy was running high because of what he was about to present. Everyone had arrived and taken their seat, cups of coffee and tea in front of them. Everyone had greeted him when they entered. Only Jeff had addressed him by *Jack*; everyone else had said *Mr. Vice President*.

Sutton called the meeting to order. "First things first, I would like to welcome Jack Gold, our new vice president."

There was a round of applause and smiles on everyone's faces. "Thank you," Jack said once the applause died down. "May I begin, Mr. President?"

"Yes. Proceed."

"First and foremost, I would prefer to be called 'Jack' if at all possible."

"Certainly, Mr. Vice President," Matheus said without irony as there was some laughter throughout the room.

"Okay, I give up. Let's talk about China. Before we get into the meat of things, I'd like to describe the societal situation in China. There is now no way for Chinese to get or share news. This makes them isolated. Virtually everyone in the country uses a texting and payment platform called WeChat. If they say or do anything wrong, the government can suspend their account which is their sacred and fundamental way of communicating socially, businesswise, and the way they pay when shopping.

"To create real change, we must communicate messages and actions to China's leadership and more importantly, to Chinese citizens. They must be empowered to share things they believe are bad in society and learn from the world. Susan, my colleague across the table is most qualified to talk on this matter. Susan, can you share your thoughts, please."

Susan took a deep breath. "In a Leninist system, the party owns all outcomes. In other countries—Russia, for example—there is always at least some open opposition to central state policy. This is not how China's Leninist system works. There can be no non-state actors who openly oppose policy. This means that all outcomes are the responsibility of the state. One huge virtue of liberal democracy is that when policy fails, the regime is never completely to blame. China's regime, on the other hand has everything to lose by losing control of protests and dissent. And it has everything to gain by maintaining its 'perfect record' of control, especially since people actually want this. They like the protection of the government. When Jack talks about a platform that exposes the government, it will attack the very foundation of China's Leninist system."

She shot a quick glance to Jack, and he nodded subtly. If she had been at all nervous addressing the people in the room, she hadn't let it show at all. "Thank you, Susan," he said. "The challenge in using a platform is that the Chinese are extraordinarily comfortable with the deep functionality and user interface of WeChat. As it turns out, we were able to get a platform similar to WeChat and we have been running tests as to its acceptability. We believe it is suitable. Secretary Matheus was gracious enough to have one of his experts review the platform. Jeff, would you mind speaking on that?"

"Yes, Jack," Jeff said from the other end of the table. "The platform is called LibertyChat. Catchy name. No posts can be removed, so there is absolute free speech. This means the government can use it too. It has a new age VPN on top of a communication platform that gets updated actively and automatically. This means through using the regular internet, other IP addresses can be used in other countries. It's automatic. When you use it, they can see outside news sites prohibited by the government. This platform is ideal for creating societal interconnectivity within China. The government cannot sensor it or remove content. It is unclear who built the platform, but the coding style suggests Israel. Jack was concerned about security, since its automatic update feature could result in the download of malicious software. I agree with that concern. But in this area, cell phones are more secure. It should not be downloaded to computers. Another security concern is that we do not know who owns this. Content is co-hosted in multiple countries, paid for by untraceable shell companies. Whoever ultimately controls this platform can turn it off at any time. Likewise, given the way it has started to grow in China, we believe it could have a valuation of several hundred billion by the end of the year. It's a good tool for its intended use."

"Thank you, Jeff," Jack said. "Chinese can share for the first time, how they feel without fear of reprisal. And—again, for the first time—they can see stories from other parts of the world . . . all in a format in which they are very comfortable. An important feature is that people can form groups with an unlimited number of members. China currently limits groups to five hundred. They can organize, they can protest . . . and share it. Yes, they will be arrested, but they can share being arrested. The Chinese will come to realize they have more control than they ever thought. This is when things will change. When people's emotions finally come out. The Chinese will come to agree with Confucius who said, *To be wronged is nothing unless you continue to remember it.*"

They moved on to discuss the key initiatives they had developed. Susan passed out the B4 sized printouts to everyone.

"What is the goal?" Jack asked. "We must be very focused, because some of you are thinking this sounds a lot like regime change. And you are correct. But what we are doing is untraditional. Traditional regime change often spirals into lengthy state-building projects or involves military action or covert operations. Those fail and are not worth the loss of blood and treasure. Examples are Iraq, Afghanistan, and Libya. What I am suggesting is not armed regime change. We will not need to invest into nation-building. A key point is that China's National Congress will start to fear chaos and remove Li Keqiang with a new election or an appointment of another. We are not imposing democracy at gunpoint. We do not have to rebuild institutions like we did in Japan and Europe. Literature and studies of regime change in those instances showed it was a mistake.

"The goal of what we are doing, and this Appeasement Plan, is a clear and free Taiwan. Stop China from buying Iranian oil and then arming terrorists. Free Xinjiang and Hong Kong, and stop the subjugation of the entire population—again. An ancillary problem was that the National Committee voted for a president who they thought could help them increase property prices so they could make money. The problem is that the population did not vote and, if they did so, they would not have been equipped to make an informed decision. The population must obtain fundamental knowledge of economics and politics before they are equipped to vote. Mistakes of electing another Li Keqiang will then be avoided. This is not an absolute certainty, however, in the long run."

Jack went through all the initiatives, explaining the rationale for each. "The key will be in how we execute our plan. No one will be informed outright that we are using LibertyChat and each initiative must be justified on its own merit so as to ensure there is no justification for military conflict. But we all know desperate times will likely generate desperate measures. I expect China will manufacture a military conflict of some sort before this is over."

The president looked around the room. "Secretary Matheus, your thoughts?"

"I thought it was a good plan before I heard everything today. I agree with Jack about regime change, and he was insightful to bring that issue up. Looks good. Depending on how China's responds, we can move assets. But I do not see any potential for China being provoked to an extent that would cause any conflict with causalities."

"Does anyone else have any feedback?" Sutton asked. No one said anything.

"Mr. President, may we have your approval to proceed with the caveat that I seek your approval prior to each new initiative?" Jack asked.

"Yes. Approved. Thank you, Jack. Thank you everyone for coming today."

As people gathered their things and began to file out, Sutton leaned toward Jack. "You brought the right people to the meeting," he said in a low voice. "Susan was impressive."

"She was. I'm thinking I may make her my China spokesperson."

"Excellent idea. Have you seen your office yet?"

"Not yet. I'll find it. Thank you for your support, Mr. President."

Jack got up and went over to Susan. "Care to see my new office? I haven't been there yet."

"I'd like to see your new office."

"You did well in there," he said as they walked out.

"I was nervous but once I got started, it was easy."

"You know," Jack said, "My press secretary isn't suitable to communicate or connect with people throughout the world. I was thinking you would be a great press secretary for China. My China press secretary. We need to communicate some things especially to Chinese in China . . . like how the election happened and what went wrong. Maybe we sit down and discuss the meeting coming up tomorrow morning." Jack stopped walking when they reached the end of the hallway. "Do you know where my office is? Because I sure don't."

"Mr. Vice President." A fit, middle-aged man with light brown hair approached Jack, a smile on his face, his hand extended. "I'm Mr. Jones Telly. I'm your secretary."

Jack shook his hand. "Could you show me to my office?"

"Certainly."

His office was furnished with two long sofas and an oval wood table in the middle. "Mr. Telly," Jack said, "can you please replace the sofas with a nice working table and chairs?"

"Certainly, sir."

Jack and Susan took a seat on opposing sofas.

"Tomorrow morning I need to attend a press conference to answer questions about the Declaration," Jack said. "I think it would be good if you described, in Chinese, what you said today in the meeting and the background of what happened in the past election. Maybe mention how if everyone voted, that wouldn't have happened. Oh, and that people can visit LibertyChat, which is not an American platform. What you say should cater to Chinese and to the press."

"I can do that." Susan jotted down a few notes on her notepad.

"I'll be right there so if there are any questions you're unsure of, just look at me and I'll answer."

"Any tips for when I speak?"

"*Sincerity and truth are the basis of every virtue.*"

"Confucius," Susan said. "Good quote. Can I draft an outline and we can review it?"

"Sure. Let me know when you are ready."

* * *

It was six-thirty in the morning when Jack, Susan, and his other staff entered the Briefing Room. In China, it was exactly twelve hours later. Since all of China shared the same time zone, it had been agreed that this was the best time to reach Chinese—just after they got off from work and just before the nightly news, *Xinwen Lianbo*, that started at seven in Beijing.

Jack walked up to the podium and surveyed the crowd. Every seat was taken. "Good morning. Apologies for the early press conference, but it is six-thirty pm in China and we wanted as many people there to view this broadcast as possible. Henceforth, all our China briefings will be held at this time. My apologies for the inconvenience. We'll make sure there is extra coffee and pastries going forward."

Though he was now speaking in his role as vice president, Jack felt completely comfortable standing up there, all eyes on him. In fact, he found it a lot less nerve-racking than when he had first made his address at the Control Center. Yes, he'd been speaking to over one billion people, but he had not seen a single one of them, and instead could recall, in crystal clarity, what the eye of the camera looked like as he spoke into it.

"Before I make a statement," he began, "I'd like to confirm that henceforth, Chinese subtitles will be placed on everything said, so that those who only speak Chinese can understand. You should also have your electronic earpieces for the simultaneous translation. Chinese will be spoken in this room. Right now, I would like to introduce you to my China press secretary. Her name is Susan Ting. She used to work for President Wang Yang and I have worked with her for some time, both in China and now here in America."

Susan stepped up next to him, a nervous smile on her face. He stood there for a moment, gave her an encouraging nod, and then stepped several feet back as she took her place at the podium.

"Hello everyone," she said in Mandarin. She turned to Jack. "Thank you, Mr. Vice President. I appreciate the appointment as your China press secretary. Today I would like to inform everyone of what happened in China. While Li Keqiang was under house arrest, he developed a plan to save the property sector in China. It was not a smart plan because too much speculation was occurring, and the country has too much debt.

But all those in China's National Congress—about 2,300—are landowners. They wanted the government to spend the money to save the property sector, using the hard-earned tax dollars that Chinese pay each year. Then, after he got into office, he did all the things outlined in the China Declaration. He repressed people's speech, imprisoned people in Xinjiang, trampled the rights of those in Hong Kong and so forth. These factual reasons are the basis for the historic document that all leaders of democratic countries signed." She held up the signed Declaration. "This document puts China on notice. Free nations will no longer tolerate the Communist Party. Please read the document. It is truthful. And, if you would like to share your personal experience, please go to LibertyChat. It is a safe place to share injustices with other Chinese. Such things must no longer be tolerated."

Several hands in the audience went up. Jack was pleased when Susan did not look back to him but instead pointed to one a woman in near the front. "In the document under *External Aggressions*, it's mentioned that the CCP conducted assignation attempts against foreign diplomats. But there is no source listed."

"Pull up the pictures, please," Susan said, in English. Then she switched back to Chinese. "Jack Gold was a diplomat in Beijing. This was the down-stairs of his home. Four armed men were let in to his compound by the state security and then broke into Mr. Gold's home. He was upstairs with his wife and kids." The next picture showed all the men on the ground and was one of the less gruesome ones. "Mr. Gold fortunately was able to neutralize them."

Jack walked up to the podium. Susan stepped back so he could address the audience, still in Mandarin. "I have it on good authority that Li Keqiang gave the order for the assassination. He was concerned that I might say something in the Chinese press to try and change public opinion away from him." Jack paused and then began speaking in English. "The China Declaration details issues for humanity and history to witness. Just the other day, China invaded Taiwan. If any of you have been there, you'll know its beauty and history. It would be similar to the United States invading Canada. This is but one more illustration of the importance to take bold actions to cripple the Chinese government. It's important you understand that the China Declaration is the basis for actions the administration takes. With that said, what is the first action we will be taking? Effective immediately, the president, in consultation with the secretary of state and me, have ordered the closing of all US embassies and consulates in China."

Hands shot up but Jack wanted to emphasize the importance of a key point. "Americans have a fondness and deep respect for the Chinese people. I want to assure everyone that visa applications will continue to be processed online. We know that the small Chinese businesses and restaurants near the consulates will suffer as we pull out our people. We regret this, but it's not our fault. It's the fault of the Chinese government."

Now Jack called on one of the reporters. "What impact do you expect this will have on Beijing?"

"It sends a message that the United States of America wants nothing to do with a country that is evil, despite its wonderful citizens."

Jack pointed to another hand. "Is this the entire US response, or is there going to be more repercussions for China?"

"We're only beginning. We do not believe in simple sanctions or diplomatic exercises. After all, China has a perfect record of never living up to what it says. I will say this—Chinese citizens, and all those in government, should start thinking very seriously how they can personally contribute to this effort of making China a more civilized country. If citizens and China officials do not try to act to rectify the ills, they too are guilty. The United States of America hereby puts China, and its malicious rulers, on notice."

More hands shot in the air. He could be here all day. "Thank you for your time today and appreciating the seriousness of this situation."

He and Susan walked off the stage to the shouts of questions.

"You did great," he said to her. "Like you've done this a million times."

Her cheeks flushed a little. "I like what you said about the restaurants near embassies and consulates. No one will have thought about that. But they will be impacted, and they will remember that you told them and be angry at the government."

"Can you help to now ramp up the review and posting of stories? Jason was in back filming. You could even get footage of you speaking and post that. Posting stories with me is useful, but you are here, Susan. You are Chinese. Everyone will be able to relate to you, to what you see and how you feel. People will trust you. Tell your stories. Consider starting a group of your own. You can be a leader online too and reach out to others. That could be powerful."

He stopped by the Oval Office to see how Sutton thought it had gone. They took a seat on the cream-colored sofas in the middle of the room, Sutton on one, Jack on the other.

"That went well," Sutton said, smoothing his tie as he leaned back into the couch. "It was firm and left everyone knowing there would be more to come. Susan was great. I could read the translation in English as she spoke. That was a really smart move. We can now switch the language to whichever country we are talking about. I expect we'll get China's message of indignation soon and they'll close their embassies. What do you suggest I do when China's ambassador calls to request a meeting?"

"You're busy with other things. It's way too early to talk to anyone. We need to wait a few weeks. Just when there is a little bit of heat, and the newspapers are carrying stories about embassy closures, *then* we can move on to the blacklisting of National Congress members. When we get to shifting America's immigration policy to take in more Chinese, that will infuriate the Chinese leadership."

Sutton grinned. "Jack, you're ruthless. Glad we are on the same team."

"I'd like to get your involvement in the next news conference and give you a chance to support all of the initiatives being taken as an outcome of the China Declaration."

"Sure, Jack. The next initiative is about fentanyl. I'd be happy to speak about that."

"That's great, Mr. President. That'll be a week from now. I'll leave some talking points with your staff."

"Perfect."

"Okay. I think I should arrange a Zoom call with other leaders to explain today and our next steps. Unless you would like to do it, of course?"

Sutton waved the offer off. "Jack, I so enjoy having you here. Best if you take the call. You're the subject matter expert."

*   *   *

"Did you see these tweets?" Susan asked as she came into Jack's office and took a seat in the chair opposite his desk.

"What tweets?"

"From the spokesperson for China's foreign ministry. They sent a series of tweets. That the US closing of embassies is *unbelievably ridicu-*

lous. That the US needs to *reverse its erroneous decision* or China will . . ." She paused and looked down at her phone, "China will *react with firm countermeasures.*"

Jack leaned back in his leather executive chair. "I wasn't aware of those tweets."

"Hold on." Susan held up a finger. "I'm not done yet. *Closing embassies can only lead to the deterioration of relationships that took many years to foster and will be lost, unless this action is reversed.*" She put her phone down. "Okay, that was it."

Jack tried not to roll his eyes but was not entirely successful. "That might sound all well and good," he said. "Kind of like when someone's trying to end a toxic relationship but the other party is saying that the person just isn't trying hard enough. We'll see if they have anything to add about that threat of *firm countermeasures.*"

"The real reason I'm here," Susan said, "is to ask about what stories I should share when the president speaks tomorrow. We have lots of personal stories about those killed by fentanyl and have shared many of them on LibertyChat."

Jack frowned. "What do you mean, which ones?"

"Well, we shared ones online that showed Chinese and other Asians being affected, as well as some who had died. Should we share those tomorrow?"

"Pick one of a white person, a black person, and a Chinese."

Susan's eyebrows shot up. "Jack," she said, then paused. "Isn't . . . isn't picking stories we know will cater to the viewers . . . isn't that like China and their influence on the media?"

"Yes, it is," Jack said. "We're picking the stories that most people can relate to. But what we are *not* doing is censoring people. That's what happens in China all the time. Content is removed, people are punished. There is no free speech."

*   *   *

For the next week, Jack had President Sutton with him when he held a press briefing about the China Declaration. It was important to involve Sutton directly, so the rest of the country—and world—would see that, and also, it would keep him personally engaged.

A week after their first press briefing, the president entered, unbeknownst to the press, who immediately stood up out of respect.

Sutton put up one hand. "Please, be seated. I'm here because of the China Declaration, which, like other Western leaders, I signed. Among other things, China's transgressions were outlined. Today, the United States is taking bold action on fentanyl. The reason for this devastating problem in America is not because of an inability to secure our borders— The reason is that the Chinese government has authorized companies to manufacture and ship raw materials to Mexico. They are then combined to create fentanyl, which is shipped to America. China is the source of the problem." Sutton paused and took a deep breath, a grave expression on his face.

"China can no longer be permitted to kill Americans each year without repercussions. China previously fought a war to prevent the shipping of opium into China. This is very similar, except fentanyl is far more deadly. The amount of fentanyl you can place on Abraham Lincoln's nose on a penny is enough to kill someone. There are over one hundred vendors who market fentanyl out of facilities across China. They have been getting around international networks trying to stop them, but they are known in China. This supply of synthetic opioids must stop."

President Sutton brought his hands up and held each side of the lectern. He let the moment stretch, the anticipation of whatever he was about to announce building until it was almost palpable.

"In conjunction with Japan, England, France, Italy, and other Western countries, we hereby recognize the shipping and selling of fentanyl as an act of war." Sutton's tone was strong, assured. "I want to make clear we are not declaring war on China—we are declaring war on fentanyl manufacturing facilities, and anyone associated with the shipping or selling of the drug. This includes transportation companies. Over the next few weeks, our security services will be collecting data on such entities and sharing the information with our partners to formulate a plan for stopping their activities. Such information will then be provided to China. If China does not act swiftly, then we will take matters into our own hands. Shame on the Chinese government for permitting this. We should all be outraged." Sutton turned from the lectern and exited the room, not taking a single question though in Jack's estimation, every hand in the room was raised.

But Sutton had done just as they'd discussed in the days leading up to the meeting; now it was Susan's turn. She began to speak in Chinese as the reporters tried to put their earpieces in to hear the translation. "There were over 70,000 deaths last year in in this country because of China manufacturing and shipping fentanyl that reached America."

She went through and shared videos of family members describing their loved ones who had overdosed. The third video was of a young Chinese man who had attended the University of Texas and went to San Diego to visit some friends. Unbeknownst to him, there was some fentanyl that had cross-contaminated his marijuana. His mother said in Chinese, "We came to America from China for a better life and look what happened to my son. China sent the fentanyl that killed my son." It was powerful. Jack could tell that Susan was moved by the video despite having already seen it.

"China has a vast pharmaceutical and bulk manufacturing sector," she continued. "Synthetic opioid vendors are shielded behind layers of interlinked companies. Hiding shipping through mail and aircraft is easy given the high concentration of fentanyl. If I know this—so does the CCP. The Chinese government has no excuse."

Jack walked up to the podium and Susan went and sat where he had just been, in the five seats against the wall to the right of the lectern. He looked out at the audience, a view he was becoming more and more accustomed to. "China is killing Chinese in America. This is not propaganda. It is the truth. All because someone in the Chinese government wants to make money. China has been killing Americans and we have been sitting idly by. That stops now. China, let this serve as a formal notice to you and to your citizens as to the nature of the CCP's character."

He paused and hands in the audience shot up. But he did not call on anyone. "I'm too disgusted with the Chinese government to answer any questions right now. Thank you for coming so early."

The truth was that the US and other countries had already compiled the fentanyl-related information. Action would begin immediately. There would be no more waiting for China, or hoping for action, as had been the consistent American policy toward China in the past. The time for that to change had come.

* * *

And now that things were set in motion, they seemed to be falling into place. There was broad support for the fentanyl initiative in Congress. LibertyChat surpassed sixty-five million downloads, which Sutton had looked thrilled about when Jack told him, though Jack did have to temper that with the fact that it was a small percentage, given the size of the country. But even Jack was pleased with the progress they were making, and Sutton was more than happy to give Jack the go-ahead for the next initiative. Jack had a meeting with Susan, David, and Jason about moving ahead with the next initiative. Susan was going to explain something very simple that most Chinese didn't know—the three independent branches of government. As it was going to be the Mid-Autumn Festival soon, everyone in China would have three days off, so it seemed the perfect time for them to push more stories since people would have the time to see them and share with others.

* * *

At six-thirty the next morning, Jack, and Susan entered the press room. Jack couldn't keep track of how many of these briefings he'd attended in the past several weeks, but everyone seemed to be getting used to the routine, which was exactly what he wanted, in both America and in China. He wanted people to expect something to happen at a particular time; then they would anticipate it and be more likely to pay attention.

There were many more Chinese in attendance than there previously had been—the networks were changing who they had cover the news.

Susan walked up to the lectern. In Mandarin she said, "Good morning. Today is Mid-Autumn Festival, also called Mooncake Festival in China. People all over China will be lighting paper lanterns and getting together with family. I want to wish them a happy holiday from afar and at the same time, share something they should know. You see, since spending some time in America, I have learned a little about other governments. This includes not just America but England, Japan, Singapore, and so forth. I think all Chinese should know that developed countries have three branches of government. One is the legislative, that makes the law. Another is the executive branch, which is responsible for carrying out, or executing, the law. Finally, there is the judicial branch that determines whether federal laws are constitutional. The key is that in developed countries, these branches are separate and equal. The president is in the executive branch and he or she cannot touch the judicial branch or influence it. In China, there is no such clear separation, and this allows for abuse. China faces structural problems, not just people problems. This is something useful for Americans and Chinese to know, but it is only part of the story. The other part is that, in Western countries, the media is completely free and polices the branches of government. Individuals, most importantly, have real free speech and can bring to light injustices. All of these together, I believe, have enabled Western countries to thrive, compared to countries with other systems. It took me a while to understand this and I hope you too will take the time to think about it."

Jack came over and stood next to Susan. "What you just said is profound," he said in Mandarin. "Thank you." It had been so simply said and Jack knew Chinese had never heard of the concept until then. They would understand it, could share it with others, and maybe even internalize it.

Susan took a seat, leaving Jack at the lectern. He switched to English. "Another week has gone by. Embassies and consulates are closed or closing. America is disengaging from China politically. The United States, along with other countries, is aggressively moving to plan for the stopping of China's poisoning of people worldwide through the manufacturing and distributing of fentanyl."

Jack surveyed the room, making sure the reporters were hearing his summary. "At this time, I would like to announce the administration's next initiative aimed at addressing those ills outlined in the China Declaration. Effective immediately, all China National Congress members and CCP members who are top management in Chinese companies are hereby blacklisted. Their assets in America and other participating nations will be seized. This applies to them and their family members. All their visas are null and void. We considered blacklisting and sanctioning all CCP members—and we still may. The Chinese Communist Party is responsible for the actions listed in the Declaration. Everyone in China should know this. Just because you have not done anything wrong does not mean your membership in the CCP is excused. Henceforth, there are no excuses when you decide to join the party. Take notice."

Hands shot up in the audience. Jack pointed. "Yes, you."

"Don't you think that is a little harsh?" a Chinese journalist asked. "What if a CCP member has a kid attending high school in America and the kid did nothing wrong."

"No," Jack said. "I do not think it is harsh. What is harsh is China placing over one million Uyghurs in concentration camps. We did however, anticipate this eventuality and there is an appeal process already prepared and it will be in place after this briefing. But what often happens is CCP members put money in family members' bank accounts. We'll be checking for that too."

He called on the next reporter, an American. "It seems like you prepared for this for some time. What else is coming up?"

"We have prepared many non-military initiatives, depending upon what China does. China is at crossroads in history. Most Chinese are happy because things have gotten better over the past thirty years. They do not know what a Western democracy is or what it looks like. They do not know of the atrocities that have been carried out by their leaders, and they do not care because it does not directly affect them. It is time for everyone in China to start paying attention. My press secretary just explained one of the most important things in the world that we *all* should learn or remember. That is an alien concept in China, given their education system. I'll take two more questions. You." He pointed to a youngish blond man in front. "Mr. Vice President, why not reveal your entire plan to China? Might that help make change come faster?"

Jack nodded. "That's a good question. We have intentionally decided not to reveal the plan in order to inject a great deal of uncertainty. Foreign investment into China and businesses already there need certainty to operate. China has no strategy to deal with America or the items listed within the China Declaration. It is only a question of time before China's economy deteriorates from this uncertainty. Our plan is extensive and thorough. China should be worried about solving the problem since our initiatives will inevitably have ramifications throughout the Chinese economy. We are being honest with the American people and they are in firm support of the administration's efforts. The American people are angry. They now know China's true character."

For the last person, Jack pointed to a woman in the middle. "Is there a conflict because China's previous president is your father-in-law?"

"I love and miss my father-in-law. I have not talked to him since leaving China. President Wang Yang has not said anything about the current situation, probably out of fear of being arrested. My sense is that President Wang was an amazing leader for the time he ruled China. It's my belief that China needs others with a fresh mindset. Truthfully, I think President Wang would rather be here playing with his grandchildren and planting watermelon. This is a sad time for my wife and me being so far away from him. Thank you, everyone." As usual, more hands went up but Jack stepped back from the podium and exited the room.

Susan was waiting for him and they walked together through the West Wing toward the Oval Office.

"Was that the truth or were you acting?" she asked.

"It was the truth, but I intentionally told it to them in a way I was hoping would get sympathy. Never mind me, though—you again did a phenomenal job. I mean really fantastic. Let's go see what the president thought."

Sutton could not have been more pleased, as was evidenced when they entered the Oval Office and he stood from his desk, an excited look on his face. "Susan!" he exclaimed, clapping his hands together. "Bravo! You just gave both America and China a lesson in civics. It was forthright, clear, and honest. Good job. And Jack—communications so far has been very good."

"Thank you, Mr. President," Susan said. "Oh—something I haven't mentioned is that LibertyChat is ramping up."

"How many members in total?" Jack asked.

"About eighty-five million. Membership is finally growing exponentially. People have realized the platform is a safe place and their identities will be protected; they know no posts will be removed. I have about fifteen million members following me in my group. Quite a bit of the content being shared by others is becoming viral. There is Zhang Li, who you've met Jack. He was on Wang's Standing Committee. He has become very vocal on the platform too."

"Sensational," Sutton said. "That's excellent."

"The reaction to the latest initiative will be interesting," Jack said. "It's a solid shot at the heart of the Chinese Communist Party. We'll have to wait and see its impact. Susan, please post your latest press briefing to LibertyChat."

"I will," Susan said. She looked at the president, "Thank you for your appreciation, sir," she said before she left.

Sutton waited until she was gone before he looked at Jack, his eyebrows raised. "She is singlehandedly having a big impact. The press loves her."

Jack knew how right he was. "She will become famous in China because of the platform and who she is. You are seeing someone who does not yet know how their life will change."

"Jack, whenever you are around it seems like things end up being rather surreal." Sutton said.

"We are borne into interesting times, Mr. President."

*   *   *

Two days later, Sutton called Jack into his office to discuss the protests that had started happening at many of the leading universities.

"It seems CCP members have kids there," Sutton said.

"Yes, sir."

He looked at Jack quizzically. "Are you worried about the protests?"

"No. Are you, sir?"

"Jack, I'm disciplined enough not to listen to the news; nor do I watch TV. I was just curious what you thought."

"We have an appeal process in place. I'd be interested to see which universities come out with pro-student statements. China has given over one billion dollars in gifts to universities over the past ten years. China never invests without expecting a return."

"That is interesting," Sutton said, steepling his fingers. "Maybe I'll give the dean at Yale a call to learn more. It'd be nice to know what the money gets China."

Sutton rose from his desk. He and Jack walked to the Situation Room in the basement of the West Wing. Jack had been there before but this time as he followed Sutton in, he felt like it needed to be reorganized. There were thirteen plush chairs around a big wooden table. Each seat had a placemat like dinner was about to be served. They were meant to protect the table. As the president walked in, everyone stood up. Jack took his chair to Sutton's right. He could not understand why the most important person was always furthest away from the monitors that would show the important information they'd need to see.

Jack looked at Matheus, who was sitting across from him, "I like it when you have to do the presenting. I get to sit back and relax."

Ron Timmons, seated next to Matheus, gave Jack a nod. "How are things going at State?"

"Jack, everyone is focused on China, but you're having all the fun."

Secretary Matheus cleared his throat. "Jeff Hern, who heads up our Cyber Division, has a direct plug into the bunker at Zhongnanhai. We wanted to share with you a meeting that happened earlier today. I believe it was four pm Beijing time."

Jack was remiss in not tracking Jeff down earlier. They were such good friends at Berkeley and now, even though they were even in closer proximity, they never connected.

Jeff stood up. "We established a link to one of their computers so we can both see and hear what happened in the meeting. Jim Tong here will translate it since it's all in Chinese."

Jack felt a strange sense as he realized he had been in that exact bunker several times before with President Wang and some generals. Now the atmosphere was much different. Li Keqiang was at the head of the table, speaking tersely to four generals. Tong began to translate: "Li is pissed off and telling them that they need to retaliate against America for what it is doing. He's telling them he wants a cyberattack. He wants everything that can be shut down that can be. 'This LibertyChat is totally out of hand. Why can't we just stop it? We cannot afford for it to grow and all the voices to be heard.'" Li pounded the table in the video. "That Jack Gold is dangerous."

That was not what he said. "Tong, make the translation accurate, please," Jack said.

"Apologies." Tong said. "Fuck Jack's mother." He coughed once, before continuing to translate. "I want all options on the table of how China can retaliate."

All the generals were quiet. Finally, one spoke up. "President Li, a cyberattack would be tracked back to us and could justly be considered an act of war. Plus, the LibertyChat is not America's. There are only a handful of white people using it. Also, a number of countries are working in collaboration. We need to think of something that does not result in repercussions that exacerbate the situation."

The fury on Li's face was visible, as was the generals' concern that they might be ordered to do something they didn't think was right.

Li pointed at each of the generals. "I want solutions. You get forty-eight hours—otherwise I will replace each of you."

"You really know how to make friends, Jack," Matheus said.

Jack looked to Jeff. "Do we have any information on what Li's Standing Committee is thinking about?"

"Nothing, yet. We had the previous Standing Committee pretty wired up. But they all got replaced and they brought in a Russian team to upgrade all their equipment and security."

"He's desperate," Jack said, glancing at Sutton. "He's about to make a mistake. The generals all looked and sounded nervous. That's good, but at the same time, this is the riskiest period we'll face, during the next few weeks."

"Is there anything we should do?"

"No. We proceed as planned. They will inevitably make a move and we'll need to call their bluff."

"Mr. President," Matheus said, "in light of these findings, I move that we reschedule poker night."

Sutton smirked. "Jack, if you keep pissing off foreign leaders, you'll never be invited."

*   *   *

The following day, Foreign Minister Zhao Lijiang held a press briefing in Beijing: "*In the strongest terms, China opposes the United States interfering in its internal affairs. The United States is closing its embassies and placing sanctions on Chinese Communist Party Members in an attempt to influence Chinese politics. We consider this an aggression and will take action accordingly.*"

The foreign ministry posted a warning to Chinese students in the US, asking them to "be on guard" as "US law enforcement agencies have stepped up arbitrary interrogations, harassment, confiscation of personal belongings and detention targeting Chinese international students in the US."

CHAPTER 23

"Could you please assist in reserving two bar seats at El Centro for Jojo and me for Saturday at seven pm?" Jack asked Telly. This was long overdue; he couldn't actually recall the last time he and Jojo had spent time together alone.

His secretary nodded. "Certainly, sir. You know it's okay if you pick up your phone and use that; save you a trip out here."

"I know," Jack said. "I guess I'm old school. And don't mind the chance to get up and stretch my legs."

He hoped El Centro would be a good restaurant; it seemed like it had a good vibe and it had been a while since he'd last had Mexican food, which Jojo also liked. He just wanted to go out somewhere with a relaxed, laid-back atmosphere so he and Jojo could enjoy each other's company.

Instead of returning to his office, Jack went to look for Davis, who he found in the Entrance Hall, chatting with a Secret Service agent. When he saw Jack, he ended the conversation and made his way over.

"I just had a question," Jack said. "Do you think it'd be okay if I ride the motorcycle with Jojo to dinner on Saturday evening? I booked us bar seats on El Centro."

Davis frowned and rubbed his chin. "Hmm. I would counsel you against riding a motorcycle. But—it's up to you."

"Would you do it if you were the vice president?"

"Hell yes."

Jack laughed. "Okay, that's what I thought. Well, that'll be our plan on Saturday. I've taken the bike out a few times, but never with anyone on the back."

Davis nodded. "It sounds like it'll be a nice time. Let me know how the food is; Rio and I will check it out if it's any good. We'll do a double date."

"Jojo would love that." It was a simple, regular thing that people did in real life. Jack was missing that sort of thing. "As a matter of fact, I would, too."

*   *   *

But that Saturday was just for Jack and Jojo. The weather was getting warmer and the cherry blossom trees, given long ago by Japan, were beginning to bloom. Their delicate pink blossoms joining a welcome change from the gray of winter.

The restaurant was less than two miles away and Jojo had her arms wrapped around Jack's midsection as they cruised the streets of Georgetown. Jack could feel the mild fluctuations in temperature as they zipped along. There would be pockets of colder air that made his eyes water and then they'd be past it, the scent of the cherry blossoms and the warmth of the milder air like a beckoning of spring.

As they pulled up to the restaurant, they parked between cars. Jack could see Secret Service agents were already stationed around the entrance to the restaurant.

They held hands as they walked in and over to the hostess. "Hi, I think I have a reservation for seven pm."

"What is the name under?"

"Jack Gold."

She found his name and they made their way over to the bar and sat with their backs to the restaurant.

Jack put his arm around Jojo and said in Mandarin, "I thought we should drink dinner and share a taco." He kept a straight face for as long as he could while Jojo just raised an eyebrow.

"You are so romantic, Mr. VP."

He made a face. "People at work are finally starting to call me Jack. I figured if I correct them often enough, they'll change. But let's not talk about that right now. I want this to be about us, about you. How is your studio coming along? I saw that lots of stuff has been arriving."

Jojo smiled. "I actually feel inspired. Having kids has made me want to capture their beauty. If I can reflect that in sculptures, that would be great. So it's coming along pretty well. Also, I'm thinking we need to utilize all the space we have—I have lots of friends who want to come visit. Is that okay?"

"Of course. That would be great." Jack recalled all the tremendous friends, actors and musicians, who he met a long time ago when Jojo threw a party and introduced all her friends to her new boyfriend. So much had happened since then, and Jack knew that Jojo would have kept in better touch with people if she hadn't had to uproot her life several times for him.

They paused their conversation when the bartender came over. They ordered margaritas and an array of the street tacos, some with steak, some with mahi, and some with pork shoulder.

"Maybe we can have a musical event of sorts," Jack said, returning to their conversation, "like you did before. I bet we could even have it at the White House."

"Are you serious? Could we do that?"

Jack shrugged. "Why not? Sutton basically said we could do anything. He would probably enjoy attending if you thought it was fitting to invite him."

"Okay, I'll think of something."

Their drinks arrived. Jack had ordered the prickly pear margarita and Jojo got the spicy mango. "Oooh, this is good," Jojo said after her first sip.

When the tacos came out, they paired perfectly with their drinks and Jack and Jojo had no problem clearing their plates. More importantly though, this dinner was like old times. Just them hanging out at a bar and enjoying each other's company. Jack could almost imagine what it was like when they first started dating and they were at Bar No. 3, where Jojo had been working when he first met her. He still marveled at everything that had taken place since then.

But when they went to leave, there was a gaggle of press waiting outside, who began yelling questions and taking pictures when they saw Jack and Jojo. "Have you seen the news?" one shrill-voiced reporter kept shouting. "Have you seen the news? What are your thoughts Mr. Vice President?"

Jack didn't respond. They got on the motorcycle and retraced their way back to the house. They held hands when they entered the quiet home and Jack grabbed Jojo, pulled her close to him. "Thanks for the lovely date. Can we do this more often?"

Jojo beamed up at him and touched the end of his nose with her finger. "You aren't kidding me, Jack. You're dying to find out what the news is that reporter was talking about. But, yes, let's do this more often."

He kissed her. "You know me so well."

Jack turned on the TV. It was splashed over all the news networks. *China's National Congress has voted to remove Li Keqiang from office. No new president has been selected.*

CHAPTER 24

Jack was looking over Susan's shoulder at a video of Zhang Li urging the National Congress to institute a fair election system, allowing all citizens to vote. He was very popular now, with about twenty-five million followers. Susan was well ahead at about sixty-million followers. "Altogether the platform has about two hundred million members. It's growing super fast."

Jack said, "That's about fourteen percent of the population. Time to move on to our next initiative. What does everyone think about Li Keqiang being kicked out of office?"

David said, "I heard mentioning he was responsible for the attempt on your life as a key reason he was kicked out."

"But it was more than that," Susan said. "The Standing Committee and National Congress realize change needs to happen. They are getting scared about our initiatives and all the voices now on LibertyChat. Discontent is growing and they need to show they are doing something."

"Is there any mention of who might be voted in to replace of Li?"

Susan shook her head. "It'll take them a while to figure that out. If they follow the same path as in the past, there will need to be all sorts of private discussions in order to build a consensus around one person. Rumor is the National Congress is considering allowing all citizens to vote. That would be a big change but they want the right ratify anyone elected. No one is sure if the Standing Committee is in support or not."

"You mean that what Zhang Yi is pushing for might come true?"

"Yes, but the National Congress might insist on having the authority to approve a candidate or not. That would not be ideal."

"No, it's not," Jack said. The others nodded. "Maybe you share your thoughts on this stuff. People need someone like you to tell them honestly how the process works. Both in China and in other countries."

Jack walked over to the Oval Office and was motioned by Madeline to go in. "Hello, Mr. President," he said to Sutton. "No formal communication from China has occurred, just press releases. I talked to CIA and Matheus. It seems like the Standing Committee is indecisive regarding what they want. Things are in a bit of disarray without a head of state. I suggest we stay on schedule and up the stakes by going with our next initiative. This will also help get more people on the platform. Membership stands at about two hundred million, which is only fourteen percent of the population. May I proceed?"

"Yes Jack, proceed," Sutton said.

*   *   *

Once again, exactly a week from the past press conference, at six-thirty am, Jack and Susan walked into a room packed full of press. Jack went up to the podium. "Thank you for coming this morning. We have all heard about Li Keqiang's removal from the position of President of China. This is good news for a variety of reasons. What will likely end up happening is China's National Congress will replace Li Keqiang with someone else like him. This does not fix the structural problems that China faces. It is like playing musical chairs. Someone even worse could come—now or later. With that in mind, I have another initiative related to the China Declaration that I would like to announce. China has some of brightest most talented people in the world. But there is a lack of opportunity in China for those potentially brilliant doctors, lawyers, athletes, chefs, inventors, businessmen, and so forth.

"America feels that the lack of opportunity in China is a form of oppression forced upon the population. America is not a comparatively populous nation. However, studies indicate that there are numerous areas within America that require more expertise that is just not available. Unfilled, this will cause a strain on America and lead to increased costs and unproductive wage inflation. Each year there are about thirty-thousand immigrants from China to America. This contrasts sharply with those from Mexico, which in recent years has been averaging about one million.

"Therefore the president, in consultation with the secretary of state, believe it is important to increase the immigration quota of Chinese to America. This is an emergency humanitarian presidential order. The quota for the next twelve months will triple to one-hundred- and-twenty-thousand people." There was some murmuring and shifting in seats. "This large increase will be for people in certain skill areas and for specific geographic regions across America to maximize the benefit to the United States. America is increasing opportunities for those from China who would like to immigrate. America wants the best and brightest. You'll find that a streamlined application process is already online. CCP members and their family members are excluded from immigrating henceforth. We expect this presidential order will discontinue when the president's comprehensive immigration bill gets passed."

Hands flew up and Jack called on a Chinese reporter, "You are intentionally taking the best and smartest from China?"

Jack had expected this line of questioning. "This is no different than what China has been doing with its Thousand Talents Plan. Except China hoped to hire people to *steal* their knowledge acquired at their institution in their home country. Fundamentally though, China is a closed society with zero percent foreigners. This contrasts with New York and LA that have about 33 percent foreigners. It's quite common here to run into someone who's Asian yet does not speak an Asian language. There is not a single such person in China. The country is closed. America is an open society where people from everywhere can flourish. Not providing such an opportunity to those who are oppressed in China takes an opportunity away from them. The United States is the land of opportunity—at least the last time I checked."

He called on the next person. "How do you think China will feel about this policy? Is this being done just to infuriate them?"

"China will be mad at the United States, though what they really should do is look in the mirror. Their real problem is in creating a real and vibrant society—they have failed at that miserably. It is their own fault their citizens want to leave China. Let me note, Chinese leave their country reluctantly. It is very difficult for them to leave their family, culture, and cuisine. It is not easy, I know. They always miss what they leave behind. Yet Chinese come to America regularly to have their children born here. They want what they cannot get in China. They want liberty for their children. They want freedom and prosperity."

He called on the next person, an Asian woman near the back. "Isn't there a way to solve this problem with China that doesn't involve these sorts of actions?"

"China caused this situation as outlined in the China Declaration. You should ask China that question. Over the years we have repeatedly to reason with China. They have stolen our intellectual property, they've signed agreements they never live up to, they subjugated tens of millions of people. The China I see now is one history will look upon with complete and utter disdain. No one has stood up to them. Everyone talks and eventually China wears them down or people want to make money there. The Sutton Administration knows China's game. Japan, England, France, and other nations are instituting similar programs. The world has recognized the nature of China. The administration will not back down. I will not back down. We are ready for a long, drawn-out process. In the meantime, we will provide more immigration opportunities to the smartest and best Chinese. Think of it as humanitarian relief. You will be hearing from me again with our next initiative soon."

Jack gave a slight nod to the Secret Service agent standing near the woman who had just asked the question. He went over and leaned in, saying something quietly to her. She shook her head and then the agent reached out and took her arm, started to pull her up out of her seat.

"I will not leave!" the woman screamed as the agent dragged her out. Heads swiveled to watch the commotion. "You can't make me leave just because I asked a question."

"Next question," Jack said, pointing. The man stood.

"How can the United States take such drastic action that effect so many?"

Jack waved to another Secret Service agent who immediately walked over to the man. The security agent whispered to the man and then took him by the arm. He yelled, "You cannot just remove me. We have freedom of the press. What is going on? How can everyone just sit there and let this happen?" His yells grew more distant as he was pulled from the room.

"Mr. Vice President, this is not right!" a woman near the front said. Jack had her removed, too.

Things were starting to deteriorate. The remaining people in the room were looking around, wide-eyed and uncertain; a few were angry.

"What the hell is going on Mr. Vice President?" someone shouted.

Jack held his hands up and gestured for everyone to settle down; the anxiety was nearly palpable. "Let's take a seat," he said. Two people from his team came in and started handing out pieces of paper, which was enough of a distraction to get everyone to sit back down.

"In China," Jack said, "the press is removed if they ask an inappropriate question. They are given a list of questions they're allowed to ask, prior to the press conference. There is zero freedom of press."

He looked to the back of the room where the three people who had just been so forcibly removed now stood, smiles on their faces. They returned to their seats, confusion now the dominant emotion in the room.

"Those are actors I arranged for," Jack said. There were audible sounds of surprise, but more so, relief. "Who in this room is very familiar with the Declaration of Independence?" Jack asked. A few hands rose immediately. The others were slower to follow.

"Can you humor me then? Let's take a thirty-minute break and please re-read the Declaration of Independence. Then read the China Declaration. You should all have a copy."

Jack went and sat in one of the five seats positioned perpendicular to the lectern. He pulled out his phone and texted Jojo. *I'll be leaving in about ten minutes. Muah.* They always texted in English because Jack's written Chinese was poor.

Jojo responded quickly. *Aren't you in the middle of a press conference? Muah.*

Yes, but I can do two things at once.

You are crazy. See you soon. I like the new upright piano in the downstairs room.

Jack smiled. He knew Jojo wanted more music in their life. More art. The Steinway piano was a small start.

When everyone had finished reading, Jack put his phone in his pocket and went back to the lectern.

"The Declaration of Independence is one of the most remarkable documents in the history of America. It carefully details what England was doing to America. It lists facts and how every person has unalienable rights. *We hold these truths to be self-evident.* But many in America have forgotten what comes after those words, and so it has really been lost in history. What came after that document was the founding of America through a great war led by George Washington. Interestingly, Washington never signed the document. The reason I bring this up is because the China Declaration closely follows that format. It has a clear argument as to the rights of Chinese and how China has trampled them and how it has been a horrible world citizen. That document was written to make Chinese aware of the situation and to bring together democratic nations in the hopes of addressing atrocities to humanity."

Jack let that sink in. He wanted the press to understand what was happening and what was at stake. He walked to the front of the podium so he could be closer to everyone and spoke slowly, with no notes. "Now we find ourselves in a non-military battle with China. America's actions and that of our partners are noble. Sometimes it is necessary to take bold steps to create bold change.

"One thing that I feel is missing are the personal stories in Western media that seem to not get reported. Stories about the Hong Kong people fleeing, those in jail in Xinjiang, the scared people in Taiwan. These and other stories are often hard to find. Case in point—Chinese press are subjugated, but if you look at them now, you can't readily see it. What happened to you tonight when some of the press was thrown out gave you an unforgettable emotional reaction. Think about how you felt before you learned it was staged. This happens broadly in China every day. The stories are never pleasant. So, we will start sharing more stories with you. Real stories. And we hope you can find ones of your own. We have a solemn duty to share, to help, and also to bring pressure. Sometimes a country's citizens cannot defend themselves. We are bound by a duty to help humanity. This is not a lofty goal. It is a moral imperative. Americans must understand this to appreciate our ultimate objective and what we are doing."

Jack left it at that. He started to walk off and a few reporters started to clap. Then, they all rose to their feet applauding. Jack stopped and walked over to a few who had their hands stretched out. The applause increased. Jack waved, then turned and left the room.

He walked in back toward his office, rather exhausted from the press conference. His staff followed him, knowing he was collecting his thoughts. Jack turned toward them. "I'm going to drop by the president's office. I'll see you in a bit."

He veered off toward the Oval Office and mudded as he walked by Madeline. Walking in, he saw Sutton talking with Matheus. "Jack, you better sit down."

Jack went over and took a seat next to Matheus on one of the sofas. There was a map on the table. "Right near the end of your press briefing, China announced the closing of the Taiwan Strait in the South China Sea to all foreign vessels, given that its territory extends now to Taiwan.

Matheus and I were just ruminating options. The British have said their navy will not enter the Taiwan Strait even if the US does, given the abundance of Chinese ships in the area and the high tensions in the region. The USS Harry S. Truman is deployed nearby. They are about a day away. So, Jack." Sutton rubbed his palms together. "Any ideas?"

Jack wasn't surprised to hear this. "China has no right to close the strait off. One-third of shipping goes through that part of the South China Sea each year, carrying about three trillion in trade. Once we give in to China by not entering the strait, it could be lost forever. It has security implications too." Jack paused, thinking. "Mr. President, my suggestion is you fly me out to the Harry S. Truman. My bet is that the Brits will then join, and China will not fire on us."

"Jack, the Chinese military head right now is a guy named Lai Kang. He's a serious communist, according to our sources."

"Fly me out. If they shoot on the Truman, they'll have more trouble internally and externally than they know what to do with. Something like this was bound to happen. Just make sure you let them know I'm on the carrier, Mr. President."

Sutton glanced at Matheus. The secretary of defense shifted so he could look at Jack straight on. "You'll miss poker night again. Marine One to Air Force Two to Japan. We have a chopper there that can get you to the Truman. We'll have it moved closer to make sure."

Sutton nodded, his gaze going back to Jack. His expression was serious, maybe even a little concerned. "Be out back in ten minutes."

*   *   *

Jack went to talk to Susan, Jason, and David. They were in their offices and he told them about the meeting he'd just had. "Jason, you're coming with me, please. Susan, you need to stay here to notify the press and hold other briefings as necessary. And—make sure you report on it and share with everyone on the platform. If I get killed on an aircraft carrier, Jojo is going to get pissed off. You also may need to announce our next initiative in two days. Get the president's approval beforehand. I'll try to keep you updated. Also, importantly, please put together a simple matrix of Russia, America, Japan, England, and China and compare their forms of government, how elections are held, laws made and then enforced.

Include economic growth. You can leave a comments area. The countries go down, and the other items across. Present that in Chinese to the press and post the story on your feed. Talk about what you personally learned."

While Jason was gathering his things, Jack went back to his own office and asked Telly to get two reams of yellow paper and twelve Sharpies, in a backpack.

"I have to leave for a few days," he explained.

"I already heard. I'll get that together right now."

The minutes were ticking down. Jack grabbed his warm jacket, then Telly came into the office with the backpack. Jack thanked him. He and Jason exited the back of the White House. Jack felt hyperaware of everything, yet things were happening so quickly it also felt like a blur.

*   *   *

Close to fourteen hours later they arrived at an American air base in Japan and were immediately escorted to a large helicopter.

It was loud. Brain jarringly loud. Fortunately, there were headsets and Jack put his on and handed one to Jason. The pilot's voice came through the headset. "Welcome aboard, Mr. Vice President."

"Thank you for the lift. Is there any update on the situation?"

"Not that I've been informed about, sir."

"What's the commute time?"

"About three hours, sir."

He had slept a little on the flight over but it had come in fits and starts. The vibration of the helicopter put him to sleep and he awoke only moments before the helicopter landed. Jack looked at his watch and saw that it was two am in Washington DC, which meant it was two pm near Japan.

He was greeted by a line of officers when he and Jason stepped out. One came up and saluted Jack. "Welcome aboard, Mr. Vice President. I am Rear Admiral Curt Grant. May I introduce you to my leadership team?"

"Certainly."

The admiral proceeded to introduce his team, and then Jack had Jason take a photo of him shaking the admiral's hand. "Send that to Susan, please."

"When we heard the news that you were coming, everyone was surprised," the admiral said. "Usually, politicians visit when we are at port."

"I hope you'll come to realize that I am not a typical politician."

"We all know that, sir. We've been watching all your news conferences. May I take you on a little walk to the PriFly. Then we'll get you to your accommodations. We can give you a more detailed tour later. I'd like to get under way."

"When will we arrive at the beginning of the Taiwan Strait?"

"I'll show you on a map where China considers the red line in their waters. We should hit it in a about twenty-two hours."

"The British still won't enter?"

"No change."

"Please communicate to the British captain that Mr. Jack Gold who is onboard, sends his best regards to the prime minister and the Queen."

The admiral stopped walking and stared at Jack. "Are you serious? You really want me to send the message?"

"As soon as you can. I met the Queen and the prime minister recently. Both signed the China Declaration. I want the Queen to tell the prime minister to grow some balls."

The admiral chuckled. "Change of plans. We'll visit the bridge first."

The nuclear-powered aircraft carrier was even more impressive up close, in person. Jack had read it was over one thousand feet long and rose twenty-four stories above the water. They took a stairway up a few floors before entering the captain's bridge. On the flight deck below, Jack could see well over a dozen fighter jets.

"Please tell my colleague what he should not take pictures of," he said. "I don't want him taking any confidential pictures or video."

"Thank you, sir. I'll let you know. Let me get that message out to the captain of the British ship." The admiral picked up the receiver. "HMS Queen Elizabeth, please come in. This is Harry S. Truman."

"*We are here, Admiral. Go ahead.*"

"Vice President Jack Gold just arrived aboard the Harry S. Truman. He would like you to forward a message. He sends his best regards to the prime minister and the Queen."

"Also," Jack said in a low voice, "please tell them to inform the PM and the Queen that I will be joining you through the Taiwan Strait when we get there."

After the message was conveyed, Jack and Jason were escorted to their small rooms, right next to each other. "There are some uniforms inside if you need a change of clothes, also something to work out in," the admiral told him before departing.

Jason said he was going to lie down and take a nap, but Jack felt he had some excess energy he needed to burn. He changed into a pair of the workout clothes then left his room and asked for directions to the gym. The aircraft was massive, a city on the water that held over six thousand people. At the gym, Jack saw people boxing, lifting weights, and running on treadmills. There was a large area for stretching. He went there first, warming up and then going through all his karate forms, followed by a bunch of combinations, each a way to counter an attacker. *Almost a better place to work out than his place in Beijing.* He appreciated the fact that though it was clear people recognized him, they let him get his workout in without any interference. When he was done, he did shake some hands and took a few pictures with people.

"Would you like to box, Mr. Vice President?" The man who asked was a tall, well-muscled African-American. He held out a pair of gloves.

"I never use those things!" Jack said. Those within earshot laughed. "I'm actually wondering if someone could direct me to the mess hall."

There were a few people who said they were headed that way now, so Jack went with them. Passing through Jack could see people hard at work. Once there, he got a cheeseburger, some fries, a salad, and a Diet Coke. They sat together at a long blue table and Jack couldn't help but notice how happy they all seemed. They were joking around but in a friendly way. Just being on the ship was giving him a respect for the Navy that he hadn't had before.

After the meal, he returned to his room, showered, and changed into the light camouflage uniform they left for him. It fit perfectly and it felt extraordinarily comfortable.

He lay down on his bunk, aware that he was in a small metal room within a bigger metal ship. The air was dry, probably to avoid things rusting. He closed his eyes in the total darkness, trying to remember where the light switch was when he woke up.

*   *   *

Hours later, a blaring alarm went off, jolting Jack awake. He got up and felt around for the light switch, then put on his shoes. An announcement came over the intercom. "*Escort Vice President to the bridge.*"

There was a flurry of commotion when Jack opened the door, people rushing in both directions. "Follow me, sir," a young man in uniform said. "I'll take you up."

Jack was grateful for the assistance since there was no way he could have remembered how to navigate back to the bridge. When they arrived, his escort announced, "Vice President on deck."

Everyone stood and saluted. Jack walked up to the admiral. "Is there something I can help with?"

"I have the president and Secretary Matheus on speaker phone."

"Hi Jack," Matheus said. "Here is the situation. You are being pinged by a Chinese submarine, which means they can shoot you. A few miles ahead there are Chinese naval ships on both sides of your path, including a Chinese Type 055 warship, their most advanced destroyer. This is not a good situation."

"Has the British ship started to move?"

"No. There has been no change to their position."

"I strongly believe we should keep our defenses down and proceed like we are taking a walk in the park. No defensive or offensive actions. Their military and country have way too much to lose."

"What should we tell them?" Matheus asked.

"Have the admiral tell them that Vice President Jack Gold is onboard the Harry S. Truman. He can then say 'The United States does not recognize China's sole right to the South China Sea. We are peacefully navigating through. Please keep your distance and weapons secured so that there are no unintended mistakes.' I can echo that in Chinese."

"Hold on, Jack."

Sutton's voice came across the line. "Jack, who should speak first? You or the admiral?"

"I should, sir."

"Proceed please."

The admiral handed Jack another phone. Jack took it and said in English, "Hello."

A voice immediately came on saying in English. "You are invading the sovereign territory of China. Please turn around or suffer the consequences."

"Hello, everyone," Jack said, switching to Chinese, and trying to make sure they recognized his voice. "This is Jack Gold. I am on the Harry S. Truman aircraft carrier. The United States does not recognize China's sole right to the South China Sea. We are peacefully navigating through. Please keep your distance and weapons secured so that there are no unintended mistakes."

Jack handed the phone to the admiral, who proceeded to say the same thing in English.

"Jack. This is Matheus." Jack turned his attention back to the speaker phone.

"Yes, Mr. Secretary?"

"You're missing poker night, again. Sorry about that. We'll schedule something for when you get back."

"You're a tease, Mr. Secretary."

"The British are moving into the strait," one of the operational specialists said.

"That's good news," Matheus said.

Jack nodded. "Long live the Queen."

"I think you're right, Jack," Matheus said. "Keep us posted."

The admiral turned to Jack. "It seems your message got through to the Queen."

"Yes."

"I must say, having you on board is different from other guests we've had."

"I hope you mean that in a good way, because I'm about to ask a favor."

"What can I help with?"

"I'd like you to make sure we sail close to the British ship. Tell them to go very slow. Then, I need as many people as you can spare to make some paper airplanes. I'd like your sailors to throw them to the British ship. To thank them."

"How many people do you need?"

"Twenty. In the mess hall."

The admiral nodded. "Sounds reasonable. They'll be there in ten minutes."

"Thank you."

Jack retraced his steps to his room to pick up his backpack. Then with Jason, went to the mess hall. There were both men and women there at the ready, all with their sleeves rolled up. Jack showed them how he wanted them to fold the airplanes, then demonstrated how to adjust the wings. Lastly, he took out the Sharpie pens and wrote on the wings *Long Live the Queen!*

"We have only 1,000 pieces of paper," he said. "With the wind, it'll be a little bit tricky but I'm sure we can get enough on the British ship."

"Mr. Vice President, we have some yellow paper onboard, at least a few reams."

"That would be amazing. We can have a wave of yellow messages. Excellent."

With that, everyone got to work. Jack sat next to Jason as they began folding paper into planes.

"British ship approaching," the voice over the intercom announced a little while later. "Ten minutes out. Permission to greet."

Over three thousand people made their way to the deck of the Harry S. Truman. Paper airplanes were distributed to nearly every person. The wings on each plane were adjusted for straight flight. As the British vessel came just near the Truman, a wave of thousands of yellow airplanes were launched into the sky and over onto the British carrier.

After the shock of seeing so many airplanes, the British started to pick up the planes and read the messages.

Cheers erupted on the British vessel and a loud chant began: "Long Live the Queen!"

Jason stood next to Jack, filming from his phone. He saw a photographer on the British ship snapping photos. He knew the message sent from the Harry S. Truman would arrive to the Queen.

*   *   *

They stood on the flight deck, about four thousand of them, wearing white uniforms. It was a sunny day in Singapore and fortunately the temperature and humidity were not too bad. Admiral Curt Grant was at the podium speaking. "And when they said the vice president was going to visit, I'll be honest with you—I was worried. I thought he was a little bit crazy to be coming at the time he did. He was an easy guest. He found his way around. When things got dicey with China, he stepped in with his insight and a determined view, which he gave to the president and the secretary of defense. They respected what he said. He communicated directly to the Chinese in Mandarin. He got the British into the game. With that said, I would like to introduce you to the Vice President of the United States, Mr. Jack Gold."

Cheers erupted. Morale was high and everyone seemed happy. The mission had been a success.

"Speech! Speech! Speech!" the crowd chanted.

Jack walked up to the microphone. "Sorry to disappoint you, Admiral. When I was speaking Chinese, I thought I was ordering dinner."

A wave of laughter rippled through the crowd. Jack smiled.

"When I found out the situation, I said that I needed to go because I knew I could help. I didn't think of the danger, but I knew of it. I'll bet that each and every one of you would have done exactly the same thing. Yes or no?"

"Yes!" the crowd yelled.

"Every politician should serve in the Navy and learn what it's like. To learn what bravery is about. To understand discipline and dedication, and how to have fun but be professional about what you do. I'm proud of all of you. I'm indebted to you. I'm grateful for your service in making America safe!"

More earnest cheering.

"Admiral, could you order everyone to turn off their phones and cameras? That goes for you too, Jason."

Jack waited for the order to be given before continuing. "Now I've been thinking about mottos for the Navy. It does not seem right not to have one. I have two I'll try out. How is: We float well because we have big balls."

There were cheers and laughs.

"If anyone thinks that's sexist, we can change it to We float well because we have big tits."

Clearly, no one expected the vice president to talk to them like that but there was laughter and cheering all around. The admiral put his hand over his face.

"I'd like to explain about the yellow paper airplanes," Jack said. "Throwing them at the British ship will be remembered for a long time.

It'll help grow and deepen our friendship. But that's not why I wanted to do it. In 1951 the Queen visited and stayed with Truman's family in Washington DC. She has nothing but fond memories of Harry Truman. And we are on that remarkable man's ship. It is only fitting on behalf of Harry Truman, that we sent our best wishes to her. He would have wanted that. And we did it. I would like to thank you all for your graciousness in hosting me. I shall remember the visit fondly, always."

Jack waved both his hands and enjoyed the ovation. He shook the admiral's hand. "Thanks, Jack."

"Thank you, Admiral."

He stepped back from the podium and looked for Jason. It was time to go.

CHAPTER 25

Roughly twenty-eight hours later, they arrived back in Washington DC. It was dark and Jack went home, not caring what might be going on. If it was important, he knew they would reach him.

He found Jojo sitting at the piano, Kai on the bench with her, resting her head in Jojo's lap. He went over and kissed them both on the top of the head.

"Welcome home," Jojo said. She ran her fingertips over the ivory keys. "I never knew that an upright piano could have such good sound quality. Thanks again. How did your trip go?"

"Just another day at the office. What have you two been up to?" Kai had sat up and held her arms out to him. He lifted her up. "You should come to work with Daddy."

"I got a strange call today," Jojo said. "Someone with an English accent was calling to confirm that we would be spending two nights at Windsor Castle over New Year's with the Queen." She gave him a quizzical look. "Was it a prank?"

"I thought I mentioned the invitation?"

"I vaguely recall something like that. Are we going?"

"We have to. You cannot refuse an invitation from the Queen."

"I need to call them back then."

"Just ask them when they would like us to arrive. We have transportation."

"That's right. That's very convenient. I'll take care of it. Is it okay if just you and I go? A nice getaway. The kids won't be staying up till midnight anyway, and we can take a nice family trip when we get back. Maybe to see your dad."

Jack looked at Kai. "Does that sound like a plan?" he asked. She smiled, reached out and grabbed his nose. "I think that's a yes," he said.

* * *

After breakfast with the family the next morning, Jack was back at the White House. He first went to Susan's cubicle, where he found her, along with David and Jason, elated expressions on their faces.

"Did someone win the lottery?" he asked. "What happened?"

Susan's eyes went to Jason. Jason looked to David. David couldn't wipe the grin off his face.

"Okay, out with it," Jack said.

Susan took a deep breath. "The National Congress voted to approve elections that allow all citizens to vote."

Jack could see all three of them were still beaming. "What else are you not telling me?"

Susan remained uncharacteristically silent. Finally, David said, "Elections will be held next month. Zhang Li and President Wang have both pledged their support of Susan."

"You mean Zhang Li doesn't want to run?" Jack asked.

"He's very open-minded," Susan said. "He wants to see China have its first woman president. Plus, I have lots more followers than he does," she added.

"So, what happens next?"

Susan's smile widened. Jack could not recall ever seeing her so excited. "I need to go to China very soon." She paused. "I was wondering about my China passport."

Jack said, "Look in your top desk drawer."

Susan opened her drawer and pulled out all three of their passports.

"Jack!" she said, holding the passports. "You put these there. Did you know all along?"

"Let's go see the president."

He and Susan made their way to the Oval Office, stopping first at Madeline's desk.

"Welcome back, Jack," she said. "Do you know why female sailors float so well?"

Jack put his hand over his face, hiding his smile. "No, I do not."

Madeline winked. "I thought so. President Sutton is inside with Matheus. Please go in."

Jack found the two men relaxing on the sofa, chatting. The demeanor in the room was markedly different than the last time he was here. "Good morning, gentlemen," Jack said.

They said good morning and Sutton told him to take a seat. He sat next to Sutton. Susan sat across from them on the other sofa next to Matheus. "Hello Susan," Sutton said. "Jack, your visit was productive. Good job."

"Is there a poker game coming up that I can join?"

"Could you believe we had to reschedule it?" Matheus said.

"There have been some developments in China" Jack said. "The National Congress has agreed to a popular election to elect the next president."

"That's outstanding news. Congratulations, Jack. Who do we think will win?" Sutton asked.

Jack looked directly at Susan, grinning. Sutton shot a quizzical look at Jack, then looked at Matheus, whose brow was furrowed as his eyes shifted from Susan to Jack.

"Susan has the support of President Wang and Zhang Li. It looks like she may become the first woman president in the history of China," Jack said.

"No kidding?!" Sutton clapped. "Susan, that's incredible. We will be rooting for you."

"Thank you," Susan said. "President Wang and Zhang Li have agreed to serve as advisors as we go through the election process and if I should be elected."

"Jack, I'm sorry but, Jason and David would like to return with me and serve in my campaign."

"Of course."

"Another thing. When can we get all those initiatives reversed?"

"Once you win and troops leave Taiwan."

Susan looked at him. "I thought you'd say that. Some of the troops may decide to stay on their own volition."

"That makes sense," Jack said, knowing Taiwan was a beautiful country where many would want to stay. "We'll arrange transport. Just let us know when you'd like to go."

"Thank you. The sooner the better please."

The president stood up. "It has been a pleasure working with you, Susan. We wish you the best of luck and if you need anything, always feel free to call."

They shook hands and Susan left. Jack closed the door.

"Did you know that would happen?" Sutton asked.

Jack gave an exaggerated shrug. "Ask Matheus. Maybe he knew."

Secretary Matheus leaned forward, shaking his head. "Some things are best not discussed."

CHAPTER 26

Six weeks later on December thirtieth, Jack and Jojo arrived at Heathrow Airport and were driven to Windsor Castle. As instructed, they arrived at five pm and were escorted to their room. Their attendance was requested at six for an audience with the Queen.

"This is extraordinary architecture," Jojo said. "It's a mix of Gothic, Baroque, Victorian . . . I'd love to sculpt here any day."

They were walking with an escort through the opulent Crimson Drawing Room with its scarlet and gold walls, gilded ceiling, and magnificent framed portraits. Jack carried a bottle of Maotai with him. The Queen was there talking to a gentleman who immediately left as Jack and Jojo entered.

"Hello, Jack. Hello Jojo," the Queen said. "I understand you speak French." Jojo did not curtsy or say *Your Majesty*; they just started chatting as if Jack did not exist. He enjoyed seeing Jojo speaking French. To him, she became a completely different person. Jack ordered a beer from one of the attentive waiters and handed over the bottle of Maotai, requesting that it be served in small cups at the beginning of dinner.

A few other people arrived and Jack went over to introduce himself. He met England's minister of defense and Betty Bao, a Chinese-American author. Two others came in and politely introduced themselves to Jack. They chatted about China. Jack enjoyed the conversation but felt the author was out of touch. Jack had seen this before—a Chinese person who thought they knew best simply because they were Chinese. But Jack wasn't going to let those things bother him, at least not tonight.

The announcement came that dinner was to be served. Jojo held hands with the Queen as they made their way to the dining room. There was a long wooden table which was set with beautiful china, crystal glasses, and fine silverware. The attendants showed everyone where they should sit. Jack found himself directly across from the Queen, who had Jojo right next to her.

Jojo showed the Queen the bottle of Maotai and she explained its background. The Queen's eyes widened when Jojo had told her the price of the bottle.

"Usually," the Queen said, "I wait until later to make a toast. But tonight, I think that should change. The last time Jack was here, I signed the China Declaration. Jack and I spoke about the wonderful time I had staying with Harry Truman and his family in Washington. At that time, I referred to the China Declaration as the *China play*—I knew it would be one—but not to the extent it was. Jack flew onto the Harry S. Truman aircraft carrier and entered where my military was too frightened to go. Right into the Taiwan Strait where there were hundreds of Chinese boats with missiles aimed at him. He had the audacity from the Harry S. Truman, to send a message to our ship, the RMS Queen Elizabeth. He said to our captain, *Send my regards to the PM and to the Queen.*"

Though he was focused on the Queen, Jack could see Jojo scowling at him. *Just another day at the office.* He could hear her voice in his head perfectly.

"Jack, I received the message swiftly. The Queen should not be in politics, but I urged the prime minister to get the ship moving and stop being a sissy. After all, what is the point of having a big, beautiful ship unless you use it in times of danger.

"Both ships sailed through the strait unharmed, thanks to Jack's bravery. But that is not all. As the American and British ships passed each other, a wave of thousands of yellow airplanes were thrown from the Harry S. Truman onto the British ship."

The Queen had one of the paper airplanes in her hand and raised it so everyone could see. "Each had written on it *Long Live the Queen!* It was as if Harry Truman himself were sending me a message. Truly one of the grandest gestures I've received in my life."

The Queen looked directly at Jack. "Jack, well done. Everyone, I understand this Chinese liquor is special. A toast to the man of the hour."

Everyone raised their glasses and said, "Hear, hear. Well done."

Jack drank himself only after everyone sat, as he knew was proper custom.

The Queen raised her glass to Jack again. "Jack solved the China problem. It was a brilliant play. We need to show our thanks to Jack."

"Your kind words suffice, Your Majesty."

Jojo said, "Ma'am, you see what I'm talking about. He always says the correct thing. He always means it. It's intolerable." She grinned.

"Jack, for the second time in my life, an American has impressed me with their grandeur. Your wife is delightful, by the way."

"Thank you, Ma'am."

"Tomorrow you will be knighted."

Certainly, he had misheard. But the Queen gave the slightest nod of her head, as if she could hear his skepticism. "Tomorrow," she said.

CHAPTER 27

On the flight back, Jack and Jojo relaxed in the glow of their remarkable New Year's experience. The Queen's humor delighted them, as did the spirit of the young lady she seemed to exude. They both felt better for having met her and having the privilege of getting to know her a little bit.

"And to think I was wondering if we should go or not," Jojo said.

"Imagine. I wouldn't have been knighted."

"A knighthood, a vice presidency . . . is there nothing you can't do?"

Before Jack could respond, his phone rang. He stood up and took a few steps away.

"Hello, sir," he said. "Yes. Yes. No problem. I think that is good idea."

He hung up and sat back down. "Who was it?" Jojo asked.

"It was the president. It seems there was a skirmish between Singapore and Malaysia. He wants us to go there for a day so I can meet Chen Leong, Singapore's president. I hope that's okay. The food there is amazing."

"I guess we can extend things for a day. I'll call Sherry."

*   *   *

When the plane landed, Jojo looked out the window. "This looks like China, not Singapore." She stood up and looked at Jack. "I thought you said Singapore."

Jack bit his lip, frowned, and looked out the window. "Hmm. Maybe it's someplace else. The pilot could have made a mistake."

They got up and started to walk out of the plane. Jack let Jojo go first. As she walked down the steps there was a group of people waiting—her dad, her kids, Susan, and the nanny. She shrieked with joyous surprise and ran to hug everyone.

As Jack descended, he saw the dog and yelled out, "Mini, come!"

The border collie bound up the stairs and jumped onto Jack, nearly taking him down.

"You're a good boy," Jack said, adjusting the dog's weight in his arms. He went up to Wang and shook his hand, Mini still in his arms. "Where's my Maotai?" Jack asked jokingly.

Wang smiled deeply and patted him on the shoulder. "All is taken care of, Jack."

"We'll have to drink some together to make sure it's authentic."

Jack went to Susan and gave her a hug. "Thank you for arranging this, Madam President."

"Thank you, Jack. Thank you for everything. Your place has been immaculately cleaned and it's ready for you," Susan said.

President Wang looked from Jack to Jojo to his grandkids. "Welcome home."

Behind him were five large Audis and one SUV. Susan motioned for everyone to get in, but Jack stayed where he was as the others made their way to the cars.

After a moment, Jojo turned and saw him standing there. "What's going on, Jack?" she asked, walking back over to him.

He took her hands. "I can't, Jojo. I'm sorry. I'm still the vice president. Go have fun. Enjoy yourself. I'll be back home waiting for you."

Tears came to her eyes but she blinked them back and nodded. "Okay Jack, I understand." They hugged and then Jack held her hand as he walked over and said goodbye to everyone.

Mini followed Jack back onto the airplane where Davis was waiting.

"It must be hard to leave them," Davis said.

"It is," Jack said. He stroked Mini's fur. "But Mini will keep me company until they come home."

The plane doors closed. They began to taxi as Jack reclined his seat, making sure there was enough room for Mini to lie down next to him.

* * *

Hours later Jack woke up, Mini still lying next to him. Davis was still asleep. Jack gingerly got up, but still woke Mini. "Stay," he whispered.

Jack stretched his legs, looking at the back of the plane for his briefcase, which he spied in a nearby seat. As he walked over to get it, an attendant came up from out back.

"Mr. Vice President, may I get you anything?" she asked.

"A cup of hot black coffee would be wonderful please."

"Coming right up."

Jack sat down in the empty seat next to his briefcase. Other administration staff and press were further back in the plane, which he was grateful for. He pulled out his laptop and placed it on the table in front of him.

"Here you go Mr. Gold," the attendant said. "Please let me know if you need anything else."

"That's great. Thank you."

Jack took a sip of the hot coffee and was grateful for the simple pleasure. He thought there were few things better than a hot cup of coffee on an airplane after a nap.

He opened the laptop and used his fingerprint to unlock the computer. Immediately it came to life and his Safari browser informed him he wasn't connected to the internet.

He hadn't put the wifi password in, but instead of doing so, he closed the browser window. Behind it was his file of the China Declaration. He remembered writing it in Florida and carrying it throughout Europe. Much had happened, in large part because of the foundation the Declaration provided.

Jack took another sip of coffee and began to read the document again.

THE CHINA DECLARATION

All men are created equal, and they are endowed with certain unalienable rights. *First* and foremost is Safety: One should face no fear of being harmed. *Second* is Freedom: No one can stop another from doing as he wishes, so long as he does not infringe upon the rights of another. *Third*, Free Speech: No one can prevent another from the freely sharing of ideas and information. *Fourth*, the Right to Vote. To secure these rights governments are instituted among men and women, deriving their just powers from the consent of the governed.

Whenever a government consistently and dramatically tramples on these liberties, the governed possess the right to alter or abolish it and lay a new foundation to protect and foster these fundamental ideals.

Should the international community witness a people being repressed and unable to rise up against their oppressors, and that government additionally has proven itself a menace to the world, other countries have a right individually and jointly to foment the changes that such a nation's citizens cannot secure for themselves.

As leaders of the Free World, we have a solemn duty to serve as the leaders of peace. Sometimes in the course of history, human events make it necessary for free nations to stand up, protest, and stop another nation's egregious actions affecting the world and that country's citizens. While nations may witness citizens' sufferance, watch as the oppressed suffer, no country may use its will to impose and create a government in place of its citizens. This guides the right and duty of free countries to act. Inaction would be immoral anc encourage other malicious governments and the subjugation of other people.

These principles apply to the Chinese Communist Party (CCP), which has subjugated Chinese since 1949. The CCP has perpetrated massive atrocities against its own people since the dark days of Mao

Zedong. When dealing with other countries, the CCP routinely acts dishonestly and illegally.

A list of the CCP's abuses is long:

INTERNAL AGGRESSIONS

- China represses its citizens' free speech through technology by closing WeChat accounts of those who do not parrot the CCP's official line.
- China arrests and jails those who dissent from the CCP's opinions and edicts.
- The CCP continuously has placed its financial interests above those of the Chinese people.
- Within Xinjiang Province's internment camps, human rights abuses include widespread rape and torture. Chinese authorities have banished some 1.8 million people, primarily Muslim Uyghurs, in these off-limits internment camps.
- The CCP demolished Hong Kong's protective shield outlined in the Sino-British Joint Declaration, which was registered with the United Nations. The CCP's obliteration of its solemn agreement with Great Britain, Hong Kong's previous protector, crushed the precious rights of citizens to speak freely, publish at will, vote for their leaders, and remain safe within their homes and property.
- Since 1951, The CCP systematically has conducted a cultural genocide against Tibet and its people in a "calculated and systematic strategy aimed at the destruction of their national and cultural identities."
- The CCP has forced women to endure 400 million abortions to protect its one-child policy. In an about face, China now increasingly

disallows abortions solely to resume
population growth.
- The CCP restricts its peoples' access to
  foreign news and opinions about the CCP's
  controversial actions within and outside of
  China.
- China closely monitors and severely limits
  religious liberty.
- China's surveillance state monitors all citizens
  through electronic devices and other means.
- The CCP denies due process and hinders the
  development of an objective judicial system.
  It applies the law selectively, to benefit
  those it favors and destroys those it opposes.

EXTERNAL AGGRESSIONS

- The CCP smuggles fentanyl ingredients and
  related dangerous pharmaceuticals via third
  countries into the USA. Each year, fentanyl
  kills more than 81,000 and has become the No.
  1 cause of death of Americans between the ages
  of 18 and 45.
- The CCP violates trade agreements including
  its 2001 signature on the pact that welcomed
  it into the World Trade Organization.
- The CCP violated its 2020 Economic and Trade
  Agreement with the U.S.
- The CCP repeatedly has stolen American and
  Western intellectual property and profits as
  its countrymen did so.
- The CCP relentlessly threatens to invade
  Taiwan, intimidates that nation with
  belligerent military actions, and sanctions
  those who support the Republic of China's
  independence.

- The CCP helped Russian dictator Vladimir Putin invade Ukraine through a "no limits" partnership and funded the war through billions of dollars of purchases in oil.
- China unleashed the COVID-19 virus or, at the least, failed to timely notify the world resulting in countless deaths that would have otherwise been substantially decreased.

Repeated attempts to remedy this situation have failed.

- Forty countries worldwide have called on China to respect the human rights of Xinjiang's Uyghur community.
- Calls between U.S. President Joe Biden and China's President Xi Jinping failed to discourage China from assisting Russia in its invasion of Ukraine.
- The Chinese subjugation of Hong Kong received global condemnation but triggered zero change from China.
- China said it would ignore international court rulings regarding its behavior in the South China Sea, particularly regarding the Philippines.

Wherefore today we make amends in the annals of history for the ills brought upon the noble Chinese people and by China on the world. Today we declare our countries are united and individually dedicated to abolishing the CCP as it stands, to allow the Chinese people to enjoy the freedoms that they rightly deserve.

We, the leaders of free nations, hereby support The China Declaration:

Jack closed the computer when he was finished reading. It now seemed implausible to him that he could have written it. Yet at the same time, it didn't matter *who* wrote it but that so many were in support of it.

The attendant approached. "Can I get you a refill sir?"

"That would be great."

After she finished pouring Jack said, "My dog may be thirsty. Also, any idea on where he should go to the bathroom?"

"We can take care of that. Just let me know when he is ready."

"Thank you."

CHAPTER 28

It was a cold morning with the chance of snow. Jack tied a black lamb's wool scarf snuggly around Mini's neck and they walked out of the manor home together to the garage. Jack started the Triumph motorcycle and then, upon Jack's invitation, Mini jumped up in front of him. Jack put his two arms on the motorcycle bars, which kept the dog safe, and then pulled out.

He braked by Davis's SUV. "I think we got this," he told him.

Davis grinned. "Awesome, Jack. Enjoy the ride. You'll be able to do it exactly once. The Secret Service will make sure of that, given security concerns. You're too important now."

"I better make it a good ride then."

He took off, trying to ignore the government vehicles that were in front and behind them, and on the sides. *So much for a casual ride to work.*

Jack had an eight-thirty meeting with the president. As they walked into the White House people looked and pointed at Mini, walking perfectly in stride with Jack. He stopped by Madeline's desk before going in to see Sutton. "Madeline, I would like to introduce you to Mini. Mini, this is Madeline. Can he stay with you while I'm in the meeting?"

"He's adorable," Madeline said. "Of course."

Jack pointed to the space next to Madeline's chair. "Mini, stay." The dog immediately went over and sat down

"You can go right in, Jack."

Jack walked into the Oval Office. Matheus was also there, sitting with Sutton on the sofas. Jack hadn't seen them since he left for England and China.

They both stood and welcomed him with broad smiles and hand-shakes. "You got knighted!" Sutton exclaimed. "Congratulations. How'd that go?"

"The Queen forced me. She can be rather persuasive."

"We heard you rode in with your dog," Matheus said. "Where is he?"

"He's outside with Madeline."

"Jack, you must bring him in and introduce us," Sutton said.

Jack went over and opened the door he had just come through. "Mini, come."

The dog, still wearing his stylish scarf, immediately walked in. Sutton and Matheus had sat back down again. Jack took a seat on the other sofa and Mini sat attentively next to him. "Mini, meet President Sutton, and Secretary Matheus."

Matheus grinned. "You know pets are not allowed at poker night."

"Don't let him hear you say that," Jack said. He looked at Mini. "Mini, smile at Matheus."

Mini turned toward the secretary and started to growl, showing his teeth.

With Mini still growling, Jack asked, "When is the next poker night?"

Matheus looked to the president. Sutton said, "How is this Thursday night?"

Matheus nodded.

"Thursday sounds good," Jack said. "Okay Mini," and the dog stopped growling.

"We're not playing with real money," Matheus said. "Just chips for fun, right Mr. President?"

Sutton guffawed. "Not in my White House. Bring cash."

Jack laughed. He liked these men. They were good and honest. He needed their company and the intellectual stimulation that came along with them. With Davis, he now had three good friends. For many years he had gone without such close friendships, and that was no longer an area of his life he wanted to neglect.

"Now, let's get down to business," Sutton said. "Matheus was just outlining Iran's progress on building deployable nukes. Israel wants our participation in a pre-emptive strike. Also, Jack, we found the guy responsible for recruiting the FBI agent who tried to kill you at that wedding . . ."

Please leave a review
and if you have any inquiries visit
www.bradleygood.com